Secrets Never Told

Books by Raegan Teller
in the Enid Blackwell Series

Murder in Madden

The Last Sale

Secrets Never Told

Secrets Never Told

Raegan Teller

Pondhawk Press LLC

Columbia, South Carolina

Copyright © 2019 by Raegan Teller

All rights reserved. No part of this publication may be reproduced, distributed or transmitted in any form or by any means, without prior written permission.

Pondhawk Press
PO Box 290033
Columbia, SC 29229
www.PondhawkPress.com

Publisher's Note: This is a work of fiction. Names, characters, places, and incidents are a product of the author's imagination. Locales and public names are sometimes used for atmospheric purposes. Any resemblance to actual people, living or dead, or to businesses, companies, events, institutions, or locales is completely coincidental.

SECRETS NEVER TOLD/ Raegan Teller. 1st ed.
ISBN 978-0-9979205-4-3

Dedicated to William Earl Craig, Jr.,
the best man I know.

> We dance round in a ring
> and suppose,
> But the secret sits in the
> middle and knows.
>
> — Robert Frost, *The Secret Sits*

CHAPTER 1

Enid Blackwell glanced at the clock on the wall and grimaced. She would have to hurry to make her deadline for tomorrow's weekly newspaper edition. She got up and shut the door to her tiny office at the *Tri-County Gazette* in Madden, South Carolina. With no interruptions, she just might make it.

The newspaper's mission, "Truth First," applied equally to all the local events and topics of interest, most of which the larger newspapers didn't carry. Today, Enid was writing about a rash of animal disappearances from the local farms. First a goat, then a couple of chickens at another location. When one of Madden's finest citizens, a steady advertiser in the paper, reported his prized miniature horse missing, the story earned its spot as front-page news. Sadly, there was nothing to report, other than the details of the missing animals and their descriptions. A reward was posted for the tiny horse, which was sure to elicit some interest.

When Enid heard the knock on her office door, she tried to ignore it. Most likely, it was Jack Johnson, her editor and the owner of the newspaper, wanting to know if she had the lead story of the week ready.

Another knock on the door. "Hold on. I'm uploading it now." Her fingers danced across the keyboard.

"It's me. Theo."

Enid's fingers stopped moving. Theo Linard managed the Glitter Lake Inn, a century-old bed-and-breakfast just outside of Madden. A year ago, Enid had helped him look for his missing daughter. Although they were close friends now, she couldn't remember him ever coming to the newspaper office to see her.

She hit the "submit" button on her laptop. "Come on in." She stood and gave him a hug. "It's good to see you, Theo."

His face was etched with the same concern as when he told Enid his daughter had disappeared. "I'm sorry to bother you, but I need to talk to Jack. The lady up front said he's out."

Enid moved some file folders off the metal folding chair against the wall and offered him a seat. "Jack won't be back until later. Is there something I can help you with?"

He took a deep breath and clasped his hands. "You know we're renovating the inn's kitchen, right?"

"Jack mentioned you were upgrading to a commercial stove and refrigerator. Since you've been doing so many events at the inn, I know you'll be happy to have better equipment."

"Jack has been generous to us." In addition to owning the newspaper, Jack owned the Glitter Lake Inn, which had been left to him in a friend's will. He mostly left the inn and its business to Theo, as he wanted no part of being an innkeeper, but he had vowed to hang onto it as long as he could. It was the least he could do for the woman who might have become his wife, had her life not been tragically ended.

Enid waited for Theo to explain further, but he was silent. "Something is bothering you, I can tell." She pulled her chair from behind the desk and sat across from him, taking his hands in hers.

"I'd rather show you, if you have time."

"Of course. I just finished the article, so I'll let Jack know I'm leaving. Give me a minute." She made the call and picked up her worn leather tote from underneath the desk. It had been an anniversary present from Cade years ago when she was an AP reporter. She kept using it, not only because of its sentimental value but because the fine Italian leather was buttery soft and the tote was big enough to carry extra shoes, her laptop, a bottle of water, her notepad, and any other supplies she might need.

"Ready? Let's go."

. . .

Fall, in all its colorful glory, signaled the change of season. Splashes of orange, red, and yellow leaves painted the woods on both sides of the rural county road. A cold front was coming through, and fallen leaves danced in the brisk breeze.

When Enid arrived at the inn, the beauty of the old mansion and the sparkling water of Glitter Lake captivated her. She never grew tired of that view. Theo parked in the area beside the inn, and Enid pulled in beside him. Lately, there had been work trucks in the parking area: electricians, carpenters, plumbers, and the dreaded inspectors. Upgrading the old house had proven to be a bigger undertaking than either Jack or Theo had bargained for. The wiring wasn't up to code and couldn't handle the demands of a commercial kitchen. The gas lines had to be moved to accommodate the new layout, and the plaster walls would eventually have to be re-mudded in keeping with the historical materials at the inn. Today, none of the usual workers were there.

Theo entered the inn's back door, and Enid followed him through the mudroom and into the kitchen. He stopped suddenly and pointed to a hole in the wall big enough to walk through. "There."

Enid peered into the dark void where the old sixty-inch O'Keefe & Merritt antique stove had once sat against the wall.

Theo held a construction light one of the workers had left, the kind that had a wire cage around it and a hook on the top for hanging. "Follow me but watch your step." He walked into the opening, holding the light out in front of him.

When Enid was a kid, her mother had taken her to see the Luray Caverns in Virginia. Stepping into the caves, she had experienced a stillness that was hard to describe. She had that same feeling now, as she looked around the big space and inhaled the dank air. "What is this? A secret room?"

"When they tore out the wall today to run the new wiring, they found this small room that had been sealed shut."

"This inn is so big, I guess no one ever noticed this space had been walled off." She looked at the wooden floor, covered with decades of dirt.

"Over here," Theo said, walking to the corner by the far wall. He stopped and held his light over a portion of the floor where the wood had some water damage and had rotted. Several of the damaged floor boards had been pulled up and piled to the side, so that an area about four feet square was nothing but dirt. The dirt floor was about three feet lower than the wooden floor, creating a shallow crawl space. "Careful, watch your step." He put the light down into the hole to illuminate the area.

Enid peered into the opening and pointed. "What is that?"

"Bones. Human, I believe."

CHAPTER 2

Madden Police Chief Joshua Hart leaned back in his chair as he listened to Theo telling about the discovery of the bones. Enid sat beside Theo.

After a few minutes, Josh interrupted. "One thing I'm confused about, Theo. Why didn't you call me immediately? You know, before you went to see Jack or Enid."

Enid started to speak, but Josh held up his hand. "Wait, I asked Theo." He smiled at Enid with a look she knew well. She and Josh had been "an item," as the Madden ladies called it, for about a year. That look meant "stay out of police work." The relationship between reporters and police was tenuous at best, but being romantically entangled added another dimension of difficulty.

"Since it's outside the Madden city limits, Enid and I called the sheriff's office right after we went back to the inn," Theo said. "I wasn't sure what to do, and Enid has always given me good advice." He looked like a child who had been scolded for misbehaving in class. "I meant no disrespect toward you."

"None taken," Josh said.

"Where will they send the bones for analysis?" Enid asked.

"I'm sure the sheriff will ask the county coroner to handle it. Can't say that I have much experience in this state on this kind of thing. It's wasn't that unusual in New Mexico to find human remains in the desert, but here, well, that's a different matter."

"Are we even sure they're human?" Enid asked.

"Can't say at this point." Josh looked at the photo Enid had taken and pointed to what looked like a ribcage. "But they definitely look human."

Theo cleared his throat. "I'm worried about what this will do to the inn's business."

Josh threw back his head and laughed. "Are you kidding me?" He waved his hand across an imaginary sign in the air. "I can see the billboards along the highway now. 'Stop at the Glitter Lake Inn and see the haunted secret room.'"

Neither Theo nor Enid laughed with Josh.

"Okay, sorry for the bad joke. Since Jack is the owner of the inn, I'm sure they will talk to him right away." Josh looked at Theo. "I'm sure the county sheriff will do what he can to minimize disruptions at the inn. His forensics team will take photographs and get whatever else they need. You know, soil samples for decomp materials and things like that."

"We have a big dinner party a few weeks from now. It's a fundraiser for Miss Madelyn's campaign. I don't want to disappoint her."

As a successful attorney in Columbia, Madelyn Jensen had been courted to run for the state senate. She was also a niece of the previous Madden police chief, Dick Jensen. Everyone who knew Madelyn said she should run for something, because she could work a room like no one else. Although she and Enid were close friends now, their relationship had begun with mistrust and accusations of

Madelyn's having an affair with Cade, Enid's ex. Enid had accepted both Madelyn's and Cade's assertions that nothing had ever happened between them. Still, there was no denying that Cade admired the strong-willed, attractive attorney.

The election was just over a month away, and Madelyn had been leading in the polls since early summer. Everyone assumed she would win. Even though the Jensen family's power was centered in and around Madden, their name was known throughout the state for their philanthropy and for their influence.

"I think you'll have more problems with the county inspectors approving your new wiring and gas lines than you will with investigators," Josh said. "The county investigator will question you, but it's pretty clear those bones have been there a while. I doubt they'll hold up the inn's construction plans until they figure out what, or who, those bones once were. If it's someone's pet dog that was buried under the floor, then you won't have to worry."

Theo nodded. "Thank you, Chief Hart. I need to get back to the inn now unless you have more questions for me."

"Nah, we're good. I'll be in touch later," Josh said. He walked Theo to the door of the small cinder block police station and locked the door behind him.

After Theo left, Enid said, "Please don't lecture me about not getting involved in police business. It's late and I'm tired."

"I'll make a deal with you. You don't meddle, and I won't lecture." He flashed a boyish grin. "That work?"

Enid reached for her tote on the floor and stood to leave without responding. "I'll see you later." She blew him a kiss. "Deal." She smiled, but her reporter's instincts were kicking in. While she enjoyed unraveling a good mystery, these bones could be the beginning of another test of her relationship with Josh.

CHAPTER 3

Thursdays were special to Enid. Especially rainy Thursdays. Cade had proposed to her on one, and she had won two awards for her investigative reporting, both presented to her on rainy Thursdays. Today held a different significance. The weekly newspaper was delivered each Thursday, so the staff took this day to catch its breath before launching into the next week's edition.

Since it was drizzling rain and dreary, she didn't feel particularly special today. Mostly lazy. Jack had run her article on the missing miniature horse with only a few edits, and she had asked for the day off. She had moved into her new house in Madden several months ago but hadn't unpacked the last stack of boxes in the corner of the living room. Today was a good day to tackle that project, but she was mostly trying to avoid it again.

After making herself another cup of Lady Grey tea, she halfheartedly opened one of the boxes. It was the smallest one, and a bad choice. Inside was a linen, lace-edged handkerchief belonging to her late mother, a small framed photograph of her, and Enid's wedding ring. After touching each one of the items, she taped the box and put it on the top shelf of her bedroom closet. She cherished both of those memories, her mother and her marriage, but she needed to move on.

This time, she would go for the biggest box, since small boxes seemed to pack the biggest gut punches. It was full of bed linens. She pulled out the handmade quilt she had bought at a craft festival when she and Josh visited Asheville, North Carolina. Running her hand across the intricate hand stitching, she marveled at the time and patience embedded in the artwork. It was almost too precious to use, but it would feel good across her feet as the cool October weather approached.

She worked her way through three more boxes before the door knocker announced a visitor. "Coming," she called out. Peeping through the translucent glass panel that ran beside the length of the door, she saw a man's shape. He had his back to the door. "Who is it?" she called out.

"Have you forgotten me already?" a male voice responded as he turned around.

Another gut punch. So much for special rainy Thursdays. She opened the door to the man holding a bunch of flowers. "Hello, Cade. This is quite a surprise."

They embraced each other with the distant politeness of strangers. "You are as beautiful as ever," Cade said to his ex-wife. "Small town life seems to agree with you."

Enid bristled at the veiled put-down. As an investigative reporter for the Associated Press, Cade traveled all over the world on assignments. That was the life he wanted and that she had wanted, at least at one time. During their life together, he had often scoffed at rural life, saying that small towns bred small minds.

"Thanks. It's good to see you." Enid hung his wet jacket on the wooden peg near the front door and offered him a cup of coffee.

"That would be great, if you have some. I know you don't drink the stuff."

"I keep coffee for my guests." Especially for Jack and Josh, she wanted to say.

Enid put the flowers in a vase and watched Cade as he sipped coffee. Memories flooded her mind; some good, some painful. "Madden is not exactly on the way to anything. I'm surprised to see you."

Cade sat his coffee mug on the low table in front of the sofa. "Actually, I'm here on business."

Enid waited for him to elaborate, but he just stared at her, as she sipped her tea. "Do you need a place to stay?"

"No, thanks. I'm staying at the Glitter Lake Inn. Got a pretty good discount since the kitchen is under renovation. No meals, but that's okay. I just need a place to sleep. And I met the new manager. Theo? Was that his name? Anyway, he speaks very highly of you."

"Yes, Theo Linard. He's a great guy. Oh, and I want to thank you for that profile you did about me searching for Theo's daughter. You made me sound like a superhero, rather than a small-town reporter."

Cade unexpectedly put his hand on hers. "You'll always be my superhero."

Enid gently pulled her hand away.

Cade apparently took the hint and broke their gaze. "I'm not trying to be mysterious, but I'm not sure how to tell you about this story I'm working on. As you know, throughout my career I've focused on corruption, both in the government and in law enforcement."

"Those stories got you fired once when you refused to drop an investigation on a powerful senator."

Cade laughed. "That's true." Then his smile faded. "Anyway, I'm working on a story about police vigilantism, and I got a tip about an undercover detective in New Mexico who is suspected of killing a perp acquitted for murder."

Afraid she might drop her tea cup, Enid gripped it tightly.

Cade shifted his weight on the sofa and continued. "The detective is Joshua Hart. I believe he's the Madden chief of police now." He picked up his coffee mug and stared at its contents. "And I believe you're dating him."

After holding her breath, Enid exhaled deeply. "Yes, Josh and I are seeing each other." She fixed her eyes on Cade's. "He's a good man."

Shifting again, Cade said, "This sofa is not very comfortable. Maybe I should get you a new one, as a housewarming gift."

"This one's okay." Josh had given her the sofa when he bought a new one for his house.

"What do you know about Josh's late wife?"

Could she trust her ex-husband? Should she refuse to discuss Josh? "He told me she was murdered in New Mexico, where she worked on an Indian reservation." The only time she had questioned Josh, he had been evasive about the details.

"Serena Hart, his wife, was killed by the estranged husband of one of her legal clients," Cade said. "As you may know, traditional Native American men are very possessive of their women."

"If you're implying that Josh is possessive, then you don't know anything about him. He can be overly protective at times, but in his line of work, that's understandable."

"Look, I have to be honest. Talking to my ex-wife about her lover is a bit uncomfortable for me."

"Then why are you?" Enid's tone was sharper than she intended.

"He may not be who you think he is. I don't want you to get hurt."

Enid put her tea cup in its saucer so hard, she was afraid she had cracked her mother's china. "And how do you know what I think of him?"

Moving over closer to Enid, Cade put his arm around her. "I'm not here to cause you problems. We might be divorced, but I'll always love you and worry about you."

She pulled away.

"I didn't want you to hear from someone else about my being in town investigating Josh. I'm trying to do the right thing." He paused. "If I don't do this story, someone else will take it."

Enid's mind was racing. "Who called in the tip?"

Cade smiled. "There's my girl. Her reporter's instincts are back." He touched the tip of her nose with his finger. "We don't know who called it in, but it came from New Mexico. All tips are recorded, but the sound quality leaves a lot to be desired. You really can't tell much. No discernible accent."

"What did he say? Exactly?"

"The tipster said he knew we were investigating police vigilantes. No, wait, he didn't use that word. He just said police killings."

Enid recalled Josh's face when they talked about his wife's murder. His dark eyes had flashed anger. "Did he name Josh specifically?"

"No, but with the information the tipster provided, it couldn't be anyone else."

"So you just jumped in your car and rushed down here to see if this tip had any merit?"

"No, I drove here to see you and talk to you in person. If you want me to hand this story off to another investigative reporter, I will. I'm not interested in writing a revenge story about Josh, even if I don't like the idea of your dating him."

Enid decided to let that last comment go. "If you do this story, will you promise to keep an open mind and not let our relationship cloud your judgment?" No matter how uncomfortable this situation might be, she trusted Cade to be fair. He might not have been the best husband, but he was an excellent reporter.

Cade leaned over and kissed Enid gently on the forehead. "Yes, of course."

CHAPTER 4

Enid sat at her desk looking at the paperwork stacked on her desk. She had begun working for Jack Johnson when the *Madden Gazette* was a small-town, weekly newspaper. Then he bought two small weeklies in surrounding counties and combined them into one paper about six months ago. Even before the acquisitions, many of the reporters had left, some leaving journalism altogether due to low pay and long hours. Others had moved on to the *State* in Columbia, the *Post and Courier* in Charleston, or one of the other daily newspapers. The *Tri-County Gazette*, like many weeklies, struggled with high turnover and low profit margins.

Today, she had a hard time concentrating, as her mind kept going back to the conversation with Cade. Could he possibly be right about Josh? If she asked Josh about it, then she could blow Cade's investigation. But if she didn't confront Josh with this information, he might think she was colluding with Cade.

She was massaging her throbbing temples when Ginger, the newspaper's office manager, knocked on her door. "There's a woman here who insists on seeing you. Right now." Ginger waved her arms dramatically, as she was prone to do when frustrated. "I tried to get her to make an appointment, but . . ." She waved her arms again.

"It's fine. I'll be glad to talk to her." Enid pointed behind Ginger. "She's already here."

Ginger turned around to face the woman. "I told you to wait up front." Ginger made a huffing sound and marched back down the hallway.

Enid motioned for the woman to come into her office. "I apologize for Ginger. She's a bit demonstrative at times. I'm Enid Blackwell." She extended her hand, which the woman ignored. "Please have a seat."

The woman's age was hard to tell. She stooped over and her shoulders slumped, but her face was free of wrinkles or lines. It was as though someone had pasted a young woman's head on an old woman's body. She was covered from head to toe in dark grey clothing that looked at least two sizes too large for her slight frame.

"I understand you wanted to see me. How can I help you?" Enid asked.

"I seen seven crows on your house yesterday."

Enid gripped her pen. "My house? How do you know where I live?"

The woman laughed softly and shook her head. "You in Madden, missy. Everyone knows you live in dat house." Her smile disappeared. "You know what seven crows mean?"

Enid glanced at the phone on her desk and was tempted to call for help. But who would she call? Jack was out of town, and Ginger might only make things worse. "No, I don't, and I'm not really interested. May I ask your name, ma'am?"

In a singsong voice, the woman replied, "Seven for a secret, never to be told."

Enid stood up. "Alright, that's enough nonsense. I'd like for you to leave. Now." Enid walked to the door and motioned for the woman to get out of the office.

The woman didn't budge. "Now, don't go getting your hackles up. Didn't you never hear that verse?"

Enid pointed to the door again. "Have a nice day. Now, please leave."

"I know whose bones them is at that big house on the water."

Enid walked back to her desk and sat down. "What bones?"

"Don't play dumb," the woman said, pointing a finger at Enid. "I know you ain't stupid."

"You mean the bones found at the Glitter Lake Inn, I presume."

The woman cackled and then mocked Enid. "You *presume* rightly."

"If you know something you need to talk to Police Chief Hart."

"He your man, ain't he?"

Enid straightened the stack of papers on her desk, as she had already done several times. "That's none of your business. How do you know anything about those bones?"

"If you want, I'll just go talk to your lover boy police man." The woman leaned forward in her seat. "But you're curious as a cat, yes, you are. That what makes you good. Figured you'd want to know first."

"I'll be glad to pass along whatever you tell me to Chief Hart."

The woman smiled, showing a beautiful set of white teeth. "My auntie once told me a woman be buried there at the inn. But she didn't die there."

"What's the woman's name, the one buried there?" Enid picked up the pen on her desk and started making notes. "Do you know anything about her?"

The woman shrugged again and stood to leave. "You're the one to know the secret. 'Seven for a secret, never to be told.'"

"Stop talking in riddles. What does that mean?"

The woman walked toward the door.

"Wait, please give me your name or how I can contact you."

The woman left without saying another word. Enid walked up front to Ginger's desk. "Do you know who that woman is?"

Ginger continued to stare at the computer screen. "Never saw her before."

Enid walked outside and looked around. The woman was nowhere to be seen. Jack's pickup pulled into the small parking area beside the newspaper office. Enid waited for him to get out.

"Well, this is nice. Having a welcoming committee, I mean," Jack said. "Or are you just out for some air?"

"I was looking for a woman that came to see me."

"Come on in, and you can fill me in."

Enid looked in both directions again but didn't see the woman. A light breeze blew, and leaves skittered across the sidewalk in a circular motion. "Seven crows," Enid said aloud, shaking her head as she followed Jack into the building.

CHAPTER 5

Enid sat across from Jack's big metal desk and told him about her encounter with the woman. She looked at her notes. "That's about all I know."

Jack leaned back in his chair. "Well, that's quite a story. Can't say that her description rings a bell at all, but I'm still a relative newcomer here. Anyone in this town less than three generations means you're new." He sipped coffee from a chipped brown mug. "How old was your visitor?"

"I have no idea. In some ways, she seemed old, but her teeth were perfect and her skin was as smooth as a baby's." She paused. "What's this rhyme about seven crows? Have you heard it?"

"As I recall, it's from an old nursery rhyme, 18th century, I think. It's been revised over the years. I did an article many years ago on the dark side of these children's verses, and I recall that being one I researched. This woman, was she white? Black?"

"She had brown skin the color of caramel and the most beautiful green eyes."

"I wish Cassie were here to tell us more about the inn's history. Although, she was a relative newcomer, too, even though the inn had been in her family for generations."

The mention of her late friend's name made Enid recall their brief, sister-like relationship. "I was thinking of Cassie, too. I'm sure there are records somewhere of the previous owners."

"I'll check the paper's archives for any mention of a killing at the inn, although if the body was hidden, it was likely not reported."

"A secret," Enid said, "never to be told."

"Seems like that comment was meant to get into your head. When she mentioned knowing where you live, did she confirm that she actually knew your address?"

"No, not really. And I admit, she did get into my head. She was just so strange. Her body was big and stooped, but her face and everything else about her was younger."

"Maybe she had on a costume," Jack said.

"Now that I think about it, her clothing appeared to be padded underneath."

Jack leaned forward. "So why would a fairly young woman dress up like an older person and come to see you? Why the game? Why not just call you anonymously?"

"Do you think it's a hoax?"

Jack leaned back in his chair. "Probably. But I'll still check and see what I can find. You might want to share all this with Josh. He may know something about this woman."

. . .

Enid walked down the sidewalk toward the small police station with the intention of talking to Josh. But instead, she walked down the street a few blocks further to the Blackwell building, named after Fern Blackwell, her ex-mother-in-law, who had made a generous donation to the town years ago. The old two-story building had been restored and now housed Madden's Women's Club, Garden Club, Historical Society, and a small art studio. The main living and dining areas of the elegant old building were often rented for bridal showers, tea parties, and other events.

A couple years ago, Enid had met the young woman with the historical society who served as the host and greeter for all visitors. But now there was a new person here, a young black man. While Enid wouldn't describe Madden as a racist town, the blacks and whites didn't mingle much. Each group was respectful of the other, but they remained separate. Since this building was the mecca of old Madden, the young man's employment was somewhat surprising.

"Hi, I'm Roscoe." His bow tie jiggled a bit as he vigorously shook Enid's hand.

"Pleasure to meet you, Roscoe. I'm Enid Blackwell."

"Oh, what a lovely name. I assume you're related to Fern Blackwell whose generous donation made all this possible," he said, waving his arm around.

"Yes, she is my ex-mother-in-law. You're new here, aren't you?"

"Yes, ma'am. I'm working on my master's in historical preservation. My thesis will focus on small towns, so I'm working here on an internship."

"That's interesting. Have you been in town long?"

"Oh, no, ma'am. This is my first week."

"I'd like to do an article on you, that is, if you're interested."

"Oh, yes. That would be wonderful," Roscoe said, straightening his bow tie.

"I came here to see if a woman I met recently, an artist, is in the studio. She invited me to drop by."

Roscoe waived his arm toward the stairway in a sweeping gesture. "Of course, the art studio is upstairs. May I escort you?"

"No, I can find it."

"Then just make yourself at home."

. . .

Enid took the stairs to the second floor where the art studio was at the end of the hallway. She knocked on the door.

A female voice called out, "Come in."

Enid walked into the high-ceilinged room flooded with sunlight from the three large windows at one end. "Hi, Lindy. I met you at your art showing at the inn recently, and you invited me to come to the studio. Is this a good time? You look busy."

The fifty-something woman's pixie hair cut was a beautiful silver grey, but she had a youthful look. She wiped her hands on a paint-stained towel before reaching out to Enid. "I told you to stop by anytime, and I meant it. So glad to see you."

After Lindy showed Enid her collection of dragonfly paintings and a few of tree frogs, Lindy said, "I get the sense there's something else on your mind today, other than my artwork. Can I help you with anything?"

Enid blushed slightly. "I did want to see your work. I particularly love this one," she said, pointing to one of the tree frogs with large eyes. "But, yes, there is something else. I think you told me you do work for two of the nearby high schools, with their drama classes."

"How nice of you to remember that small detail." Lindy went to the back of the studio and got a large black portfolio from the cabinet. "Here are sketches, and some photos, of the stage backdrops I created for their plays."

"These are great. Looks like a lot of hours go into creating these canvases."

"Yes, and I do it to help the kids and the arts, so it's all unpaid work. A labor of love, as they say." Lindy closed and zipped the portfolio. "Are you involved in plays or stage work?"

"Me? Oh, goodness no. Do you meet the students or others involved in the plays?"

Lindy cocked her head slightly. "Well, sometimes. Why do you ask?"

Enid told her about the woman that came to the newspaper office. "I'm not sure, but it may have been someone in costume. She looked so young, maybe not as young as high-school age though. She was stooped over and appeared to have a hard time walking. Except when she left the office. I'm just wondering if maybe she's involved in plays or acting."

Lindy leaned back in her chair. "You're a reporter, right?"

Enid nodded.

"Do these questions have something to do with a story you're working on?"

"No, well, maybe. At this point, I'm just trying to follow up on her visit."

"Jack speaks highly of you. Otherwise, I would be leery to talk to a reporter about something so vague. But, as I said, Jack thinks you're wonderful, so how can I help?"

Enid relaxed the tension in her shoulders. "I'd like to find this person to ask her more about what she told me. Or maybe it was all just a prank."

Lindy went to her work table and picked up a sketch pad and pencil. "Describe her for me."

Enid closed her eyes and tried to remember as many details as she could about the old, or perhaps young, woman that came to see her. As she shared those details with Lindy, the artist sketched away feverishly. When she stopped drawing, she picked up a handful of colored pencils and began filling in more details to the sketch. After a minute or two, she held up the sketch pad for Enid to see. "Is that her?"

Enid's hand flew to her mouth, "Oh, my gosh. Yes! That's her." Enid studied the sketch more closely. "You're amazing."

"Well, it was your detailed description that made it possible. You have a good eye. Ever think of trying art?"

"Thanks, but I think I'll stick to writing. Do you recognize this woman?"

"No, I've never seen her, at least not in this outfit. What makes you think she was in costume?"

"I think most of all it was because her face didn't match the rest of her."

"Maybe she just had a young face."

"Perhaps. May I keep this?" Enid asked.

Lindy tore the page from her sketch pad. "Of course. I'll just take a photo of it. If anything comes to mind, or if I see her anywhere, I'll let you know."

Walking back to the newspaper office, Enid's mind wandered more often to Cade's comments about Josh than to the strange encounter with the woman in her office. She pulled out her phone and left a message telling Ginger she'd be back later. The second call she made was to Cade.

"This is a surprise. A pleasant one." Cade said, answering his cell phone.

"Can we meet? Just for a few minutes."

After a brief hesitation, Cade replied. "Sure. Meet you at Sarah's in a few."

. . .

Most of the locals referred to the only restaurant in Madden, Sarah's Tea Shoppe, as Sarah's diner. The exceptions were the town's finest ladies who took tea there in the afternoons. If a place could have a split personality, this one certainly qualified. The early morning and lunch crowd was typically a mixture of retired locals, mostly older white men, and a few commuters who drove to Columbia or other places to work each day. The latter group often ordered coffee to go or something that could be eaten with one hand while driving. Sarah's bacon and egg sandwiches cut in quarters, with no mayo to drip, were popular for mobile eating.

After decades of declining population, Madden was growing again, mostly because of a retail distribution center recently built on the outskirts of town. Many of the center's jobs were filled by locals, but the high-tech and management positions attracted mostly newcomers. Many of them chose to live in Columbia, but a few had built large homes in and around Madden where the land was relatively cheap. While the locals were happy with the job opportunities and the influx of business for the local stores, they were wary of the fast-walking, smooth-talking newbies in town.

The split personality of Sarah's little restaurant revealed itself after lunch, when it became the kind of environment its owner had envisioned. Teas and scones replaced pancakes and the meat-and-three lunches. Paper napkins were nixed for pressed linen ones favored by the afternoon ladies who often gathered there, sipping tea and sharing tidbits of information. It wasn't gossip, one of them told Enid, when it was mostly true.

When Enid walked into Sarah's, the transition was in progress. A few men were finishing lunch, but the scones were on the counter, displayed on doily-lined plates under glass domes.

Cade was sitting at one of the tables, sipping coffee. He stood when he saw her come in. They hugged, but Enid resisted a full embrace. "Have a seat," he said, as he pulled out a chair for her.

A waitress showed up immediately, her blonde ponytail swinging side to side as she walked to their table. Enid ordered a glass of iced tea. "We got unsweet for you today, Miss Enid."

"Thanks. I'll also have a fried green tomato and bacon sandwich. No mayo."

"We got some whole grain bread, too. Miss Sarah keeps it in the freezer 'cause not too many people want it here other than you and some of the new folks. But it toasts up fine."

Enid smiled. "Perfect."

When the waitress was out of earshot, Cade threw back his head and laughed. "You've become a local. And you're ruining a perfectly good diner."

Enid made a face at him. "Very funny."

Cade looked at the time on his phone. "I have to make this quick. Got an appointment in Columbia this afternoon."

Enid wanted to ask if it was with Madelyn. "This won't take long."

Before she could continue, Cade asked, "This is about Police Chief Hart, isn't it?"

"Before you get defensive, let me say something. You showed up, unannounced, in Madden, claiming that someone who is a close friend of mine may have killed his wife's murderer, vigilante style. Did you stop to think what kind of position you've put me in?"

Cade cleared his throat, something he did when nervous. "Yes, of course. I mean, I didn't intend to complicate your life, but I thought you needed to know what I was doing." He reached out and put his hand on top of hers. "I still care about you, you know, as a friend. We had some good years together." He withdrew his hand. "What was I supposed to do? Say nothing and snoop around in your boyfriend's life without telling you?"

Enid laughed, while Cade looked at her with a surprised look on his face. "I'm sorry, it's just that . . ." The smile left her face. "Never mind, this conversation feels all too familiar, just a different subject." This time, Enid put her hand on Cade's. "I realize you're in an awkward situation too. But now, we've got to figure this out, for all our sakes. Mine, yours, and Josh's. No matter what you think you know about him, or how much he may have wanted to kill the man who shot his wife, he wouldn't have. He's not like that. And if you don't tell him about your investigation, I will."

"You've always been hardheaded. It's a trait that's both admirable and frustrating. So, I assume you want to be the one to tell him."

Enid jerked her hand away.

Cade reached into his leather portfolio and pulled out a business card. "After you've talked with him, give him my card and ask him if he'd be willing to talk with me. On the record, of course." He stood up. "I gotta go."

CHAPTER 6

After a good night's sleep, Enid no longer dreaded having a conversation with Josh. She pushed the nagging doubts aside, assuring herself that her defense of Josh was warranted. But did she really know him? Every time she brought up his wife and Josh's past, he was evasive.

She Googled Joshua Hart and found it to be a fairly common name. When she added "wife's murder" to the search, several articles appeared. The earlier ones focused on the tragedy of Serena Hart trying to help Native Americans and then being killed by one. Later articles mentioned the suspect was killed after being released on a legal technicality. Josh was questioned by the police, but no charges were ever filed.

She closed her laptop and switched her attention to another reason she needed to talk to Josh. While he wasn't involved in investigating the bones found at the inn, he might be able to give her an update. After a cup of jasmine tea and a honey-drizzled English muffin, she dressed and drove to the Madden police station.

Pete, the young police officer at the front desk, greeted her. "Hello, Ms. Blackwell. How are you today?"

"I'm doing well. Is Josh here?"

"Yes, you can go on in. I know he'll want to see you." Pete grinned.

Enid felt her stomach muscles tense when she walked into Josh's office and saw him smiling at her.

"Hey, gorgeous. What a nice surprise." They had agreed on no touching, hugging, or other intimate gestures while in the police station or newspaper office. It was hard enough for them to keep boundaries around their respective duties without adding further complications. "Uh oh. You've got your reporter face on. What's up?"

"I'd like to get an update on the bones found at the inn." She decided not to mention Cade's investigation until after she got the information she needed.

Josh sat up in his chair. "As far as I know, they don't have any solid information yet. The county coroner took the bones, and Boogie and his men processed the crime scene for anything obvious. They called in SLED to do a more detailed crime scene investigation." SLED, the State Law Enforcement Division, was routinely called in to assist local agencies, like Sheriff Bernard Waters' office in Bowman County. Locally, the sheriff was known as "Boogie," a nickname given him for his shag dancing at Myrtle Beach's Society of Stranders conference every year. He routinely won the local dance contests, and now in his sixties, he could still put the younger shaggers to shame. When Josh first came to Madden, Boogie had taken Josh under his wing and acclimated him to small-town policing and politics. The rumor around town was that Boogie would retire soon, and Josh would run for sheriff.

"How long will it take to get the results? I assume they'll do a DNA test."

Josh nodded. "If we were in Richland County, the results would be quicker. They have a forensic anthropologist on staff. Our county crime lab is much smaller, so we'll have to depend on SLED for our crime scene work. Or we'll have to get Richland County to step in and help. The DNA results will be run against the FBI and NamUs databases. Maybe we'll get lucky and get a hit."

"What if you don't?"

"The sheriff's office is looking into missing persons also. The problem is, until we get a better idea of how old those bones are, we can't narrow the timeframe. Right now, the search parameters are too broad."

"I know you often help Sheriff Waters. Are you assisting him on this one?"

"He hasn't asked for help yet, but one of his female deputies is out on maternity leave, and the ex-Gamecock football player he recently hired fell off a ladder cleaning his house gutters. He's out for a while. Being down two deputies, I expect to get a call from Boogie any day."

"Thanks. I'll check with you again in a few days." Enid hated being so formal with Josh, but they were still trying to figure out how the local police chief and the senior reporter for the local newspaper could work together and protect sources without stepping over boundaries of professionalism and confidentiality.

"Yes, ma'am. I'll be glad to tell you what I can."

"Do you have a minute? There's one more thing I need to discuss with you."

Josh leaned back in his chair. "Sure."

Enid pulled Cade's business card from the ever-present leather tote. "Here," she said, handing the card to Josh.

He took the business card and studied it, reading aloud. "Cade Blackwell. Reporter. Associated Press." Josh looked up at Enid. "Ah, the infamous ex-husband."

"You probably knew he was in town." No one came into town without Josh knowing about it. Madden was still small enough that a stranger stood out among the locals and word spread fast.

"Well . . ." Josh hesitated. "Yes, I guess I heard a reporter was staying at the inn, but I didn't know it was your ex."

"I'd like for you to call him as soon as you can."

"Because . . . ?"

"Because he's investigating you."

Josh put his hands behind his head and rocked back and forth in the old wooden banker's chair. "Gee, I guess I should be flattered. It's my understanding Cade Blackwell only casts bait for the big ones."

Enid played with the notepad in her lap, bending and unbending the corner of the paper. "I don't think this is a joking matter. He's . . ." She stopped to think about what she could or shouldn't say. "He's looking into a police vigilante killing in New Mexico. Your name came up."

The crease on Josh's forehead deepened. "Is that all you can say?"

Enid shifted in her seat. "That's about all I know." She leaned back and squared her shoulders. "I hope you understand what an awkward position I'm in. Please don't make it any harder for me. I'm trying to do what's right for both of you. Cade knows I'm talking to you."

Josh stood up abruptly. "Well, thanks for that. I'll give him a call."

Enid remained seated. "I asked you once about your wife's murder, and you were vague about what happened. I'd like to know more."

Josh walked to his office door and stood by it. "So that's what this is all about. I think we need to keep our boundaries on this subject. I said I'd call Cade, and I will."

As Enid was leaving Josh's office, she turned to him. "Oh, I almost forgot." She pulled the sketch the artist had done of the old woman who had come to see her at the newspaper office. "Do you recognize this woman?"

Josh took the drawing from her and studied it. "No, I can't say that I do. Is she local?"

"I have no idea. She just came to see me, and I'm trying to figure out who she is."

"Didn't you ask her?"

"I did, but she never told me."

Josh handed the sketch back to Enid. "Sorry I can't help you."

As Enid left Cade's office, Pete called out. "Bye now, Ms. Blackwell. Always good to see you."

CHAPTER 7

Enid logged onto the website for NamUs, the National Institute of Justice's National Missing and Unidentified Persons System. It was a national centralized repository and resource center for missing persons and unidentified remains. She put in search parameters for anyone missing in the surrounding areas during the last twenty years. The bones could be older, but at least it was a place to start.

After inputting the necessary information, her efforts produced no results of missing persons in Bowman County, but there were twenty-three people in the surrounding counties and more than a hundred statewide over the last two decades. Since she didn't know the sex or race of the bones, she couldn't narrow the search by either. Rather than spend more time guessing, she closed her laptop. Once she got more information, she would try again.

What she needed was a local historian, someone whose memory rivaled NamUs. She glanced at the time on her phone. It was nearly lunchtime, so she went to the kitchen of her small cottage and checked the refrigerator. A small plastic container of hummus sat on the top shelf with a half bottle of water. On the next shelf down was a white Styrofoam container. She opened it and an unrecognizable glob of something with green on it emitted an onerous smell. "Ugh," she said aloud. After dumping the container in the trash, she pulled the car keys from her tote.

A short drive later, she parked in front of the Blackwell Center where she had visited Lindy at the art studio. When she rang the doorbell, Roscoe greeted her. "Ah, Ms. Blackwell. A pleasure to see you again. Please come in."

Enid followed Roscoe into the large entrance foyer. A large bouquet of fresh flowers was sitting on a round mahogany table. The smell was sweet but overpowering.

"Is there anyone here today from the Madden Historical Society?" She stepped back, away from the flowers.

Roscoe clapped his hands silently. "Oh, yes. Miss Murray is down the hall. Shall I accompany you to her office?"

"Yes, thanks." Enid followed Roscoe, being careful not to slip on the freshly waxed floors.

Roscoe tapped on the closed door. "Miss Murray, are you there? You have a visitor." Roscoe turned to Enid and produced a smile that took up his entire face. "You're just going to love her. She's so full of it." He laughed, but after Enid didn't respond, he added, "Information, I mean. You know, she's just full of information."

The door opened, and a stooped, grey-haired woman stood with the aid of a wooden cane. "Yes?" She eyed Enid from head to toe.

Roscoe waved toward Enid. "Miss Murray, this is Ms. Enid Blackwell. Her family—"

Miss Murray interrupted. "Yes, I know Ms. Blackwell." She stepped aside slowly. "Come in." Looking at Roscoe, she added, "Thank you."

"Oh, yes ma'am. Anytime." He turned to Enid. "Bye now."

Miss Murray closed the office door and slowly made her way to a large chair covered with faded floral chintz and stuffed to point of bursting. The arms were covered by crocheted doilies.

After Miss Murray got settled in the chair, Enid sat in the wooden Windsor chair across from her. "Thank you for seeing me. I hope I'm not interrupting anything."

Instead of responding, Miss Murray just stared at Enid.

"I can come back later, if—"

"Not at all, dear." Miss Murray smiled. "I've known of you and your work since you got here. Anytime we get newcomers in town, the buzz intensifies, if you know what I mean. I love small towns, but we do tend to amplify everything." She laughed. "Probably because we're all a bit bored and self-consumed." She paused. "Or perhaps I'm just talking about myself." She crossed her legs at the ankles, the way women were trained to do in earlier times when they wore mostly dresses and skirts. "Now, what can I do for you?"

"I'm doing some research on missing persons in the area. I've searched the online registry, but of course it only contains people who are reported missing. I would imagine that not everyone gets reported."

"You mean poor or black people."

Miss Murray's bluntness was both refreshing and disconcerting. "Well, yes," Enid said.

"This is about the bones found at the inn, isn't it?"

"Do you know something about them?"

Miss Murray uncrossed her legs and held her hands in her lap. "I don't know anything."

"But do you have any thoughts or suspicions you can share with me?"

Miss Murray eyed Enid again. "You're no fool, are you, Ms. Blackwell?"

"Sometimes I feel foolish, but I hope I'm not a fool. Why do you ask?"

"We have a lot of fools in and around these parts, as I'm sure there are everywhere. With enough power and money, even fools are deemed to be normal."

"Are you talking about someone in particular?" Enid asked.

"As I said, I don't know anything, but if I were you, I'd look at the inn's history. You know, who lived there and worked there. The workers, in particular, are the sort that wouldn't have the connections needed to do an extensive search, should someone just up and disappear, you know."

Enid picked up her tote and fished in it for a business card. "Well, thank you for your time. If you think of anything, please give me a call." She handed the card to Miss Murray, who took it without glancing at it.

"Fools eventually reveal themselves. Take care of yourself, Ms. Blackwell. I hope you find who you're looking for."

CHAPTER 8

Theo Linard managed the Glitter Lake Inn with an efficiency of a five-star kitchen, mostly because he had been a chef in a Boston, Michelin-rated restaurant for years. The inn had never had problems filling reservations, but since Theo had taken over its operation, it stayed booked nearly a year out. Instead of offering only the usual breakfast and afternoon wine to guests, Theo served a different soup and homemade breads for lunch each day and opened the dining room to visitors for the mid-day meal. His take-out soups were so popular with locals that the inn consistently showed a profit for the first time in decades.

Enid drove up the long driveway to the old mansion, admiring its beauty. The previous owner had done extensive renovations throughout but had done nothing to the kitchen. Since these improvements were overdue, Theo had asked Jack to upgrade the appliances, wiring, and plumbing. A few construction workers milled around in the front yard. One was smoking a cigarette, and another was gulping a Mountain Dew. Enid smiled when she recalled the renovations she and Cade had done to their home in Charlotte, North Carolina, years before their divorce. One finish carpenter stood out from all the rest, because he was able to work magic with wood. He could recreate any molding or fit any two pieces of wood together seamlessly. Later, he confessed to Enid that he was an alcoholic, and the

Mountain Dew he seemed to always have nearby was half filled with vodka. When he began going to AA meetings, his work deteriorated, and he seemed unable to do the intricate work any longer.

Enid looked around to see if Cade's car was in the parking area but didn't see it. Cade was likely around town gathering information on Josh. But it was Theo she wanted to see today.

"Hello, Enid. How are you?" Theo asked as he kissed her on both cheeks, Euro style. "To what do I owe this honor?"

"I was wondering if I might spend some time in the library. I'm hoping to learn more about the inn's history."

"Of course, look at whatever you like. There are some very old materials there. Fascinating history. Is there anything in particular you need?"

Enid filled him in on her visit to Miss Murray.

"Ah, yes. Miss Murray is one of my best customers. She is particularly fond of my asparagus cream soup for her soirees."

"I don't want to keep you from anything, so I'll just look around on the shelves and see what I can find."

"Do you think the bones are someone who lived or worked here?"

"I have no idea. This search may not reveal anything, but it's worth trying. By the way, it looks like work has resumed on the kitchen."

"Yes, we had some people here from the University of South Carolina anthropology department taking soil samples. I'm not sure exactly what they were looking for. And the police gathered whatever evidence they needed.

Although, I understand there's not much to go on." He took Enid's hands in his. "You must stay for lunch. I insist."

"So your kitchen is operational again?"

"We're making do. The county inspector gave his approval on the upgraded gas line and electrical service so we could get the inn's kitchen operating again. They sealed off the room where the bones were found with plywood. Later, when the county sheriff's office gives us the go-ahead, an historically appropriate wall will be constructed."

"What about your new stove?"

Theo's face lit up with a smile. "It's been hooked up and approved for use. Jack also did a little persuading with the county inspector." His smile faded. "If it weren't for the sad discovery of that victim behind my kitchen, I would be thrilled."

• • •

The inn's library was impressive for a private home. It housed valuable, leather-bound first editions, as well as paperbacks guests had left behind. But Enid wasn't interested in the literary collection. She wanted to go through the volumes of photo albums and journals some of the previous owners had kept. Cassie, Enid's friend who had managed the inn before Theo, had been an avid journal keeper, but what Enid wanted was likely to be much older than those recent entries.

What was even more impressive about the library was that there was no dust hiding on the shelves. Theo had insisted on hiring a husband-wife team who helped keep the place in order, leaving his time free to focus on the guests and the food. The place was always immaculate.

For the next two hours, Enid poured through photos of the annual picnics hosted by the inn. Most of the pictures were of people standing by the lake, smiling, drinks in their hands. Notably, all the guests were white, mostly middle-aged or older. In one photo, a black man in a white jacket and dark bow tie was serving drinks on a silver tray.

She also recognized the previous police chief, Dick Jensen, along with his niece Madelyn. Another person showed up often in the photos. His back was usually turned to the camera, but in several images, his full profile was in view. Some of the photos were old and grainy, but it was easy to recognize the portly figure of Sheriff Boogie Waters. Considering how much he enjoyed good music with free food and drink, and not particularly in that order, Enid wasn't surprised to see him often in attendance.

She was about to close the last album when one of the photos caught her eye. Since it wasn't attached to a page, it appeared to have been tucked in the album later. A younger and slightly slimmer Boogie had his hand on the arm of a young woman. He seemed to be holding her at a distance, although he was smiling. She was not. But what caught Enid's eye was the color of the young woman's skin. She was black and not dressed in a servant's uniform, which made her an oddity in this setting. The other two people near them appeared to be engaged in their own conversation. Except that one of the women was casting a sideways stare at Boogie and the attractive woman.

Enid pulled out her phone and made a copy of the photo. It was probably nothing, other than just interesting.

She tucked the photo back in the album and replaced it on the shelf. The smell of fresh baked bread wafted from the kitchen. Theo had wasted no time trying out his new stove.

Cassie had once told Enid that most of the previous owners had kept journals. Each owner was expected to preserve as much history and stories of the inn as he could. It was easy to see from the journals' contents which owners enthusiastically accepted the responsibility and which ones made only obligatory entries. Cassie had been the first female owner, having inherited the inn, and Jack was now the only person in the line of succession who owned the inn but didn't manage it. He was also the first owner not in the family lineage.

When Cassie passed away and left the inn to Jack, he searched extensively for more suitable heirs but found the family had virtually died out. After investing time and money toward the search to no avail, Jack succumbed to the responsibility of keeping the inn operational. He didn't want to be the person who closed the inn after nearly a hundred years of operation. Enid made a note to talk to Theo about continuing the journaling tradition, as Jack was a hands-off owner and would have no opportunity or reason to document the inn's activities, special guests, and events.

A stack of journals sat on the top shelf of the bookcase. She pulled the mahogany library ladder toward her on its metal track and climbed up to retrieve the eclectic mixture of leather-bound volumes and less expensive journals. The handwriting in the older journals was ornate and articulate. As the dates progressed, the handwriting styles deteriorated, but at least they were still written in cursive. Enid mourned both the lost art of handwriting and the keeping of journals.

She understood the trend, however, as she hadn't written in her own journal for more than a year, and nowadays she was much more likely to grab her iPad instead of a notepad. What would the world be like in another fifty years? Enid shook her head to clear the thoughts and returned to her research.

She stacked the journals on the library table in chronological order. The oldest journal was dated 1900, and the inn had been built sometime around 1885, just twenty years after the Civil War ended. She made a note to ask Theo if he had seen any earlier ones. Without knowing the age of the bones that were found, it was hard to narrow her search. Cassie had once mentioned to Enid there was a lot of "stuff" in the inn's huge attic that she had intended to go through but never got around to. There were several time gaps between journals, which Enid noted. Perhaps those journals never existed or had been destroyed or were stuck in a chest in someone's home. Most of the journal entries were about parties, weddings, births at the inn or in the owner's family, and other events. A few entries noted the growing debt at the inn and the difficulty of staying afloat. But nothing that would help identify the bones found in the secret room behind the kitchen. Enid pushed the older volumes aside and focused on the newer ones.

She randomly started reading entries from about forty years ago. Renovations and rising operational costs were frequently mentioned. In most of the newer journals, the entries were monthly or even less frequent. While these owners were honoring the tradition, their entries lacked the insights the earlier ones revealed. Because of the infrequent postings, many of the volumes covered several years. The entries got shorter as time progressed, and Enid was tempted to abandon the idea of looking at the journals. She had gotten nothing for her efforts other than a dull headache. But she flipped through the pages and then went to the next journal.

The next book was one of the bigger volumes. The leather cover was a more modern design, and the quality wasn't as good as the older editions. The reddish-brown leather was dull and cracked from age. Instead of the traditional stitched binding, this one was glued and coming apart. Some of the pages had detached from the spine. The handwriting was written in a hybrid version of print and cursive. Different people appeared to have made the entries. Perhaps husband-wife owners had alternated this chore. This particular journal contained multiple entries about the Jensen family, who had, until a few years ago, been the most revered family in the area. A few years earlier, Enid had several encounters with then Police Chief Dick Jensen and witnessed firsthand the power of the Jensen dynasty.

As Enid flipped through the pages, references to a "trial" kept popping up. She turned back the previous pages until she found the beginning of these entries. Approximately ten years ago, someone had been on trial in Bowman County for murder. She began making notes.

A knock on the library door startled Enid. "Oh, Theo, it's you."

"Sorry to interrupt you, but lunch is being served if you'd like to join us."

Enid whiffed the smells coming from the kitchen. "I'm starved, but I think I'll keep working."

Theo looked disappointed. "I'll make you a container to take home. It'll be on the kitchen counter in case I'm busy when you leave."

Before Enid could thank Theo, he had left the room. As tempting as it was to stop and eat Theo's delicious meal with the inn's guests, she resumed taking notes. Her reporter's instincts had kicked in. Perhaps this trial had nothing to do with the bones, but one thing had jumped out in the journal. The body of the missing person had never been found.

CHAPTER 9

By the time Enid returned home, her eyes were dry and irritated from staring at journals all day, and her neck ached from leaning over the library table at the inn. She needed a hot shower.

Her phone rang just as she was about to step into the warm spray of water. Jack's name and cell number appeared on her screen. She was tempted to let it go to voicemail, but not only was he her best friend, he was also her boss.

"Hey, Jack. Sorry I've been out of touch today."

"I was worried about you. Did you check your messages?"

Enid had been so absorbed in her research at the inn that she had ignored any distractions. "No. Sorry. Why didn't you text me? Is everything okay?"

"You know I hate texting. But how about I answer that in person? I've got a great pinot grigio chilled. I'll stick it in the cooler along with some smoked salmon."

Enid hesitated briefly. All she really wanted was to shower and crash. "Sure, that sounds good."

"Be there about thirty minutes?"

"Yes, that's fine. And, Jack, while you're here, can we talk about what I found at the inn?"

"Of course. After all, I am the owner of the place where the bones were found, although I don't think of myself in that role, except when the repair, insurance, and tax bills are due." Jack sighed. "Oh, and don't forget you've got an article due tomorrow morning."

Enid groaned. "No, I didn't forget. See you soon."

• • •

Enid and Jack sat at the small table on her screened back porch that overlooked a small pond. Tea candles sat around the framing of the porch, casting flickering shadows.

"I really love this place," Jack said. "You've fixed it up nice."

"With a lot of help from my friends."

Jack raised his glass. "To Enid, a talented reporter and dear friend. May your life always be filled with love and laughter."

Enid tipped her wineglass to his and they laughed together. Not for the first time, she noted how comfortable she was with Jack. Over the past couple of years, they had settled into a comfortable relationship built on mutual respect and a common mission: finding the truth. She and Cade had once been that way.

While Jack talked about the possibility of selling his horse ranch, Enid's thoughts drifted to Josh. Where did he fit into all this? Or did he fit at all? Not too long ago, she had fantasized about their life together. But the realities of keeping boundaries between the local law enforcement and the local news had proved to be challenging. And now Cade's investigation was making their lives even more complicated. She wanted to believe Cade, just as she wanted to believe Josh. But she would keep an open mind on both men.

"Enid, what's going on in that head of yours?"

"I'm sorry. Too much on my mind tonight. Thanks for bringing the food and wine. It's delicious, and just what I needed."

"You said you wanted to talk about what you found today. Or would you rather get a good night's sleep and wait until you're up to it?"

Enid sipped the last bit of wine from her glass. "I'm fine. It's just that . . ."

"I haven't said anything about Cade being in town, but that must be upsetting, or at the least confusing, for you."

Jack's sympathetic tone brought tears to Enid's eyes. "Are you aware that he's investigating Josh?"

Jack rubbed his neck. His telltale sign of anxiety.

"Never mind," said Enid. "Of course you know. I keep forgetting there are no secrets in Madden."

"I've known Cade for a long time. As you know, we worked together on a couple of reporting gigs back in the day." Jack laughed. "He can be a self-righteous prick at times. But he's a good reporter." He paused. "And a decent guy, as far as I can tell. I think we can take him at his word until we learn anything to the contrary. Life has a way of thumbing its nose at us sometimes. Keeps us humble." Jack pushed his chair back slightly. "Now tell me what you learned today. I need to know. The rest of this stuff will work itself out."

Enid filled Jack in on her search at the inn, finishing with her discovery of the trial. "What do you know about the trial?"

"I remember reading about it. Happened here in Bowman County, as I recall. The victim was white, as I recall, and her boyfriend was black. That didn't go over too well around here. Anyway, I don't know anything other than her boyfriend was tried for her murder. Supposedly, he killed her because she was pregnant. What made the trial newsworthy was that the body was never found. I remember being surprised that the county prosecutor would try to convict someone without a body or more substantial evidence. But it worked."

"So the boyfriend was convicted?"

Jack nodded. "Life sentence, as I recall."

The fatigue that had debilitated Enid earlier had vanished. "Do you think the Madden news archives would have any information?"

"Maybe. We can look tomorrow. It would still be paper archives in storage. Local newspapers weren't too sophisticated about data storage. The *Madden Gazette* skipped right over microfilm and went from paper to digital. Besides, ten year ago, the fine citizens of Madden didn't care much about anything outside the town, so the story might not have even been carried here. Or it might have been a short paragraph or two. The *State* would be more likely to have good records on it."

"I'll check with them first."

Jack cocked his head slightly to the side. "Are you thinking this trial might be connected to the bones found at the inn?"

Enid put her napkin on the table and pushed back her chair. "Right now, all I know is that I need a good night's rest." Even as she said it, Enid knew sleep would be elusive.

CHAPTER 10

Since the Glitter Lake Inn was not actually in Madden, but on its outskirts, and far more private than Sarah's Tea Shoppe, Josh had agreed to meet Cade there. When Josh pulled into the gravel parking area beside the old mansion, he saw a nondescript four-door car with a black and green Enterprise logo on the bumper. Since it was probably Cade's car, Josh made a note of the make, model, and license plate number. Just in case he needed it later.

Josh flipped his notepad shut and put it back in his pocket. Time to get this little chat over with.

In the inn's entrance hall, Josh was met by the wife of the caretaker team. "Mr. Linard sends his regrets that he couldn't be here to greet you, but I'll be taking care of you and Mr. Blackwell during your meeting." She gestured toward the open library door. "You can meet privately in there. Mr. Blackwell is waiting, and I've put out coffee and muffins. Is there anything else you need?"

"Thanks. That'll be fine."

"I'll be in the kitchen if you need me." She walked so lightly that she appeared to float down the hallway.

Cade was sitting in an overstuffed leather chair, its hide mellowed with age, as only fine saddle leather can pull off. He stood to greet Josh and held out his hand. "Thanks for coming. I know you're a busy man. Please, have a seat."

Cade returned to his chair and Josh sat across from him in a wing chair upholstered in a hunter green velvet. "Coffee?"

"No, I'm good," Josh said. "Thanks."

"I know this is awkward for both of us. I'll be as brief, and as fair, as possible."

"Thanks," Josh said. "Enid speaks highly of your integrity."

"I typically record interviews. Is that okay with you?"

"Actually, I'd prefer that you not. But you are welcome to take notes."

"Sure, no problem." Cade slipped the small recorder back into his large canvas backpack. "I know Enid has filled you in on why I'm here, but I'd like to be sure you understand my motivation."

For now at least, Josh didn't think of Cade as the enemy, but things could change. Josh needed to know as much about Cade as Cade needed to know about him, so the two men were cautiously studying each other.

"A couple months ago, my senior editor at the Associated Press asked me to do an article on police vigilantism. I focused primarily on white cops strong-arming black or brown suspects, mostly gangbangers, dealers, and pimps who had managed to escape punishment. When the system failed to punish, the local police had their own code of justice. I gathered enough cases and information to write volumes of articles."

"I've never punished drug dealers and such by taking the law into my own hands."

"No, I'm sure you haven't. In fact, your record is stellar." Cade paused. "With this one exception."

Josh stiffened. "And what's that?"

"I got an anonymous tip one day that a former undercover agent in New Mexico had killed an unarmed man. Both men, the shooter and the victim, were Native American, so I decided to ignore it. The story, although intriguing, didn't fit the pattern for my articles."

"And besides, red men killing each other won't sell as many papers as white cops killing black thugs." Josh immediately regretted his own tone. He believed in the free press and had always cooperated to the extent that he could share information. But news coverage about Native Americans was mostly negative. The sad truth was his people were forgotten, often abused, and living in abject poverty, especially those still on the reservations.

"I didn't mean to offend. I was merely saying I didn't jump on this story immediately. And I didn't know you were involved or that you were seeing Enid, not until sometime later."

"So why did you decide to pursue this story?"

Cade put his pen down and looked at Josh. "Do you know what made me fall in love with Enid when we first met?"

Josh shifted his weight. This conversation with not going the way he had envisioned. "No," he said, shaking his head. Enid had shared very little with him about her former spouse.

"When we met in journalism school, we were both working on the campus newsletter, but we both freelanced for a local paper as well. Enid had a nose for finding a good story. That was impressive enough. But she also managed to find humanity in everything she wrote. If it was about a local robbery, she had to learn more about the perp's life and why he did it."

Josh smiled. "Yes, that's Enid. But what does she have to do with this tip you got?"

Cade picked up his pen again, poised to write. "This is where it gets interesting. While the man that called me talked about a cop going rogue, what I heard was really a great love story. A cop's wife tried to help Native American women with their legal issues, and the spouse of one of her clients killed her in a rage because she interfered in their personal business. But due to a legal technicality, the man got off. The man who shot the cop's wife in cold blood became a free man."

"The system isn't without its flaws."

"But that's not the story, is it?"

"So what is the story, in your opinion?" Josh asked.

"The cop allegedly killed his wife's killer. Was it a primal act of rage and revenge because the system failed? Or a poignant act of love? Or both?"

"You're sure it was an intentional shooting, like an act of . . ." Josh decided not to characterize the incident for Cade.

"There were no witnesses. Only hearsay and speculation."

"So how did this tipster know what happened?"

"It was a confidential tip. I can't discuss those details, as it might identify him."

"Sounds like the tipster may have been taking revenge also. Could be a hoax." Dozens of names went through Josh's head—people who would like to see him punished for sending them to jail.

"Maybe. But the guy said the cop resigned and left New Mexico, landed in a small town in South Carolina as a police chief."

"And then that cop became involved with your ex-wife." The cliché of "cutting the tension with a knife" popped into Josh's mind. "Because of my wife's murder, my resignation and leaving the state was reported in the Albuquerque Journal, so it wasn't a secret. And I'd be pretty easy to track here."

"Are you admitting the undercover policeman was you?" Cade reached over and poured himself a cup of coffee. "This inn has the best coffee." He added cream and stirred slowly.

Finally, Josh broke the silence. "What is it you want from me?"

"I'd just like to hear your side of the story."

Josh sat his coffee cup on the tray. "Just write a fair and balanced article—and be sure you get your facts straight. Isn't that what they teach you to do?"

Cade closed his notepad and put it in his backpack. "Much to my regret, Enid and I are history, at least as a couple. That doesn't mean I don't still love her and want her to be safe."

Josh smiled. "She can take care of herself. I found that out pretty quickly."

"Enid takes things seriously. Meaning, she's as committed to her relationships as she is to her job. Just remember that and don't hurt her or drag her into anything illegal, like lying for you." Cade paused. "Our marriage failed because I failed her. I will continue to investigate this story, and if and when you're ready to talk to me about it, you've got my cell number there on my business card. Call anytime. In the meantime, if I think Enid is in any danger because of you or your past, whatever that may be, don't think I won't hesitate to do whatever I can to bring you down."

Josh watched Cade walk out of the library, his stride long, his shoulders squared. Josh pushed an errant strand of hair from his eyes. A good haircut would solve that problem. But there was no quick fix for the rest of this mess.

CHAPTER 11

Enid sat in her office and logged onto the county library's NewsBank database. Since almost all articles were stored digitally now, accessing historical information about the missing woman and the resulting trial of her boyfriend would be relatively easy.

In about fifteen minutes, Enid had found the few scant articles related to this incident. Most of them focused more on the unusual nature of trying someone for murder without a body than it did on other details. She printed copies of the articles and put them in her folder. While it was fresh on her mind, she jotted some notes for herself. One thing she had learned was that the woman, Angelina Peterson, had been dating a man named Reggie Long for more than a year. According to the victim's brother, when the boyfriend found out she was pregnant, he got angry and claimed he wasn't the father. A few weeks later, the woman was reported missing by her brother in Bowman County. Sheriff Boogie Waters led the investigation.

After changing the search parameters and trying again, Enid found another article. Sheriff Waters was hailed as a "hero" for the boyfriend's quick arrest. It was an "ironclad" case, according to the sheriff because they had physical evidence to tie the man to the missing woman, who was presumed dead.

The photo of the missing woman's boyfriend revealed a young man who looked scared. He had repeatedly claimed he had nothing to do with the woman's disappearance and knew nothing about her being pregnant. His court-appointed attorney, Alonso Keen, declared that Sheriff Bernard Waters had "rushed to judgment" for the sake of headlines—and his upcoming re-election bid. Even though a black man was accused of killing his white girlfriend, racial tension was not mentioned but lurked between the lines.

Enid put her notes away. Perhaps it had happened exactly as the sheriff had claimed. Enid reminded herself that this case might not have anything to do with the bones found at the inn. On the other hand, even if it proved to have no connection to the bones, it would make an interesting follow-up article. People's perceptions changed, especially after ten years. It would be interesting to revisit the boyfriend's trial and conviction.

The first step was to talk to the boyfriend's attorney. In South Carolina, reporters are not allowed to interview prisoners, but she could do some digging around on him. Once she had more information, she wanted to talk to Sheriff Boogie Waters.

. . .

After leaving Columbia, Enid called Jack to check in. The grandson of one of Madden's prominent citizens, Mrs. Hathaway, had been awarded a scholarship to Clemson to study livestock maintenance. The Hathaway Farm had been modeled after their family's estate in Lancashire County, England. The family represented old money and, along with the Jensen family, were considered Madden royalty. Enid agreed to interview Mrs. Hathaway and to duly uphold the family's standing in the community.

The Madden Historical Society was Enid's next stop, and about thirty minutes later, she parked at its front door. There were no parking meters in Madden, at least not yet. The town council had considered it, but the older members insisted there was no need to change anything.

Inside, Enid was greeted by Roscoe. "Why, Ms. Blackwell. What a pleasant surprise. How can I assist you today?" He pushed his black-framed, retro-styled glasses up on his nose, his smile consuming his face.

"Do you know if Miss Murray is in today?"

Roscoe made a sweeping gesture with his hand toward the hallway. "She certainly is. Right down there in her office. And I'm sure she'll be delighted to see you. Have a nice day."

The door was closed, so Enid knocked lightly. "Miss Murray, it's Enid Blackwell. Do you have a minute?"

Hearing no sound inside, Enid decided Roscoe had been mistaken and that Miss Murray had stepped out. As she turned to leave, the hinges on the heavy door squeaked loudly. "Please come in. I was just pouring tea. Will you join me?"

"I'd love to." Enid followed Miss Murray into her office. Between two chairs, a tray held a teapot, two cups and saucers, cream, sugar cubes, and a small plate of butter cookies. "Were you expecting someone? I don't want to intrude."

"Oh, no, my dear. I just think it's depressing to put out only one place for tea, so I always add an extra. Sometimes I get lucky, like today, and get an actual visitor." Miss Murray poured cream in the cups before asking Enid, "You do take cream, I assume?"

While Enid did not, she didn't want to spoil her host's mood. "That's fine. Thanks."

After a few minutes of chatting about the weather, the Hathaway Farm, and other town news, Enid pulled out the copies of the articles she had printed from the *State's* archives. "Are you familiar with this trial?"

Miss Murray put on the half-frame reading glasses that hung around her neck. "Ah, yes. Such a tragedy."

"Are you referring to the trial? Or the victim?"

Miss Murray chuckled and removed her eyeglasses, letting them dangle from her neck again. "I like the way you think. Actually, the whole mess was a tragedy."

"Did you know either the victim or her boyfriend?"

"No, I didn't. I'm ashamed to say I know very few of our younger citizens, especially the non-white ones. My grandson says I live in a bubble. He works in the Research Triangle in Cary, North Carolina. Some kind of biochemical scientist. His husband is a Vietnamese photographer." Miss Murray shook her head. "He says I have a lot of catching up to do."

Enid weighed her next words carefully. "You are one of Madden's most respected citizens and the keeper of its history. The telling of that history is often influenced by many factors, like money, power—"

Before she could finish Miss Murray interrupted. "My dear, I'm not a fool. I might be an old white woman in a small Southern town, but I'm not cut off from reality, no matter what my grandson thinks. The truth is often blurred by both well-meaning and nefarious individuals. That's why you have a job, isn't it? To determine the truth as best you can."

Enid smiled. "Yes, it is. Then let me rephrase my question. Do you think this man killed his girlfriend?"

"Or was he framed? Isn't that your real question?"

"Perhaps. What do you know about Sheriff Boogie Waters?" Enid asked.

Miss Murray leaned back in her chair and briefly closed her eyes. "I dated Bernard Waters once, you know. He asked me to go to a movie in Columbia. We shared popcorn and then had dinner at Mary's Supper Club. It was a nice place over on Two Notch Road, but it's closed now." She opened her eyes again. "I thought we had a pretty good time, but he never called me again. Later, I found out he told someone I was boring. It crushed me, at the time." She shrugged. "Now, not so much." Miss Murray closed her eyes again, as if replaying a movie only she could see.

Enid waited for Miss Murray to refocus to their conversation. "Have you had any contact with Sheriff Waters since then?"

Miss Murray chuckled. "Oh, no. I follow whatever news about him gets reported in the newspapers, but no more than any other citizen would. My brief relationship with him is ancient history. In fact, I shouldn't have even brought it up. But, back to your question. What makes you think the boyfriend could have been framed?"

Enid took a deep breath. The question was simple; the answer was not. "I guess I've seen too many situations where small law enforcement agencies, many of which lack the personnel and experience to complete comprehensive investigations, often zero in on a suspect and fail to look beyond that person. Sometimes cases are simple and a speedy arrest is warranted. Other times, hasty and erroneous decisions are made."

"History has shown that power is obtained in two ways. One, the easy way, is through money and blood lines. That's pretty much how the Jensen and Hathaway families came to power in Madden. They had the most land and money."

"And the second way to gain power?"

"Brute force and bullying."

"What are you saying exactly? I mean, in relation to the sheriff."

"Bernard's daddy was sheriff before him. He used his office to clean up crime—and to enrich himself. We had some illegal operations around here, like bootleg whiskey, cock fighting, and pimping at truck stops. Most of the victims of these crimes were willing participants. But it made good headlines when the arrests were made."

"So how did he get rich or powerful arresting these criminals? I'm not sure I understand your point."

"If you follow these stories, these folks usually managed to get off with probation or a small fine. Few did actual jail time. Meanwhile, Sheriff Waters and his family seemed to be doing alright for themselves."

"I see. Just one more question. Do you know if the boyfriend, Reggie, is still in prison? Do you know anything further about him?"

Miss Murray began putting the tea cups on the tray, signaling an end to their meeting. "No, dear. I'm sorry, but I haven't followed the story."

Enid put her notepad and pen in her tote. "Well, thanks for the information. I appreciate your time—and the tea and cookies." As Enid was walking out the door of the historical society's office, Miss Murray stopped her. "Ms. Blackwell. I do applaud your quest for the truth. While I haven't followed this particular case in the news, I have followed your stories. You're making a name for yourself."

"Thank you."

"But you're also making yourself a target. People with something to hide are dangerous folks. Not that I have to tell you that. Just a reminder from an old woman. Be careful, my dear."

CHAPTER 12

Enid glanced at the time on her phone and saw that Josh had texted her while she had been at the historical society. They were going to an Empty Bowls event at the Glitter Lake Inn tonight to raise money for the soup kitchen where Theo had previously worked when he came to Columbia searching for his daughter. Several local artists had made ceramic soup bowls, which were for sale. Some were fairly simple and cost around twenty dollars, but some were exquisitely ornate and typically went for a hundred dollars or more. The bowls would be on display, where guests could bid on the bowl of their choice. Everyone who participated was then treated to unlimited helpings of Theo's famous chowders and soups, wine or other beverage, freshly baked breads, and heavenly desserts. All proceeds went to the soup kitchen to feed the homeless and the soup kitchen's patrons. Jack footed the food bill for the Empty Bowls event.

Josh's text reminded her that he was picking her up in a few hours. She had just enough time to do a little work, shower, and get dressed.

Thanks to Madelyn Jensen's clothing donations to Enid, she had several "little black dresses" in her wardrobe now. Although Madelyn was a good friend, Enid felt uneasy knowing that Cade would also be at the event, as he had mentioned he was invited. At any rate, Enid and Cade were divorced now, so she had no reason to stand between Madelyn and her ex-husband if there was any spark there.

Enid finished her notes from the conversation with Miss Murray. What had she learned that she didn't already know? Not much, other than Boogie preferred women more exciting than the historian. Hardly a crime or evidence of framing someone. But she still wanted to check into Boogie's past. Josh wouldn't be happy if he found out what she was up to. Keeping secrets from Josh made her uncomfortable. But, because of their work and the inherent conflicts, it was necessary for both of them.

After finishing her notes, she texted Jack to ask if he was going to the Empty Bowls event. Jack and Madelyn had dated off and on, mostly off lately. They had not argued or had any problems, but they lived in different worlds. Jack was happy in his cowboy boots, tending his ranch where he had once boarded horses. Before his quasi-adopted daughter Rachel had left for college to study cyber forensics, she had helped him tend the ranch and care for the horses, but without her there to help, he had stopped taking boarders. Now, he focused exclusively on the *Tri-County Gazette*. News was in his blood, and he had won awards at a large Chicago newspaper before coming to Madden. He told Enid he had tried several times to retire, but the allure of reporting had overcome him.

Jack responded by text that he would be attending, so this would be an interesting night. Unlike Madelyn, Jack hated parties, small talk, and fundraising. But sometimes opposites make good bedfellows. The focus was supposed to be the charity, but Madelyn's attendance would certainly shake things up.

. . .

Josh bought two Empty Bowls for himself and Enid that reflected their characters: sturdy and not-too-fancy. His was dark green, the color of a pine forest. Enid's was the color of eggplant, with touches of yellowish gold and brown around the rim. Josh immediately filled his bowl with Theo's famous tomato-based fish chowder. Enid opted for the shrimp and corn chowder.

As expected, Madelyn was the center of attention, other than the spread of food, of course. She purchased the most expensive bowl for five hundred dollars, although Enid never saw her eat anything the entire night. Instead, Madelyn went from guest to guest, shaking hands and finding a disarming and discreet way to ask for their votes.

As the police chief, Josh was also obligated to make the rounds, talking to the locals and introducing himself to the large number of attendees from Columbia and other parts of the state who didn't know him. He was less comfortable than Madelyn in this political role. The few times Enid caught his eye, she tried to convey with a smile that she was proud of him. And she was. Josh cared about Madden's citizens and, as far as Enid could tell, had impeccable principles and values. Cade would learn this about Josh, too, she was sure. Yet, for Cade to come to Madden meant something wasn't adding up.

Enid refilled her wine glass and walked out on the porch to get some air. The gentle sounds of nighttime were a soothing antidote against the chatter inside. A few of the hundred or more guests had started to leave. The crowd wasn't particularly diverse, which was usual at such events in this area, so when the young black woman walked out onto the porch, she caught Enid's eye. There was something in the way she carried herself that seemed familiar. "Thanks for coming. I hope you enjoyed it," Enid called out. The woman seemed startled, as though she had not noticed Enid sitting in one of the porch rockers. The woman turned to face Enid and the two women locked eyes.

Had Enid's wine glass not been supported by the arm on the rocker, she would probably have dropped it. The woman ran down the steps toward her car.

"Wait," Enid called out and she ran toward the woman. "Please. Stop."

The woman turned to face Enid. "Hello, Ms. Blackwell."

Enid stood back several feet, as she didn't want to alarm the woman any further. "Good to see you again. You look a lot younger than you did when you came to my office. In costume."

The woman dropped her head slightly. "I'm sorry for concealing my identity. I just wanted to make you curious enough to follow up on our conversation."

Enid held out her hand. "You know my name. Now, what's yours?"

The woman took Enid's hand. "My name is Phyllis."

"So why the charade? Not only were you in costume, you spoke in riddles that day. Was that part of the game?"

"I know you're upset with me, and I don't blame you. I was afraid that if you knew who I was, you might not listen."

"Why is that?" Enid asked. "Who are you exactly?"

"I teach English and drama at Waters Middle School. I'm also a pottery artist and donated two of my bowls for this event. That's why I'm here." She smiled. "It's rewarding to see people appreciating your work."

"That doesn't sound too sinister. So why didn't you think I'd listen to you?"

"You wouldn't understand, but I've spent a lifetime being afraid to speak up. I'm also the sister of the man who went to prison for murdering his missing girlfriend. But he didn't do it."

Enid felt like someone had hit her in the stomach. "That's interesting." Enid took a deep breath. "Can we talk, later I mean? And this time, no games." She pulled a business card from her tote. "Here's my personal cell number. Call me tomorrow."

Phyllis put the card in her purse and nodded. "Goodnight, Ms. Blackwell." She opened the car door but turned back to Enid. "My brother didn't do what they said. I need for you to help me prove that."

CHAPTER 13

Enid walked into the Richland County coroner's office in Columbia. After signing in, she took a brochure from the rack and read about their operations. While she was reading, a relatively young man, at least younger than she had expected, came into the lobby to greet her.

"I'm Dr. Vents, Steve Vents. Come on back."

Enid followed him down the hallway to a room where bones were laid out on a stainless-steel table. "Thank you for agreeing to see me."

"Of course. Always glad to educate the public on what we do here." He pointed to the bones. "These remains were found at a construction site. We're trying to identify them, so they can either be returned to the family or properly interred."

"What happens if you can't identify the remains?"

"Eventually, they'll be buried in an unmarked grave, if they are never claimed."

Enid looked at the bones carefully arranged across the lab table. "Why are the pieces so small?"

"This person was cremated. Modern cremation methods would have reduced this person to mere ash, but years ago, larger bone fragments survived the process." He pointed to a group of similar fragments. "These are all skull bones." He pointed to the jagged edges and explained their particular characteristics. He pointed to another group of bones. "These are probably from the ribcage." Pointing to the next group, he added, "And these are likely leg bone fragments."

"This looks like putting a jigsaw puzzle together. Some of these pieces are smaller than an inch long."

Dr. Vents smiled. "Exactly. We have a young woman, an intern from the University of South Carolina anthropology department, who is helping us with the work."

"How often do you partner with the university on identification work?"

"If it's a large project, for example, where an entire cemetery is discovered, we'll work with them. Or if it's a particularly challenging project, we might consult with them. I'm also a guest lecturer at USC, so we work closely together."

Enid looked down at the bones again. "Can you do a DNA analysis on a cremated body?"

"Hopefully. That kind of analysis is fairly new, and there's some interesting work being done in the field."

Enid flipped a page in her notebook and continued taking notes. "What can you learn from a DNA analysis?"

"We get a biological profile that includes age, race, and sex. We run that information against the FBI database. We also post the information in NamUs. If we're lucky, we get a hit and can identify the person. If not, then we have to rely on other means to identify the remains. But you had questions about a specific case, I believe. How can I help you?"

Enid told Dr. Vents about the bones found at the inn.

"We haven't been called in on that one, at least not yet. Bowman County, where your bones were found, is a much smaller agency than Richland County. They have to rely on

SLED for their analysis or ask for assistance from a larger county, like Richland, Greenville, or Charleston. If the need is urgent, we're often called in to assist. SLED has to serve the entire state, and as you might imagine, they get backed up at times."

"What kind of investigation would be done at the scene?"

"Of course, we're talking hypothetical here. I can tell you what's typically done, but not in this specific case."

"Of course, I understand."

"We would send out crime scene investigators to process the area. They would take soil samples and we would do a lab analysis."

"What can you learn from the soil?"

"A lot, actually. For example, soil samples can indicate whether the person died in that same spot or if the body was dumped. The soil is like a sponge and would absorb body fluids and other chemicals."

Enid looked up from her notepad. "What kind of chemicals?"

"Poisons or other toxins."

"I know you're busy, so just one last question. For the bones found at the inn, will they be able to determine the cause of death?"

"Without seeing the actual bones, I can only speculate. If there's soft tissue left on the bones, definitely. But you said they were dry bones, so unless there's a skull fracture, broken ribs, or a bullet or knife nick on the bones, or unless something shows up in the soil analysis, it would be difficult. The cause of death would simply be listed as undetermined."

Enid thanked Dr. Vents and returned to her car. Before starting the engine, she sat there a moment, reflecting on what she had learned. She had to get more information about those bones from the inn. This time she wasn't going through Josh.

She looked for a number in her contacts. After three rings, a man answered. "Sheriff Waters' office. How may we help you?"

CHAPTER 14

Boogie Waters sat at his desk across from Enid. "I must admit, Ms. Blackwell, I was surprised when you called for an interview. Being that you're Josh's girl, I figured he'd tell you whatever you wanted to know."

Enid stiffened. "Thank you for seeing me."

Boogie chuckled. "So what can I do for you?"

"I'd like to know more about your department's investigation into the identity of the bones found at Glitter Lake Inn. Has any progress been made?"

Boogie appeared to be studying Enid. He reminded her of Senator Sam Ervin from North Carolina, who investigated the Watergate scandal. Boogie had that same "I'm just a country lawyer" air about him. But his eyes told a different story. "Well, of course we've made progress. This department is partnering with SLED—that's the State Law Enforcement Division. You know, since you're not from around here, didn't know if you were aware of that."

Enid nodded. "Yes, I'm aware of SLED. Please go on."

"We're working with SLED to do a DNA analysis."

Enid had studied her notes from the meeting with Dr. Vents and was glad she had done her homework. "Have you received any information from the soil analysis?"

Boogie's smile faded. "Those are old bones, as you know."

"Yes, but it's my understanding there's a lot to be learned from the soil around the remains. You know, decomp material or the absence of it, poisons or other toxins." Enid stifled a smile when Boogie looked surprised.

"Yes, well, the results are not in yet."

"Do you have any idea of the age of the bones?"

Boogie repositioned himself in the big wooden chair. "As I said, we don't know anything yet." He smiled broadly. "This department cooperates with the press, and we'll be happy to provide any information when it's available." He leaned forward and lowered his voice. "Unless you get it from Josh first."

"And when do you expect those results?"

"That depends on SLED's workload. Could be a week. Could be several weeks. Can't really say at this point."

Enid slammed her notepad shut. "Thank you for your time, Sheriff Waters." She stood to leave. "Oh, by the way, is Waters Middle School named after your family?"

Boogied looked surprised. "Well, yes, actually. My father contributed the land it's built on. Why do you ask?"

Enid shrugged. "No particular reason. I just met a teacher who works there. When she mentioned the name of the school, I was just curious, that's all."

Boogie ran his hand through his silver mane. "I know quite a few of the teachers there. Who did you talk to?"

"I'm afraid I can't reveal a source. You understand, I'm sure."

Boogie stood up abruptly. "I think we're finished here. Couple things I need to take care of, but you have a nice day now."

• • •

Enid had agreed to meet Phyllis at the McDonald's near Waters Middle School. The fast-food restaurant wasn't an ideal setting, but there wasn't much else nearby. Enid had just ordered an unsweetened iced tea when Phyllis came in and joined her at a booth. "Sorry I'm late. One of my students needed help on an assignment."

"You're not late at all. Thanks for coming. Do you want something to eat or drink?"

Phyllis shook her head.

"I'm happy to talk with you," Enid said, "but I need to make one thing clear. I am not agreeing at this point to investigate your brother's case. I'm a reporter, not a private eye. Contrary to what you might see in the movies or read about, most of my work is pretty mundane. I attend community events and engagement parties and write about everyday things in the tri-county area. The more prominent the family, the more I write about them. If a company buys an ad, they get special coverage of their company picnic. That's just the way it is. Occasionally, I get to write about a break-in or a domestic dispute that ends up with someone arrested. All pretty common stuff for a weekly newspaper. The stories about the two cold cases I solved were exceptions. Understand?"

"Yes," Phyllis said, nodding.

"Just because I'm here doesn't mean I'm committed to doing a story for you. I'll do some preliminary research, and then my editor and I will decide if it's something we need to report on."

"Okay." Phyllis dropped her gaze, staring at her hands in her lap.

"I don't mean to sound harsh or uncaring, but since those articles were published . . . well, you know what I mean. I'm just a weekly reporter who gets lucky sometimes."

Phyllis smiled for the first time. "Don't sell yourself short, Ms. Blackwell. But I do understand what you're saying. All I ask is that you hear me out and then decide if justice has been done." She paused. "And I apologize again for misleading you when I came to see you. I was just scared, too scared to come as myself."

"Fair enough. When we talked at the inn, you said your brother was in prison for killing his girlfriend." Enid put copies of the articles about the trial on the table. "I assume this is the case you're referring to."

Phyllis nodded. "Yes, that's his case. But my brother is no longer in prison. He caught pneumonia, or so they said, and died not long after being incarcerated."

"I'm sorry for your loss. And that also presents a problem. Without being able to talk with him, I'm not sure how we'll be able to get all the facts and clear his name posthumously."

Phyllis nodded. "I understand the situation, but we can try, can't we?"

"We never like to believe those closest to us are capable of anything like this. What makes you so sure he's innocent?"

"They never checked his alibi or tried to look at anyone else. It's almost like they wanted him to be guilty from the beginning."

"Who's 'they'?"

Phyllis glanced around the nearly empty restaurant. A couple of teenage girls sat in a booth, smirking conspiratorially about something on one of their phones. An elderly man sat behind them, munching on fries slathered in ketchup. "The Bowman County Sheriff's Department," Phyllis whispered.

"Specifically, do you mean Sheriff Waters?"

Phyllis nodded.

"Look, Phyllis. I've only had a couple of brief encounters with him. I admit he's a throw-back to an era when the county sheriff was king. He rubs me the wrong way sometimes, too. But I don't have enough information to doubt his integrity or motives. I need something more substantial from you if you expect me to take your allegations seriously." Enid paused. "I want to help you, but I also don't want to get your hopes up."

Phyllis made direct eye contact before she spoke. "My brother Reggie did make a serious mistake, but it wasn't murder." She paused, appearing to collect her thoughts. "He dated a girl, a white girl, who was known around town as Angel. She supposedly got the nickname from being 'heavenly' in bed. But then, that's just gossip. When I learned Reggie was dating her, I confronted him."

"How old was your brother at the time?"

"He was twenty. Angel was a bit older."

Enid scribbled a note on her notepad. "I can understand why you were worried about your brother. He was dating an older woman with a questionable reputation."

"All that's true. But that's not why I warned him to stay away from her." Phyllis chewed on her bottom lip as she paused. "Angel got around, but it was who she was seeing that worried me." Phyllis looked around the restaurant again. "I'm sorry, I'm just not sure this is the right thing to do. It's not that I don't trust you, it's just that . . ."

Enid refrained from pushing Phyllis to get to the point. The woman was obviously distressed and needed to process her thoughts. Enid put her pen down. "You came to me, so if you're not comfortable telling me what happened, I understand. I'll tear up my notes and this meeting never happened."

Phyllis' eyes widened. "No, please don't do that. I mean, you're my last hope. I need to tell you, for Reggie's sake."

Enid cringed at the idea of being anyone's last hope. That's how she had gotten involved in two stories that had cost innocent lives. Enid knew all too well that law enforcement agencies often made mistakes, although not always intentionally. Lack of training, heavy workloads, and human bias were often to blame. Although, in this case, the reason for Reggie's guilty verdict could be something else—something more sinister. "Who was Angel seeing?"

"Mind you, much of what I'm telling you was just the talk around town, so to speak. But we're a small community, and much of the gossip you hear is either true or mostly true."

"I understand. Go on."

"Angel dated deputies at the Bowman County Sheriff's Department."

"Was Angel a prostitute?"

"If you're asking if they paid her money, then no. But she got paid in other ways. No matter what kind of trouble her family got into, they seemed to walk away scot-free."

"So in return for Angel's heavenly treats to the sheriff's department, the family was protected."

"That's right."

Enid rubbed her temples with her fingertips. "Whew. I must say, this is a lot to take in. Is there anyone who can corroborate your allegations?"

"No one that will talk. And the guys who were involved are either retired or moved on." Phyllis leaned forward slightly. "Look, even though it was just ten years ago, it was a different era then. Things were, let's say, tolerated in law enforcement then that might not be overlooked today. And all of the deputies were white then, so no black person would dare come forward to accuse them."

"None of this explains why you came to see me in disguise, spouting riddles."

"When I said things are different now, that's not totally true. Black people like me are still afraid of interacting with the police. I wanted to get your attention but not get involved." She paused. "And I do realize how shallow and cowardly that sounds. I apologize."

"What about the riddles, all that stuff about seven crows?"

"Honestly, I don't know. My mother used to recite that nursery rhyme to me when I was a child. After Reggie went to prison, she would sit in her rocker, going back and forth, reciting it over and over. All I can remember is 'seven for a secret, never to be told.' When I asked her about it, all she said was beware of seven crows. You need to understand that when Reggie was convicted and went to prison, my mother was never the same." Phyllis looked out the window and blinked her eyes several times. "She passed a couple years ago. I was thinking about her the day I came to see you, and I just said what popped into my head. I was nervous and didn't know what else to say."

"I'm so sorry for your loss. Your family has been through a lot." Enid flipped through her notes. "Tell me about Reggie's conviction—how he ended up in prison."

"When I warned Reggie that he was a young black man dating a white woman who provided sexual favors to white policemen, he told me Angel was really a nice girl and just wanted a friend."

"Your brother sounds like he was a sensitive, if not a sensible, young man."

Phyllis smiled slightly. "He was a dreamer. Wrote poetry all the time."

"Do you still have any of his work?"

Phyllis shrugged. "It's probably around somewhere. I hadn't given it much thought until now. Anyway, Reggie kept seeing Angel despite my warnings. And then one day he told me she had left town. Less than a month later, he was arrested for her murder."

"If she just disappeared, why did the police assume she was murdered? Was there any evidence linking Reggie to a crime?"

Phyllis sighed. "I'm afraid so. They found her bloody underwear in his car, under the seat. But he swore to me it had to have been planted there."

"I remember reading something about physical evidence linking him to the crime. Did they do a DNA analysis?"

"Yes, and it was Angel's blood," Phyllis said.

"If you don't believe Reggie killed her, then who do you think did it?"

"I don't know enough to name a specific person, but I know Reggie did not kill her. And I'm sure Sheriff Waters knew that."

Enid put her pen down. "Why do you think the county sheriff's department would deliberately frame Reggie?" Enid rubbed her temples again.

"Because they didn't want the real killer identified."

Enid pulled an article from her folder and pointed to the headline: "Bones Found at Glitter Lake Inn."

Phyllis stared at the headline briefly before looking up to meet Enid's gaze. "That's why I contacted you. I think those are Angel's bones."

CHAPTER 15

Josh reared back in his desk chair at the police station. Twice he had put his hand on the phone to call his old police captain in New Mexico, who was now retired. And twice, he stopped short. He pushed back his chair and called out to Pete at the front desk. "I need to make a personal phone call. I'll be out back if you need me."

"No problem, Chief. Got you covered."

Josh mused about why so many people responded to everything with "no problem." What did that mean exactly and how did the phrase become so popular? He walked out the heavy steel door separating the small area that housed two cells, both empty now, from the outside. The door was always kept locked from the inside. "Bolt this door behind me. I'll come back in the front."

"No problem," Pete called out.

Josh sat at the wooden picnic table behind the police station. When it was originally donated to the station by one of the Madden citizens, its purpose was to provide a place for the deputies to take a smoke break. Now that almost no one smoked, it was rarely used, other than for the occasional office picnic on pretty spring days. The wood was nearly bleached white by the harsh summer sun, and a fire ant colony had built a large mound right under it. Josh was careful not to get near it.

He scrolled through his contacts until he found the number and tapped it. Several rings later, a woman answered. "Hello."

"This is Joshua Hart, police chief in Madden, South Carolina. I'm looking for Captain Walsh."

"I remember you, Josh. I'm Mildred, his wife. Good to hear from you."

"Likewise, Mrs. Walsh. I hope you and the captain are doing well."

"I'm sorry, Josh. I thought you knew. Cappie died about six months ago. Stomach cancer."

"No, I didn't know. I'm very sorry for your loss." Josh felt like he had just stepped into a black abyss. It was like hearing his own father had died.

"I'm sorry you didn't get to say goodbye." There was a brief silence before she continued. "Is there anything I can help you with?"

"No, thanks. I just needed to run something past him. Do you need anything? Is there anything I can do for you?"

"No, dear. I'm just fine. A bit lonely at times, that's all. Good to talk to you. You take care." She hung up.

Josh walked around to the front of the police station. When he went inside, Pete was staring at the computer screen, as usual. Josh relied more on instinct and experience than on technology, but it was no doubt that officers like Pete were the future of law enforcement.

"I'm going up to see Sheriff Waters. He may need some help on the bones case."

"Okay, Chief. No problem."

Josh smiled and shook his head. "Right. No problem."

• • •

Sheriff Bernard Waters was drinking coffee at his desk when Josh arrived. "I could smell that coffee from the parking lot. Whew!"

Boogie's face lit up with a smile. "That's why we don't need no capital punishment here. We just pour 'em a cup of coffee." The two men embraced in a man hug.

"What brings you up here? Life too boring in Madden?"

Josh sat in the chair in front of Boogie's desk. "Yeah, but I kinda like boring. I wanted to talk to you about something, if you've got a minute."

Boogie sat his coffee cup on the desk. "Of course. What's on your mind? Want a soda or some water? That is, if you're too much of a wuss to handle my coffee."

Josh waved his hand. "I'm good."

"Then let's have it. Spill your guts."

Josh hadn't rehearsed what he was going to say. The two were close, and Josh assumed it would be an easy conversation. But now, he wasn't sure where to start. "Serena was a good woman."

"So you've told me. Sorry I never got to meet her."

"But we should never have married. I've spent many a sleepless night, tossing and turning, and thinking about her. We were opposites in almost every way, and I guess that's why we were attracted to each other."

Boogie chuckled. "I get that. Sometimes it works, but sometimes the differences become magnified over time and tug at the marriage."

"I often ask if she were alive, would we still be married?" Josh clasped his hands and stared at his feet. "I think we would have. And that, oddly enough, makes it even harder for me to accept what happened." Josh's chest tightened to the point that he was having problems breathing.

"You said the husband of one of her clients shot her. Too bad I didn't get a chance to confront that SOB."

"Serena was infatuated with the reservation. Where others saw poverty and desperation, she saw history and beauty. Native American men who have never had a life off the rez often become alcoholics and have a misogynistic view of the world. They can't find work and eventually get into trouble. Wives were often regarded as property, Serena didn't understand that by helping that man's wife get away from him, she had, in essence, stolen from him. Mind you, I'm not saying I agree with that viewpoint, but I know it exists. And I also know she was trying to do what she thought was right."

"You said the man was arrested and tried. Right?"

Josh nodded. "The tribal police arrested him on the reservation and held him a week before calling in the FBI, who had jurisdiction for murder on the reservation. The tribal police knew better but claimed it was just an oversight by an inexperienced tribal cop. The man's attorney argued the detention was illegal and violated his civil rights. He got him off."

Boogie shook his head. "That just don't sound right. It's a shame."

"The feds committed to look into it further, but nothing came of it."

"Where's this guy now?"

"Six feet under. Got himself shot after he was released."

Boogie laughed. "Well, now, that's poetic justice if I ever heard it. Good for the bastard that took that scum off the street."

Josh stared at his feet again, silent.

"Uh oh. I don't care for that look. Perhaps the obvious question here is 'Did you do it?'"

Josh waited briefly before responding. "I was responsible."

"What the hell does that mean?"

"For one thing, I should've stopped her from working on the reservation."

"You couldn't have known what would happen," Boogie said.

"I'll fill you in on the rest of it later. Right now, the less you know, the better off you'll be until all of this is settled."

"How long ago did this happen?"

"Several years back. Right before I came here."

"So what's going on now that brings all this to the surface?"

Josh filled Boogie in on Cade's trip to Madden and his investigation into police vigilantism.

"Crap, man. That sounds like one of those Lifetime movies on TV. Police chief falls in love with local reporter, whose ex-husband comes to town to expose an old murder." Boogie took a sip of the cold coffee on his desk and made a face. "Ugh. Just let me know the date and what channel this movie is on."

"Sure thing." Josh managed to smile wanly. "I'm thinking of going back to New Mexico to settle a few things. I guess I knew this day would come. I'll probably be gone a month, at least. But if you need backup on this bones case, I'll delay my trip."

"Oh, hell no, son. You do whatever you need to do to put this thing behind you. I'll keep an eye on Pete. Guess he'll be running the show for you. Don't you worry about anything here."

"Thanks, man. I appreciate it. While I'm here, can you fill me in on the bones investigation?"

"Not much to tell. The bones are at SLED, but they're backlogged. So we're just waiting."

"Can't imagine they're too excited about old bones, what with all the new stuff coming in," Josh said. "Any idea yet how old the bones are?"

Boogie threw up his hands. "Can't tell anything until they do the analysis. Might be a few weeks or more before we get the results."

"Do you have any theories of your own?"

"We're still checking all the missing persons reports and with the nearby towns. Nothing has turned up yet."

Josh stood up to leave. "Listen, don't say anything about my going to New Mexico. I've got to talk to Pete, Enid, and few other folks, including the mayor."

"Good luck with that. That new mayor, I hear she's a pistol."

"She's alright. Just a bit impatient. Wants everything done yesterday."

"I hear 'ya. Keep me posted on the outcome of this trip. It'll all work out. You got a good heart."

CHAPTER 16

Enid assumed finding Reggie Long's defense attorney, Alonso Keen, would be easy. And it was. The first thing that popped up on her search screen was his obituary. Apparently, Keen died a year earlier from sudden cardiac arrest. His wife, Ophelia Keen, lived in Columbia, and a quick online search revealed a phone number.

Enid called the number and a recording said the number was no longer in service. She looked at the time on her phone. She had time to get to Columbia before dark.

About forty-five minutes later, her phone navigation announced she had arrived at her destination. The house was in an older part of Columbia, not too far from uptown. The house was a two-story brick with ivy growing up the front of it. The yard was meticulously maintained, and a Range Rover was in the driveway.

Enid got a business card from her tote and walked to the front door. When no one answered the doorbell, she knocked on the door. No one appeared to be at home, so Enid pulled out a pen to write a note on her card. The oak door opened, a heavy chain allowing only a small crack, and a woman peered out. "Who are you and what do you want?" the woman asked.

"I'm Enid Blackwell, a reporter for the *Tri-County Gazette*." She offered her card through the door opening. "I'm trying to locate Ophelia Keen, the widow of Alonso Keen."

The woman studied the card and then looked up at Enid. "Why are you looking for her?"

"I'm doing some research on a case Attorney Keen handled, and I was wondering if Mrs. Keen might be able to help me. He represented a young African-American man accused of killing his girlfriend in Bowman County. It was an unusual case, because the victim's body was never found."

The door shut, and Enid heard the chain guard sliding. The door opened. "I'm Ophelia. You're welcome to come in if you'd like." Enid followed her to a formal living room that looked like a spread in Southern Living.

"You have a beautiful home, Mrs. Keen."

"Please, call me Ophelia. And thank you. My late husband and I spent a lifetime making this house our home. Now that he's gone, it's just a house again." She sighed. "Please have a seat." She motioned to a sofa upholstered in a gold damask material. "And then tell me how you think I might help you."

After Enid settled on the sofa, Ophelia sat across from her in a large French-style chair, similar to one Enid had admired in a store once, although it was too formal for her needs. "I'm sorry for your loss." She paused. "Do you recall the case?"

"I do. In fact, I was my husband's law office manager during the time he represented that young man."

"His name was Reggie Long," Enid said.

Ophelia nodded. "Yes, I remember him. A nice young man. My husband tried to persuade Reggie to hire a white attorney, but his family insisted on hiring Alonso." Ophelia looked down and shook her head from side to side. "That was a sad, sad situation."

"I am aware of attorney-client privilege, but I thought since both Reggie and your husband are dead you might feel free to talk to me."

Ophelia's eyes widened. "I didn't realize Reggie died. When? How?"

"He died of pneumonia while in prison. What I need to know is if there's anything about the trial that your husband mentioned, or that you might have observed, that would make you doubt the trial or verdict was fair."

Ophelia clasped her hands. "First, I want to know why you're writing about this trial, and then I'll decide if I need to help you. If you're about to do something that would cast doubt on Alonso's good name, then I will decline."

"Fair enough." Enid then told Ophelia about the bones being discovered at the inn and Phyllis' claim that the bones were Angelina Peterson's.

When Enid finished talking, Ophelia took a deep breath, so deep her shoulders rose nearly to her ears. "I don't know about you, but I need a drink. May I offer you something?"

"No, I'm fine thanks."

Ophelia left the room momentarily and returned with a cut crystal whiskey glass in her hand. "Before Alonso died, I never touched this stuff. And I still don't drink often. But sometimes, I'm hit with memories that are just too heavy to handle." She laughed. "I realize how pathetic that sounds." She sipped from the glass and set it on the table. "Reggie's case was troubling to Alonso . . . for many reasons. Mind you, he didn't tell me everything about his cases, but I knew this one was keeping him up at nights."

"What was so disturbing about Reggie's case?"

"I think what bothered him the most was that Reggie was so sincere and credible. Alonso wasn't gullible, and he knew he had to keep an open mind about Reggie." She paused. "But Alonso believed him."

"Other than his gut feelings about Reggie, what made Mr. Keen uneasy about the case?" Enid asked.

Ophelia took a sip of whiskey. "All the witnesses against Reggie were somehow connected or related. He told me at one time that the case felt like a conspiracy between the sheriff's department and the victim's family, especially her brother. But, of course, Alonso had no proof."

Enid scribbled notes on her pad. "Did Mr. Keen ever mention Sheriff Waters specifically in relation to this case?"

Ophelia shook her head slowly from side to side. "That was what hurt Alonso the most. He had always said that Sheriff Waters was not a perfect man, but at least he was an honest one."

"Are you saying Sheriff Waters wasn't honest about this case?"

Ophelia took another sip. "I don't know. All I know is that Alonso went to him about the evidence found in Reggie's car."

"You mean the bloody underwear?" Enid asked.

Ophelia nodded. "He was convinced Reggie was telling the truth, and anyone could have put it there."

"How's that?"

"Reggie drove a Jeep Wrangler, you know, one of those with the soft top. All you had to do was unzip the window to get in."

"What did Sheriff Waters say when Mr. Keen confronted him?"

"The sheriff was sure his men would never do such a thing."

"Did Mr. Keen believe him?"

Ophelia smoothed the creases in her black silk slacks. "I don't want to speak for Alonso." Ophelia stood. "I don't mean to be rude, Ms. Blackwell, but there's nothing else I can tell you. I'm sorry for the tragedy of Reggie's life, but what's done is done. My husband did all he could to help Reggie and filed an appeal, but it was denied. Life isn't always fair."

Enid stood to leave. "Thank you for your time. I'm sorry to make you relive those memories. Take care, Mrs. Keen."

CHAPTER 17

Enid and Jack sat in the small conference room at the newspaper office. She had spent the last hour filling him in on what she had learned so far.

"So you evidently think there's something about Boogie worth investigating," Jack said.

"I don't really know at this point. But based on what Reggie's sister Phyllis and Mrs. Keen told me, there's reason to doubt Boogie's integrity. On one hand, he is an effective sheriff. By that I mean, he usually catches the bad guy. The crime rate is lower in his county than in many others."

"And on the other hand?" Jack asked.

Enid laughed. "He's a chauvinist who loves to goad at me about my relationship with Josh. I don't think he approves of me, for Josh, I mean." Her smiled faded. "And he may have helped frame an innocent man, or at least looked the other way."

"Granted, Boogie Waters is about as old-school as they come. But I've never heard of any serious scandal. Then again, I'm not from around here, so I missed some of the history, and I've never had a reason to investigate him."

"It's funny about Madden. Everyone here has been welcoming and friendly. But I do sense at times that I'll always be an outsider," Enid said.

Jack laughed. "Maybe that's not all bad."

"If you're not busy, can you help me do some research on Boogie?"

"Sure. Anything in particular you're looking for?"

"No, just poke around a bit." She pulled up the copy of the photo on her phone that she had taken from the inn's photo album. "I'd like to know who this woman is with Boogie."

Jack took her phone and spread the photo with his fingers to enlarge it. "Could this be Phyllis?"

"Look at Boogie. He's got to be at least twenty years younger in that picture. Phyllis isn't old enough."

"So let me get this straight. You want me to find anything on Sheriff Boogie Waters that you can use against him. Is that about it?"

Enid laughed. "Stop it. Just see what you can find out, and I'll do some checking too. Then we can compare notes."

"All kidding aside, I think you're onto something. Let's get to work."

• • •

Jack Johnson considered himself a blessed man. He had been married to a wonderful woman for many years before cancer claimed her. He had also had a storybook career. First as an investigative reporter at some of the country's largest newspapers and now as the owner of a weekly newspaper that covered three counties. He also owned a horse ranch in "God's country," as he often called it, because it had some of the most serene and beautiful acreage around.

A couple years ago, Jack had taken in Rachel Anderson, a young woman with nowhere else to turn and no close relatives. She loved animals and had briefly planned to be a veterinarian. In exchange for Rachel's taking care of the ranch on weekends and summers, Jack had paid her college tuition. After a year, though, Rachel realized her love of animals wasn't enough to get her through the grueling biology classes. With Jack's approval, she dropped out of school to figure out what she wanted to do with her life.

While Rachel worked at the ranch, she was great with the boarders—the horses and their owners. But then she and Pete at the Madden police station became friends, and he encouraged her to consider cyber forensics. Like Pete, she had a knack for coding, so eventually she grew restless filling oat buckets and mucking stables. Jack helped her search for a good school, and it was Theo who suggested she check out Boston University, near his home town. After an exploratory visit, Rachel enrolled, and Jack had to hire someone to handle the horses. He had tried out a few but still hadn't found a true replacement for Rachel. He missed her, too, as she was the daughter he and his wife never had.

Another blessing in his life was Enid. They had hit it off as friends from the beginning, and at one point, he thought they might have a chance at a romantic relationship. He was a little older than she, but in all other ways, they were a perfect match. But, before anything serious happened between them, Enid fell for Josh. Not that Jack could blame her. Josh was closer to her age and handsome enough to be a model. If Jack had a son, he would want it to be someone with Josh's qualities: kind, honest, and humble.

Jack and Enid had settled on having a deep friendship, that space somewhere between love and respect. She was strong—much more so than she gave herself credit for. And like Josh, Enid was also kind, honest, and humble—too much so at times. As a journalist, she had excellent instincts for honing into the truth, often at a high personal cost.

Jack forced his attention back to his search on Sheriff Waters, browsing all the articles he could find and making notes to share with Enid. Surprisingly, Boogie's public life was nearly tarnish free. His old-school approach to law and order seemed to fit the county's needs. But Jack wasn't interested in Boogie's public persona.

Two hours later, Jack took off his reading glasses and rubbed his eyes. Nothing but the usual stuff on Boogie. What he needed was a skilled research assistant. Jack glanced at his watch. Rachel would be out of class for the rest of the day. He decided to text her.

Jack: Miss U. Call when U can. Need a favor.

A few minutes later, his cell phone rang and Rachel's smiling face appeared on his screen. "Hey, you," he said. "How's the future world's-best forensic expert doing?"

For a few minutes, they caught up on family news, teachers, and dorm drama.

"I'm so glad you're enjoying school," Jack said. "I need to ask you a question. How can I find information on someone outside of the mainstream stuff? Legally, of course. No hacking."

Jack filled Rachel in on Sheriff Bernard Waters, explaining that he was looking for any crack in the veneer—anything that might be worth checking further. "Now keep it legal. Promise?"

After the call ended, Jack thought about the brief infatuation Rachel once had on a hacker with a codename Tommy Two. Tommy eventually left town, especially after the relationship started heating up. Jack hoped Rachel was no longer in contact with him, but he had to accept that she was a grown-up now with a mind of her own, and he trusted her to make the right decisions.

CHAPTER 18

When Enid received a call from Josh asking her to come to his office, she assumed it was an update on the bones. They had made a pact not to discuss business while they were together socially, so even though they had seen each other last night, nothing was mentioned about the investigation.

Walking into his office, the first thing she noticed was how tired he looked. Usually, his eyes sparkled when she walked in. Today, he seemed to avoid eye contact. "Are you okay?" she asked.

"Yeah, just got a lot on my mind. Want a cup of tea while we talk?"

"No, thanks. Do you have something for me on the bones?"

Josh looked startled. "Bones? Oh, right. No, nothing yet. Boogie mentioned you had talked with him. I was a bit surprised."

"You're not the only lawman around. Maybe the best one, but not the only one."

Josh ran his fingers through his dark mane. "Thanks. I guess."

"What's on your mind? I can tell something is bothering you."

"We need to talk. There's something I need to tell you."

Enid was trying not to panic, but Josh's behavior was alarming her. "Just tell me. What's going on?"

"I've got to go back home, to New Mexico, for a while. Maybe a month or so."

Enid sat down to control all the emotions and thoughts swirling in her head. "Is this about the story Cade is doing?"

Josh stood up and motioned for Enid to follow him. "I can't do this here. I need to hold you. Come on."

Confused, Enid put her notepad back in her tote and followed Josh to the front of the police station.

"Pete, I'm going to be out for a little while. Try to handle anything that's not an emergency."

"Sure thing, Chief. No problem."

Enid followed Josh out the door. "Let's take your car," Josh said. "I'll drive."

. . .

Enid and Josh rode in silence during the drive to Glitter Lake Inn. When they arrived, he said, "Let's go sit down by the lake."

"You go on down. I just want to let Theo know we're here. He might wonder what's going on."

Josh nodded.

A few minutes later, when Enid walked down the path to the bench by the water, Josh was sitting, slumped forward with his forearms resting on his legs and his face in his hands. When he heard her footsteps, he sat upright. "Hey, Babe." He patted the bench. "Come sit beside me."

Enid sat down and leaned her head against Josh's shoulder, as she had done so many times. They sat in silence for a few minutes before he spoke.

"I don't mean to worry you. It's just hard for me to find the right words. I have some unfinished business back home that I need to take care of." He kissed the top of her head. "I know you have lots of questions, but please don't worry. Everything will be fine."

"I can't help but worry." She sat up and turned to look at him. "Can you understand that? If you don't tell me what's going on, it means you don't trust me. That hurts." She paused. "And you'll force me to make up my own stories about what's going on. You don't have to tell me everything, but you've got to do better than just riding off into the sunset."

Josh gently pulled her back into his arms. "Don't you ever get tired of being right?"

Enid smiled. "Not really. And, by the way, I need to put something in the *Tri-County Gazette* about why the Madden police chief plans to disappear for a month."

"I hadn't really thought about a public statement, but I guess you're right. Just keep it short. Tell them Pete will fill in, with assistance from Sheriff Bernard Waters, and that I'm taking accrued vacation time to handle some family business. How's that?"

"You've already talked to Boogie about this?"

"Yes, why?"

Enid didn't want to admit that she was hurt that Boogie knew more about what was going on with Josh than she did. "It's nothing. I'll get that in the next edition, assuming you're leaving soon."

"Tomorrow."

Enid sighed. Josh was not one to procrastinate. That's what made him good at tending to the needs of Madden's citizens. "Now that we've got the official statement out of the way, what else can you tell me?"

"From the minute Cade showed up, I knew I'd have to face this moment."

Enid's mind was racing. "Are you saying that you did something wrong? Did you kill the man who shot your wife?"

Josh was quiet for what seemed like a long time, but it was actually only a few seconds. Funny how much a mind can fill in during that short amount of time.

"No, but I think I know who did."

CHAPTER 19

Sitting down at the big farm table at Jack's ranch with him brought back many good memories for Enid. Rachel was on Jack's phone, and he had the speaker on. While none of them were biologically related, they had become a family. After briefly catching up on each other's lives, Enid reached for her notepad and pen.

"I'm ready, Rachel. What did you find out?"

"Okay, here's what I learned. Boogie isn't clean, but he has managed to avoid any serious consequences."

"What exactly do you mean?" Jack asked.

"He's been accused of numerous bad-boy things like bribery, mistreatment of prisoners, even misappropriating taxpayer money. But he was never convicted or even tried for any of these, as far as I could find. And most of it was ten or more years ago. None of it recent. Each time something came up, the sheriff came off looking like he had done a good thing by cleaning up a mess. One person in an interview even said that, and I quote, 'Sheriff Boogie Waters has his own methods of law enforcement, but he keeps this county safe. That's what we pay him to do.'"

"Was Boogie ever married?"

Enid could hear Rachel flipping through her notes. "Yes, he was. Briefly, at least. But his wife died. That was a long time ago."

"Any girlfriends?" Jack asked.

Rachel grinned. "Glad you asked. That was kinda interesting. You see, he allegedly dated a black woman. But it seems that was where the county drew the line. According to, let's just say, some information I found—"

Jack interrupted, "You promised no hacking. Remember?"

"Let her go on," Enid said. "I'm sure she wouldn't do that."

"As I was saying, Boogie allegedly dated a black woman who worked at the inn."

Enid stopped rocking. "At the Glitter Lake Inn?"

"Yep."

"Rachel, how you could have possibly found this . . .," Jack began. "Never mind. Go on."

"This woman worked for the owner. Of course, that was before Cassie inherited the inn. This woman Boogie dated practically ran the place. She cooked and managed the staff. Want to hear the best part?"

Enid and Jack exchanged glances, and Rachel continued before they could answer. "I found an out-of-state marriage record. He married this woman, and I found a birth certificate. They had a daughter."

CHAPTER 20

Still reeling from Rachel's revelations about Boogie's second wife and a child, Enid sat in her office and put the finishing touches on the brief article about Police Chief Joshua Hart leaving town to handle a family matter. There wasn't much crime in Madden, and Pete, for all of his youthful quirkiness, was a capable officer. More importantly, he wouldn't hesitate to ask for help if he got into something over his head.

She uploaded the article, but she had already told Jack about Josh's leaving. Since Jack didn't seem surprised, she assumed Josh had already told him. If so, Jack didn't mention it. Even though she and Jack were close friends, he usually steered away from talking about Josh with her.

After turning her attention to a few other assignments about community events, Enid glanced at the clock on the wall. Perhaps she would write an article about the disappearing wall clocks and analog watches. Recently, she had read where young people couldn't even read the time on a traditional device. These days everything was digital. When someone had asked Jack why the old schoolroom-style clock was still hanging in the newspaper office, he quickly replied, "Because I like real clocks." Nothing else was said on the matter.

Enid pulled out her notes from her interview with Phyllis. Her brother had been in a South Carolina prison, so Enid pulled up the incarcerated inmate search screen. She input

Reggie's name, and the results came back quickly. Reggie had been in the Lee Correctional Institute. A quick Google search revealed a number of articles about the facility. One reporter from Charleston had dubbed it as "the worst prison" in South Carolina. The fifteen-hundred-inmate facility had recently received a lot of media attention when seven men were killed and another seventeen were seriously injured during a prison riot. According to the *Post and Courier's* article, the facility had a serious shortage of guards and was run by gangs.

Why would Reggie have been put in this particular prison when there were other options? It seemed like additional punishment. The site also showed any disciplinary actions against inmates. Reggie appeared to have had a clean record. The search screen also included a photo and physical description. Reggie was an attractive black man, but his eyes were those of someone without hope or purpose.

Enid decided to search for more information on Reggie's trial. After a few minutes, she found an interesting article in the *State* newspaper, published two days after the guilty verdict was rendered.

Juror Now Regrets 'Guilty' Vote

COLUMBIA, SC—Lester Brown, a juror in a recent Bowman County murder trial, said during an interview he now regrets his guilty vote against convicted killer Reginald Long. Long was on trial for the murder of his missing girlfriend,

Angelina Peterson. According to Brown, he first argued to acquit the accused but then succumbed to fellow jurors after lengthy deliberations. When asked about the reasons for his doubt, he thought the evidence was insufficient to overcome "reasonable doubt" and that the sheriff's office had rushed to convict Long without exploring other suspects. Long also said the victim's sexually promiscuous habits were factors in the "hasty trial." "It was like they put the woman who got killed on trial instead of her boyfriend, and he became guilty by association," Brown said. Although Brown regrets his role in Long's guilty verdict, he plans to make no further statements about Long's trial. "What's done is done," he said.

Enid printed a copy of the article and put it in her folder. A quick search revealed twenty-seven people with the common name of Lester Brown in and around Columbia. Besides, there was no guarantee Brown was still in the state. She printed the list.

Starting at the top, she called each one until she had either talked to or left messages for each Lester Brown. Enid then looked in her contacts and called Phyllis.

"No, I don't know who he is," Phyllis said. "I remember that article, but he never contacted anyone in our family that I'm aware of. I'll check around and see if anyone knows him."

"Thanks, I'll do some more checking, too," Enid said.

The next call she made was to Madelyn Jensen. They made plans for lunch at the inn the following day.

Enid rubbed her eyes and temples. What did she hope to gain by talking with Brown? Were the bones at the inn even related to Reggie Long? There were too many questions and not enough answers.

• • •

At the Glitter Lake Inn, Theo had made a special lunch for Enid and Madelyn. They were seated on the balcony off the library at a small table for two, which was covered in a crisply pressed white cloth. The poached salmon salad was topped with Theo's family-recipe vinaigrette and served with small buttery biscuits. An assortment of chocolate and lemon cookies finished the meal.

Madelyn pushed back from the table and put her napkin beside her plate. "Only Theo can make a salad a memorable meal. That was delicious."

"I agree. He's amazing," Enid said.

Madelyn glanced at the time on her Apple watch. "You said you had some questions."

Enid pulled a folder from her leather tote and handed the article to Madelyn. "Do you remember this trial?"

Madelyn scanned the article again. "Yes, vaguely. Why?"

"Do you recall if there was talk around town about the verdict?"

Madelyn wiped the condensation from her iced tea glass with the starched linen napkin before taking a sip. "I hate to sound cynical, but you know how it works. If this Long guy had been related to the mayor or was a prominent businessman, this revelation might have been big news. But, you'd got a black man dating a white woman, which I don't have to tell you is still frowned upon in many places, and the young woman he supposedly killed got around a bit. She was hardly a model citizen."

"Her name was Angelina. And what you're saying may be true, but it's still not right. Long deserved a fair trial, and the victim's family should be confident that the right person was convicted."

Madelyn paused briefly before responding. "What's this really about? What are you crusading for?"

Her bluntness was one of the things Enid respected about Madelyn, but today, after Josh's departure, her emotions were jagged. "I'm just looking for information, not a lecture, thank you."

Madelyn's face softened, and she put her hand over Enid's. "It must be difficult for you to have your ex show up and accuse your beau of murder."

While Madelyn was trying to be supportive, the words cut through Enid like a sword. "So you've talked to Cade, I see."

"We had drinks at Bourbon in Columbia not long after he arrived. He's worried about you."

Enid didn't trust her voice, so she just nodded.

"I don't know Police Chief Hart, but I understand he's a good man. And you know Cade. He'll get to the truth. If Josh is innocent, Cade will report it."

There was no point in arguing with Madelyn. Eager to change the subject, Enid asked, "What do you know about Sheriff Bernard Waters?"

Madelyn seemed to pick up on her friend's signal to change topics. "Boogie? Well, I've known of him for a while, and I met him almost a year ago in connection with Theo's missing daughter. As far as I know, he's a law-and-order guy who likes to dance the shag. That's about the extent of my knowledge. I haven't lived in Madden or Bowman County for a long time." She paused. "But I'll ask around discreetly, if you'd like. I have to be careful about these kinds of things now that I'm running for office."

"No, don't do that. I wouldn't want you to risk your campaign by asking the wrong person. But thanks. I'll keep checking around. By the way, how is it coming along, the campaign?"

Madelyn shrugged. "After the last presidential campaign, I have a problem believing any of the polls. But, supposedly, I'm ahead of my opponents by five points in the latest."

"I'm sure you'll win. Jack says you're a natural." Enid immediately regretted interjecting Jack into their conversation, since she wasn't sure about the status of Madelyn and Jack's relationship.

Madelyn flipped her wrist to check the time. "I need to get back to the office. Somebody wants to interview me. Those pesky press people who are always looking for some little crack they can expose." She laughed. "You know I'm just kidding about that, although I really do have an interview. I respect you and all members of the press. And that's my official stance on the matter."

After the two women said their goodbyes, Enid watched Madelyn leave. If Madelyn did win the election, these girlfriend lunches might be a thing of the past. Enid would no longer fit in Madelyn's world, or if she did, it would be as a member of the press.

When Theo came to check on them, Enid was staring out toward Glitter Lake. "I don't mean to disturb your thoughts but is there anything I can get you?" he asked.

"No, everything was delicious. Madelyn had to get back to Columbia. She asked me to thank you also."

"Miss Madelyn is going to be a great senator for this state, I'm sure of it."

After Theo's departure, Enid continued to gaze at the sunlight shimmering across the ripples in the lake. As she had done so many times, Enid considered keeping the story simple: remains found at inn and the police are investigating. Yet, it was becoming obvious that this story was anything but simple.

CHAPTER 21

Enid returned to the newspaper office to wrap up a couple of stories when Ginger tapped on her door. "Somebody named Phyllis is here to see you."

Glancing at the clock on the wall, Enid replied, "Ask her to give me a few minutes. I need to finish this article and send it to Jack."

Ginger looked annoyed. "Oh, alright."

"Just send her back in ten minutes. I'll be ready then."

Exactly ten minutes later, Phyllis Long and a middle-aged man appeared at her door. "The lady at the front desk told me to come on back. Is this a good time?"

Enid glanced at the files stacked on the only other chair in her tiny office. "Let's go to the conference room down the hall where we'll have more room."

Enid sat on one side of the table, and Phyllis and the man sat across from her. "I'm sorry I didn't make an appointment." Phyllis smiled. "But I guess you're used to me showing up here unannounced."

"It's fine. Sorry to have kept you waiting." Enid held out her hand to the man across from her. He was a middle-aged white man, dressed in khaki slacks and a golf shirt. "I'm Enid Blackwell."

"I'm sorry for not introducing you," Phyllis aid. "This is Lester Brown. He was a juror in my brother's trial. You said you wanted to talk to him."

Enid sat down. "Mr. Brown. Thank you for coming in. I must admit I'm a bit surprised to see you."

"As I told Ms. Long, I don't want to be involved in any of this. But it's been on my mind for years now. After today, I'm finished with all this. I wish there was something I could do to right this wrong, but I can't. Anyway, Miss Phyllis begged me to talk to you. It's the least I can do for her."

"Mr. Brown, may I record this interview?" Enid asked. "I want to be sure I get all the details."

Brown looked at the iPhone in front of Enid like a man staring at a snake, wondering whether to kill it or walk away quickly. "If you tape it, can we still do this confidentially? I don't want any more articles about me."

"Of course. Besides, I'm not sure how, or even if, this information will be used. I'm doing a series of articles on the bones found at the inn. Ms. Long seems to think the remains may be those of Angelina Peterson, whom her brother was convicted of killing. But we don't know yet whether the bones and the case in which you served as a juror are even connected. At this point, I'm just digging for information."

Brown nodded. "I understand."

Enid tapped on the recording app on her phone and did a quick test to be sure it was functioning properly. She then noted the date, time, and subject being interviewed before beginning. "Mr. Brown, tell me why you think Reginald Long was wrongfully convicted."

"I'm not an attorney, Ms. Blackwell, just a God-fearing insurance salesman in a small town. I live over in Florence County now and most of my clients are soybean or poultry farmers. I have a good life and serve as a deacon in the church. I live quietly. No trouble. Know what I mean?"

"I understand. Please continue."

"The first thing that bothered me in the trial was that all the witnesses against Mr. Long were either related or knew each other. All their stories matched, almost too good."

"Recognizing that, as you said, you're not an attorney, do you think Mr. Long's attorney cross examined the witnesses adequately?"

"The defense attorney went through the motions alright, but the other attorney, the county prosecutor, and the witnesses had an answer for everything. I have to admit they were pretty convincing. When I think back on it, it seemed too rehearsed." Brown shook his head slowly.

"What else bothered you about the trial?"

"That sheriff, Mr. Waters, everybody seemed to treat him like a god. He had command of that courtroom. The prosecutor all but bowed down before him."

"Can you give me some examples?"

"When Sheriff Waters talked about how it happened, it just didn't add up. There were holes in his explanations big enough to drive a truck through."

"Are you saying he lied?"

"I'm just saying the sheriff's story didn't add up. Like the pregnancy. That girl was supposed to be pregnant, but there was no confirmation of that. But everyone seemed to know about it, other than the man who was supposed to be the father. It was accepted as fact by my fellow jurors. And the underwear found in Mr. Long's car. It was just too convenient. Nobody would leave that kind of evidence behind." Brown shook his head again.

"I understand they did a DNA test on the underwear, and it belonged to the victim."

"Yes, they showed the jury the report. It was hers." Brown paused. "I know what you're thinking, that nothing I've said seems so unusual." He asked Enid, "Have you ever served on a jury?"

"I have, but not a murder trial. They would hardly let a reporter be on the jury. But why do you ask?"

"The judge said that it was our job, the jury's, to evaluate the evidence presented and make our own determination about who was telling the truth. I can tell you what was said, but you had to be there to understand why I feel this way. The body language, the little glances I noticed between the deputies. Just little things. I had a gut feeling that Reggie Long was being railroaded. But then I told myself that gut instincts are often wrong. Later, as I kept replaying that trial in my mind, I knew I should have held out. Maybe if I had . . ."

Enid thought about how many times she had wrestled with her own gut feelings. "I understand. Given what you've told me, do you think Sheriff Waters purposefully convicted the wrong person?" She wasn't sure she wanted to hear the answer.

"Honestly, I don't know. He had pat answers for everything and never showed any doubt about his deputies or that they were telling the truth. I guess that's his job, to trust his men." Brown paused and seemed to be gathering his thoughts. "I read a book one time about an innocent man that was convicted. They kept using the phrase 'rush to judgment.' That keeps popping in my mind when I think of Reggie Long's trial."

CHAPTER 22

Enid was about to close her laptop and call it a day when her vibrating cell phone danced around on her desk. She picked it up and turned it over to see the screen. Josh. "Are you in New Mexico yet?" she asked.

"Yes. Just got in. Everything okay with you?"

"Sure. Just doing some checking around for the follow-up articles on the bones." Withholding information from Josh about her conversation with Lester Brown felt necessary but uncomfortable.

"With all that's going on, I forgot to tell you. The DNA results are back. Boogie texted me earlier today."

Enid grabbed her pen to take notes. "What did they determine?"

"His message just said they had the results." He paused. "I hope I don't have to remind you that whatever I tell you is confidential."

There it was again, that boundary they had agreed on. Except now it was a wall. Perhaps there was no way around it, but it didn't feel good. "Of course."

"I'll give you a call later. Love you."

"Me, too." Enid packed her notes and laptop and then called a number in her contacts.

After a couple of rings, a familiar voice answered, "Bowman Sheriff's Department. How can I help you?"

Enid identified herself. "I'd like to get some information on the DNA tests for the bones found at Glitter Lake Inn."

"I'm sorry but we can't reveal that information at this time."

Enid recalled her journalism professor criticizing her in a mock interview for not being more assertive. But that was years ago, and she had learned the lesson well. "I'd like to make an appointment to see Sheriff Waters. I'm sure there's something he can tell me. And the public has a right to know."

"Hold, please." The phone went silent, but in less than a minute, the woman returned. "Come on over. He'll give you five minutes."

. . .

Sheriff Boogie Waters stared at Enid sitting across from his desk. He looked both amused and annoyed.

"Thank you for seeing me," she said.

He chuckled. "I've seen you shoot, so I wasn't about to say no."

Enid winced at the memory of the shooting incident where two men had been killed. Although it was self-defense, shooting another human being was a serious matter. "I'll get right to the point, since you've only given me a few minutes."

"Well, go ahead then." He leaned back in his chair.

"Do you have the DNA results on the bones found at the inn, and if so, what can you tell me?"

His eyes narrowed into a squint. "News travels fast. Did Josh have a good trip to New Mexico?"

Enid refused to take the bait. "I assume you know the race, sex, and approximate age of the victim." Her pen was poised in her hand.

"Seeing as you're Josh's woman and all, I guess I can tell you that much."

Enid slapped her pen down on the desk. "Sheriff Waters, let me be clear. I'm a reporter for the *Tri-County Gazette*. I'm not here as Josh's friend or in any other capacity. I ask you to respect my position, as I do yours."

Boogie sat up in his chair and slowly clapped his hands. "Well stated, Ms. Blackwell." His tone was jovial, but his eyes were not. "The remains appear to be a young woman, approximately twenty to thirty years old."

Enid scribbled a few notes. "And her race?"

Boogie opened a folder and flipped through some notes. "Says here she's white." He closed the folder and looked at Enid. "That's about all we know at this point."

"Have you run the DNA against the national databases?"

Boogie opened his mouth to speak but stopped. He then said, "No match yet. Now is there anything else, Ms. Blackwell?" He stood up, but Enid remained seated.

"There's just one more thing. A confidential source has suggested to me that the remains may belong to a young woman named Angelina Peterson, known around town as Angel. She disappeared, and her boyfriend was convicted of murdering her. Can you comment on that?"

"DNA results don't give you a name, just a biological profile." He drummed his fingers on the desk. "But you know that, don't you, Ms. Blackwell?"

"What will happen next if the bones are Angelina Peterson's?"

Boogie stood up. "I think your five minutes are up. Have a nice day."

CHAPTER 23

The EverLife Center for Memory Care was just outside of Columbia near Lake Murray. The drive was over an hour from Boogie's house, but he made it once a week or more, never complaining about the distance. After parking his SUV, he continued on the walkway with the small lawn sign that said, "Buildings 5 through 10." An arrow pointed toward his destination: Building 10.

The groundskeepers, most of them Hispanic, nodded in recognition as he walked by. "How's your arm, Pepito?" The elderly man, whose arm was in a soft cast from hand to elbow, smiled at Boogie. "Gracias a ti, todo está bien."

Boogie took several twenty dollar bills out of his pocket and gave them to the man. "Here's a little more for your medical bills." The man shook his good hand to refuse the money, but Boogie stuffed the bills in the man's pocket. "Take care of yourself, Pepito."

Inside Building 10, Boogie was greeted by a nurse. "Mr. Waters, how are you today?"

"Still dancing to the music," he said. "Is she awake?"

The nurse nodded. "Even if she doesn't know anything else, she always seems to know when you're coming. I caught her smiling at the mirror this morning."

The facility was clean and didn't smell like some of the places Boogie had checked out. This one had a good rating, but it wasn't cheap. And each year, the cost of care increased. Last year, he had to sell some of his farmland to make the payments to the center. He tried not to think of what would happen if something happened to him or he could no longer afford this place. What would happen to her?

At the end of the hall was her room. He had picked that room for its expansive windows and slightly larger square footage. Inside was a hospital bed, a large chair and ottoman, a dresser, and a bedside table. A large rocking chair, which he put there for himself, sat empty on the other side of the bed.

Miss Lillian, as she was known at the center, sat in the large chair holding a child's stuffed animal. She spent most of her day there with her feet on the ottoman, refusing to join the others in the recreation center. Several months ago, Boogie had brought her a small, flat-screen television, but it agitated her, and he had to take it away. The stuffed toy she held was so worn that it was hard to tell it was a donkey. Boogie had won it for her at the fair, right after they first started seeing each other. They often went out of the county on dates to avoid prying eyes. Lillian liked the annual State Fair in Columbia, especially the corn dogs slathered in mustard and ketchup and fries soaked in malt vinegar.

"How are you today?" he asked her as he leaned over to kiss the top of her silver head.

She looked at him with her large dark eyes, but he knew she had no idea who he was.

"I brought you something." He reached in his pocket and handed her a small box. "Here, I'll take it out for you." He pulled out a necklace, a sterling silver dragonfly on a chain. "You always liked dragonflies, didn't you?" He didn't expect her to answer.

After putting the necklace around her neck, Boogie fastened the clasp. Since the patients weren't allowed to wear jewelry for fear of other patients stealing it, he'd have to remember to tell the nurse. He was pretty sure they'd make an exception for Miss Lillian. "That looks good on you."

Lillian's expression rarely changed. She always seemed to have a slight smile on her face, like she knew something no one else did. The doctor assured Boogie that Alzheimer's patients didn't suffer from the knowledge of their illness. They were oblivious to their condition, unlike their loved ones who suffered as they watched the people they love slip into another world.

For the next hour, Boogie sat in the rocker and read poetry to Lillian. He wasn't particularly fond of poems, and she had not been either, as least not that he could remember. But it seemed fitting when he was with her. He avoided overly sad verses, instead focusing on poems about hope, love, and gratitude.

Boogie looked up from the book in his hands. "I'm grateful for having known you. Do you know that?" He had once asked Lillian's doctor if she could understand what he said to her. The doctor replied that no one knew for sure, but it couldn't hurt to keep talking to Lillian. Boogie had convinced himself that she was trapped inside the shell that was once his beloved wife. He was pretty sure Lillian knew exactly what he was saying but just couldn't respond.

Boogie regretted he had made his wife live in the shadows all those years. She deserved better than that, but if she resented him for forcing her to keep their marriage secret, she never showed it. Decades ago, mixed-race marriages were not welcomed, even though the Loving v. Virginia Supreme Court case in 1967 had removed all legal barriers. Boogie had just been elected sheriff, and at the time, the good citizens of Bowman County were not ready to accept Lillian into that prominent position.

By the time social mores changed, Boogie and Lillian continued to keep their secret. Otherwise, he would have had to admit lying to the people who elected him. Boogie was willing to take that chance, but it was Lillian who insisted they continue the lie. She told him that no law could force society to accept what they weren't ready for, and Bowman County wasn't ready for their sheriff to be married to a black woman.

Even now, the lone picture on her nightstand didn't include him. He could have put one there that included both of them, but old ways die hard. Instead, the picture Lillian saw each day was of her and a young woman. The family resemblance was evident, but the young woman's skin was much lighter than Lillian's. Boogie picked up the framed photo and held it for a few minutes. "Two beautiful women," he said to Lillian. For a brief moment, her eyes shifted to the photo and a flicker of cognizance lit up her brown eyes, then died again.

Boogie put the picture back on her nightstand. "I'll see you in a few days. I found this new book of poems I want to read to you. I think you'll like it." He kissed the top of her head again and left Lillian in her own world.

CHAPTER 24

When Enid answered her cell phone, she was surprised when the caller identified herself as Miss Murray from the Madden Historical Society.

"I hope I'm not disturbing you," Miss Murray said.

Enid glanced at the clock on the wall of her office. Her deadline was an hour away. "No, of course not. How can I help you?"

"Are you aware that the Cherokee, Catawba, Pee Dee, Chicora, Edisto, Santee, Yamassee, and Chicora-Waccamaw and other tribes are all still present in South Carolina? At least twenty-nine distinct groups of indigenous people lived within South Carolina at one time."

Enid glanced at the clock again. "That's very interesting. I'll do a little research and perhaps write an article."

"Thanks, dear, I agree it's an interesting story. But that's not why I called. I had a visit today from Karla Burke. She's a descendant of the Cherokee tribe, and a resident of Bowman County. On more than one occasion, she's helped me with research on tribal history."

Enid tapped her pen on the desk nervously. "I'll be glad to interview her as well. Can I drop in to see you in about an hour? I'm sorry, but I need to finish this article."

If Miss Murray was offended, nothing was reflected in her voice. "Of course, dear. But I think you'll want to hear this. Karla has some information that you will at least find intriguing. You can decide if it's credible."

Enid hung up and turned her attention to the soon-to-be-late article on one of Madden's finest citizens whose grandson had been accepted at the Citadel on a full scholarship. But Enid's mind was on Miss Murray's call. Once the article was finished, Enid uploaded it for Jack to review. She grabbed her tote and told Ginger she would be out for a while.

Enid nearly ran to the Madden Historical Society building just down the street. When Roscoe answered the door, she was slightly out of breath. "I have an appointment with Miss Murray."

Roscoe beamed. "Of course you do. She told me you were coming."

But Enid was already halfway down the hallway before he finished. "Thanks," she called over her shoulder. She knocked on the door. There was no answer and no sound, so she knocked again. "Miss Murray, it's Enid Blackwell. Are you there?" This time she heard the unmistakable sound of a spoon clinking on china. Miss Murray was having tea.

"Do come on in. We're waiting on you."

Enid opened the door, unsure who "we" meant. Miss Murray was sitting at the small round table where she served tea. Across from her was a beautiful dark-skinned woman with short, black hair, stylishly cut. The woman smiled and nodded a greeting to Enid. Miss Murray had set a third tea cup at the table, so Enid sat in the empty chair.

Miss Murray gestured toward the other woman. "Enid Blackwell, I'd like for you to meet Karla Burke."

Enid offered her hand. "I'm pleased to meet you." She turned to Miss Murray. "I didn't realize Karla was already here when you called earlier." She turned to Karla. "I'm sorry I kept you waiting."

"I've enjoyed talking with Miss Murray," Karla said.

Miss Murray poured Enid a cup of tea. "As I said, Karla is Native American."

Karla smiled at Enid. "You may be thinking that Karla Burke doesn't sound much like an indigenous name." She didn't wait for Enid to reply. "You see, my ancestry is Cherokee, and many years ago, my family's name was Ko Tut Tih Nih. In the early 1800s, most of our tribal members were required to adopt European surnames, like Smith, Johnson, Burke, and so on. The ministers who converted, or tried to convert, our people to Christianity often picked the new Anglo family names. The minister in my family's area gave them the name Burke, after his relatives in Scotland."

"That's very interesting," Enid said. "Thanks for explaining it."

Karla nodded and glanced again at Miss Murray.

"Go on, Karla, tell Enid what you told me."

Karla seemed to be studying Enid's face before she spoke. "Have you ever heard of the Black Warriors, or perhaps of Spiritual Warriors?"

"No, I can't say that I have. Why?"

"These are people whose purpose is to seek the truth, to bring the truth from the darkness to the light, for all to see."

Enid nodded, unsure of how to respond. "Is this a Native American belief?"

Karla laughed. "No, actually it's not. But we have similar ideas."

"What does this have to do with me?"

Miss Murray spoke up. "It's not just you, dear. It's also the people who are around you."

"Is this some kind of warning?" Enid asked.

Karla reached out for Enid's hand and held it with both of hers. "Oh, no. Just the opposite. You, Jack, Josh, and Cade are all warriors looking for the truth."

Enid gently withdrew her hand from Karla's grasp. "Considering that Jack, Cade, and I are reporters and Josh is a police chief, it's reasonable to expect we're all looking for the truth."

"I know this all sounds strange to you, but I'm not trying to play with your head."

"Then why are you telling me about black warriors?" Enid asked. "And how do you even know about Josh, Jack, and Cade?" When Karla remained silent, Enid mulled over several excuses to leave. She glanced at the time on her phone. "I really need to go, unless you have something further for me."

"Please don't be upset," Miss Murray said. "It was my idea to have Karla meet with you. She's an intuitive."

Enid looked back and forth between Miss Murray and Karla. "A psychic, in other words." She reached down for her leather tote.

"No, I'm not a psychic," Karla said. "I can't tell you what's going to happen, or even if anything unusual will happen. But I keep having dreams about the four of you. The fact that it's four warriors is significant. As you probably know from Josh, four is meaningful to Native Americans.

There are four directions, and we believe there are four dimensions, not three, if you include time. Also, there are four seasons and four stages of life. I could go on." She paused. "Look, I know all this must sound crazy to you. I knew about you from your previous reporting on the two cases you solved."

"I didn't solve them alone. I was simply the reporter."

"I appreciate your modesty, but without you, those cases would not have been solved," Karla said. "When I began having these dreams, the other three warriors were presented to me. And I sensed that I needed to meet with you. I talked to Miss Murray, and she called you." Karla paused to smile. "There's no ulterior motive, and I don't mean to alarm you. Quite the opposite. In my dreams, you were filled with doubt about your role on this earth. My spirit guide instructed me to assure you that you are doing what you are supposed to do, along with the other warriors on your team."

Enid sat silently, trying to make sense of Karla's comments.

"You don't have to worry about Josh. I don't know all the details, only that you are worried about him. He is strong and wise. Trust in him."

Enid stood up. "I have to go now. Thank you for meeting with me. I need to think about all you've said. How can I reach you if I need to?"

Karla and Miss Murray exchanged glances again, and Miss Murray spoke. "Just let me know. I'll be glad to connect you again."

• • •

By the time Enid got to bed, she had rationalized Karla's comments as both meaningless and harmless, and a bit kooky. Yet, she tossed and turned, unable to get the conversation out of her mind. She glanced at the clock. It was after eleven o'clock. Jack would still be up, sitting in his favorite chair and reading. She reached for her phone but then stopped herself.

After a few more minutes of tossing and managing to pull the fitted sheet off the end of the mattress, she reached for her cell phone and called Jack.

When he answered quickly, she was surprised. "Hey, I was just sitting here thinking about you," he said.

"Why is that?"

"I don't know. You were just on my mind. What's up?"

"Now I'm feeling a bit foolish. I just couldn't sleep, and I didn't want to call Josh. He's got enough on his mind."

"Why don't you just tell me what's bothering you," Jack said.

Enid told him about meeting Karla at Miss Murray's office. "It's all baloney, right?"

"First, let me ask you why her comments were disturbing to you. You talk to people all the time and shake off anything they say that you don't believe. Your instincts are what make you a great reporter. Although, I admit, these comments were more personal, so I'm not surprised it's rattled you a bit."

"Do you think there's anything to what she was saying?" Enid asked.

"I think your response to her was spot on. With the nature of our jobs, we are warriors in a sense, each in our own way."

"But do you think we were destined, all four of us, to work together?"

After a long pause, Jack replied, "Yes, I do think so. I've thought about this before. After all, Cade and I knew each other before I met you. Then you came to Madden, and you and I work closely together. And now, Josh is . . ." Jack's voice trailed off.

"So what does this all mean?"

"It means I'm one damn lucky guy to be on your warrior team. And I think that Karla lady was right that you need to accept your role and quit fretting about it." He paused. "The only thing I worry about is that one day, you're going to move on without any of us. In a sense, you're the queen warrior, and we are along for the ride." Before Enid could reply, he added. "Now I need to get some sleep, and you do, too."

CHAPTER 25

The next morning, Enid arrived at the office early. She had slept well and awakened refreshed after pushing the previous day's conversations out of her mind. What she did have on her mind, however, was her conversation with Rachel about Boogie's marriage to the woman who used to manage the inn.

Enid walked next door to Jack's office. He was drinking coffee and studying the paper's next edition on his screen. "Are you busy?" she asked.

He took off his reading glasses. "Never too busy for you. What's up?"

"When you took over the inn, what happened to all the old paperwork? Is it still in the attic there, or did you get rid of it?"

"I cleaned out all the old paperwork from the inn. It was a fire waiting to happen in that old house."

Enid's shoulders slumped. "Oh. Well, thanks."

Jack grinned. "But I kept all of it. It's in storage at my house."

Enid's face lit up. "Really? That's great. Do you mind if I go through it? I'm going to see if I can find anything about a woman who ran the inn for a while."

"Is this just gossipy interest, or do you think there's some connection to the bones found?"

"Honestly, I have no idea yet. I won't waste a lot of time on it, if that's what you're worried about. Maybe I'll get lucky."

"You could just ask Boogie, you know."

Enid laughed. "Sure, take the easy route."

Jack pulled a key from his key ring and gave it to Enid. "Everything I got from the inn is in the storage area in the back of the barn. Just be careful. Last time I was in there, the field mice were scampering around. And there's a copperhead that shows up occasionally."

Enid shuddered. "Ugh. Thanks for the warning."

. . .

The barn smelled like barns should: fresh but earthy. The horses were in the pasture, so Enid had the place to herself. At least she hoped she was alone, after Jack's warning. She unlocked the padlock on the heavy steel door and pushed it to the side along the overhead track.

She breathed a sigh of relief when she saw the storage area. She had been expecting a disorganized mess of boxes on a straw-strewn floor. Instead, the storage area had a clean concrete deck and sturdy metal shelving. At this time of the year, it wasn't hot, but it would have been unbearably warm in the summer months, as there were no fans to cool it or windows to open.

A small wooden table and a red painted stool sat in the corner of the space. She put her tote on the floor beside the table and pulled out her notepad and pen, an optimistic gesture, with hopes she would find something worth noting in the old paperwork.

All the containers were fairly new banker boxes, the kind you get from the office supply store and put together yourself. The uniformity of the boxes made the space look neat but also eliminated any way of distinguishing new paperwork from older content, as none of the boxes were labeled. Enid sighed and started peeking inside the boxes for a clue of where to start. The first couple of boxes looked like invoices for food, supplies, landscaping services, and other expenses for maintaining the inn. So far, at least, the contents were consistent as to topic and not mixed up, which would have been a nightmare to go through.

The next couple of boxes she looked at contained old guest registers, some dating back to 1920. Enid made a note to talk to Jack about donating those to the Madden Historical Society for preservation.

Instead of going methodically across the shelves, she looked at the bottom of the next shelf. As she pulled the box out, she noticed where mice had chewed into the cardboard. Pushing the thought of critters out of her head, she pulled out the box and examined the contents. "Yes!" she yelled out loud. The box contained old employment records for the inn's staff.

She took the box over to the small table and carefully removed the contents. Much of it was in order, date-wise, but some of it had been randomly thrown in the box.

After nearly an hour, she had the contents stacked in chronological order. There were several gaps in time, so she began looking at other nearby boxes for more employment records. After looking at all the boxes on the bottom row, she began looking at the next rows up. Finding nothing more on employment records, she sat at the table to go through what she had.

Based on the information Rachel had given her, Enid looked for documents from at least thirty years ago. She guessed Boogie to be in his late sixties at least. Having separated the files in this timeframe, she put the other files aside to clear the small table. Unfortunately, the records were often only a couple of lines: name, address—or at least a town, and a record of wages paid. No photos or other ways of identifying the workers. The records didn't even show the workers' job responsibilities. If the woman Boogie allegedly had an affair with had managed the inn, she would likely have made more money than someone who was kitchen help. Then again, it was likely that none of them were paid enough for their hard work.

Separating the workers' records by male and female should have been an easy task, but some of the names could go either way. Enid put the obvious female names in one stack and the obvious male names in another, and the go-either-way names in a third stack.

Despite the fact it was early fall, sweat trickled down Enid's back between her shoulder blades. She had been working for hours, so she took a stretch break. She noticed a small refrigerator in the barn and was relieved to find cold bottles of water inside. She uncapped one and walked outside for her break.

Several horses were in a fenced area near the barn. The black thoroughbred caught her eye. She recognized it as Rachel's favorite, though he belonged to a friend of hers. Rachel cared for the horse, whose name was Escape, as though he were her own.

Escape was difficult to ride. Jack said he wouldn't even try to get on him. But Rachel had a way with animals, and she and Escape had bonded immediately. When she came home from college, the two were inseparable. Often, Rachel even slept in the barn on a cot near the beloved horse.

Enid stretched her shoulders and shook the tightness from her legs and arms before heading back to her task. Escape whinnied and vigorously shook his head up and down. "Time to get back to work," he seemed to be saying.

For the next two hours, Enid read the employment records of anyone with an obvious female name who had been employed by the inn during the past thirty years. Nothing on anyone named Lillian Waters, although if the marriage was secret, the sheriff's wife could have been using a pseudonym. Maybe she was compensated in other ways—with food and lodging, or in unrecorded cash payments. Perhaps there were other missing records in boxes Enid had not looked in. After looking at the time on her iPhone, Enid started packing the materials back in the box. She made a small note, "employees," near the bottom of the box. If she decided to come back later, she'd be able to find it easily.

Enid put everything back the way she had found it and pulled the heavy steel door shut. She replaced the padlock and tugged on it to make sure it was secure. That's when she heard footsteps. It was probably Jack, although he had said he would be in Camden all day. Perhaps he changed his plans. Enid looked around but didn't see anyone.

Suddenly, Escape started whinnying non-stop. Enid walked out of the barn and over to the white painted fence surrounding the pasture area. The horse was tossing his mane and stomping the ground. "What's going on, boy? Are you okay?"

Escape began pacing back and forth, running a few yards and then turning around to retrace his steps, all the while shaking his mane. Enid was admiring the beauty of the horse's muscular strength when she heard something behind her. She turned quickly and saw a man standing there.

CHAPTER 26

Enid involuntarily screamed when she turned and saw the man standing behind her. It took a moment for her mind to register that he was wearing a uniform. "God, you scared the crap out of me."

The deputy identified himself. "May I ask what you're doing on this property?"

Even though Enid had only lived with Jack and Rachel a short time, she always thought of the ranch as her home, too. "What do you mean?"

The deputy put his hand on his holstered gun. "Please put your bag on the ground and identify yourself."

Enid dutifully put her tote on the ground. "This is my friend's house, Jack Johnson's. I used to live here. Are you new to the sheriff's office?"

The deputy looked at her with an icy stare. "I'll need to verify your identity."

Now Enid was annoyed. "Fine. My name is Enid Blackwell. Call Jack if you must." She gave him the number, but he made no move to write it down or put it in his cell phone.

The deputy removed his hand from his gun. "I'll check with Mr. Johnson later. I suggest you leave now."

"No, I suggest you call Jack now. And I'll leave when I'm ready. This is ridiculous."

The deputy pushed the button on the radio on his shoulder and said, "Subject refuses to leave."

Enid threw up her hands. "Now what? You're going to arrest me." She put her hands together and held them out in front of her. "Go ahead. Cuff me and take me in."

Before the deputy could reply, a black SUV drove up the dirt road leading to the barn. A silver-haired man got out: Sheriff Boogie Waters. He grabbed his belt and pulled up on his pants as he got out and then slowly walked over toward Enid. "Ms. Blackwell," he said, tipping his hat.

"Sheriff Waters, what is going on here? Why am I being harassed?"

Boogie motioned to the deputy. "You can go on now. I got this." When the deputy hesitated, Boogie added, "It's fine. Go on."

As the deputy was walking back to his car, Enid asked, "You got here awfully quick. Were you waiting down on the highway?"

Boogie seemed to ignore her question. "As I recall, you've got a carry permit. Is there a gun in your tote?" he asked.

"No, I don't carry it unless I think I'm going into a dangerous situation. Visiting Jack's house certainly didn't cause me any alarm. At least not until your deputy showed up. What the hell was that all about?"

"I don't believe Jack's here today." Boogie walked over to Enid's tote and picked it up. After inspecting the contents, he held it out for her. "Here you go."

Enid took the tote from him.

"We've had some break-ins in the area. I told Jack we'd keep an eye out for anything suspicious."

Enid started to speak, but Boogie held up his hand. "Before you say anything, let me explain. Ricky, the deputy that was here, is my great nephew—my sister's grandson. His father was killed serving our country, and I became his surrogate father. He's a good boy, just a bit overly protective."

"Protective of what? Or whom? And why was he even here?"

"I apologize for the inconvenience and will talk to Jack also, as I'm sure you'll give him a full report."

"Damn right, I will." Enid was now shaking with anger.

"As I said, I apologize. You can go on now."

Enid turned to leave but turned to face Boogie. "I'd like to ask you a question before I go."

Boogie just looked at her.

"Did you know an African American woman who ran the inn for a while, probably about thirty years ago?"

Boogie face visibly tensed. "It's a small town, Ms. Blackwell. I'm sure I probably did."

Enid waited for him to ask her why she wanted to know. But he didn't. "Have a nice day," he said. "Tell Jack I said hello. I'm just going to check around a bit and make sure everything's okay here."

. . .

"I'm sure that upset you, having the deputy confront you like that." Jack handed Enid a glass of wine. "Here. This will help." They sat on her porch, not as big as Jack's but welcoming and comfortable with its wicker chairs and large plants.

Enid sipped her wine. "Why do you think he was there? Have there really been break-ins around your place?"

"Boogie did mention it in passing when we spoke recently at the diner. But that was a couple weeks ago."

"Do you know Ricky, his deputy?"

Jack shook his head before taking a sip of wine. "You got any cheese? I missed lunch today."

"I'm sorry I messed up your plans. It's just that—"

Jack interrupted. "I'm glad you called. I admit this whole thing is perplexing. And I haven't heard a word from Boogie about the incident. I'll give him a call. He and that deputy had no right to harass you like that anywhere, much less on my ranch."

Enid leaned back in her chair, resting her head on the soft cushion. "I wish Josh were here."

"I'm sure you miss him. Have you talked with him since he arrived in New Mexico?"

"Once or twice. I got the impression he needed time alone to sort things out." Enid sat up and put her wine glass on the table beside her. "Do you think Josh is coming back?"

"Why do you think he wouldn't?"

"I don't know. Just a feeling. Or maybe it's a fear."

Jack reached over and poured more wine in Enid's glass. "You look like you need this. By the way, did you find anything on the woman that worked at the inn?"

Enid shook her head and then filled him in on her search through the paperwork. "I also asked Boogie about her."

Jack threw back his head and laughed. "I'll bet that got his attention."

"He claimed to know nothing, of course, so I don't know how we can find her. The inn's past owners didn't keep great records, and some of the information appears to be missing."

"They've got tax records at the inn on the current employees and those for the past decade or so. I'm guessing they didn't worry too much about FICA and other record-keeping years ago. I'd ask Rachel to help us, but I worry that she might cross the line with all this cyber forensics stuff she's doing. I don't want to encourage her to do anything illegal."

Enid reached out and took Jack's hand. "She's a smart girl, and even though you didn't raise her, you've had such a positive influence on her life. Even if she were tempted, she wouldn't do anything to hurt or disappoint you. She worships you, you know."

Jack squeezed Enid's hand. "I wish she were my daughter. But then, I couldn't love her any more if she was. I just want her to have a good life and to be happy. I'll talk to her tonight and see if she can find anything."

Enid didn't tell Jack, but she had a plan, too. It was a long shot, but anything was worth a try.

CHAPTER 27

Using Miss Murray as the intermediary, Enid called to set up a meeting with her and Karla at the inn. As usual, lunch was beautifully presented and delicious. Several guests joined them in the dining room. After they finished eating, Karla and Enid walked down to the edge of Glitter Lake to talk. There was a nip in the air, signaling winter wasn't far away.

"Is it too chilly for you out here?" Enid asked Karla.

"Oh no, I came prepared." Karla pulled her wrap closer. "And I love this cooler weather. Change is good, even seasonal change."

"Thanks for having lunch with me today," Enid said.

"My pleasure."

"Now that we're here, I feel a bit foolish for asking, but you've been in the county for at least several years. Right?"

"That's true."

"What can you tell me about Sheriff Boogie Waters?"

"In what respect? I can answer you better if you're more specific about what you're asking."

"He was married, is that correct?"

Instead of responding immediately, Karla looked at Enid long enough for her to become uncomfortable. Karla finally replied, "Yes. His first wife died not long after they married."

"So you knew there was more than one wife?"

"Before I answer you, may I ask what you intend to do with this information about his private life?"

Enid was surprised at Karla's resistance, even though it wasn't unusual for reporters to be regarded with suspicion. "You told me the other day that I was a Black Warrior, and that my role was to seek the truth. I admit I'm still skeptical about that whole conversation, but I do know that people come into our lives for a reason. Maybe you are supposed to help me find the truth."

Karla smiled and clapped her hands twice, slowly. "Well done, Enid, well done. Perhaps you're right. For now, at least, I'll accept that reasoning. And you don't strike me as someone who wants to hurt people unnecessarily."

Enid cleared her throat. "Right now, I'm simply trying to uncover the facts, so I'm poking around. Sometimes the path to the truth is accidental. Does that make sense?"

Karla nodded slightly. "Of course."

"None of the information about his second wife will be used unless it's verified and germane to the story. I understand his second wife, Lillian Waters, worked at the inn."

"I don't pay much attention to gossip, as most of it is mean-spirited. But factually speaking, I believe that's true. My mother, who is no longer with us, knew the woman, the sheriff's second wife, but not well. She said the woman was foolish for seeing a white man, because people can be mean."

"A source has told me she believes the bones at the inn are a woman called Angel. What do you know about her?"

"Angel was well-known in the community. While she was frequently on the wrong side of things, her spirit was benign." Karla paused. "In other words, I didn't detect anything mean or evil about Angel. She appeared to be a lost and troubled soul, searching for something."

"What else do you know about her?"

"Most of her family were agitators who looked for trouble."

"Are they still around here?"

"Not that I'm aware of. They moved on after the trial, but the farm is still there."

"Can you tell me how to get to it?"

Karla waited briefly before responding, appearing to be studying Enid's face. "I was right about you, you know." She stood up. "Come on, I'll ride with you."

. . .

The farm that belonged to Angel's family was nearly thirty miles from the inn. Once they left the main county road, they took a series of narrow back roads, lined on each side by worn wooden fences or barren fields. Most of the farmers planted seasonal crops, but these farms looked to be idle.

"How do you even know how to get there?" Enid asked.

"It's been a while, so I hope I'm remembering correctly." Karla pointed to a dirt road to the left. "There, turn by that big oak."

There was no sign indicating the name of the road, just a rotted wooden post that could have once been a marker. The dirt road had not been maintained, and Enid had to drive slowly to avoid the potholes.

A few minutes later, a large house came into view. A metal arch, rusted with age, towered above the driveway, defining the entrance. Two empty hooks at the center of the arch had likely held a sign showing the name of the farm.

Enid parked a short distance from the house, so as not to alarm the residents, if there were any. She blew the horn, but no one came out. After a couple minutes, Enid asked, "I'm going to the door. You can stay here if you like."

Karla released her seatbelt. "No, I'll go with you. But be careful. They may have a dog. If you have an umbrella or something to fend one off, better take it with you."

"Good idea." Enid looked in the car and removed a golf umbrella that Jack had left there.

Enid and Karla walked slowly up to the house, keeping an eye out for a dog that might come racing from behind the house or out of the nearby woods.

The house appeared to be abandoned and in need of repair. The wooden siding had darkened with age, and a few pieces were hanging loose. Weeds had overtaken a neglected flowerbed. Enid knocked on the door. No answer.

"Well, I guess there's no one here." Enid turned to leave.

"Wait." Karla closed her eyes briefly and then tapped on the door.

Within seconds, a young blonde woman answered. "What do you want?" she asked.

Enid gave her a business card. "I'm researching a story about a young woman who used to live here. She was known as Angel. Do you know anything about her?"

The young woman ran her hand through her long hair and shook it away from her face. She appeared to have just awakened from a nap. "That was a long time ago. I heard somebody talk about her a few times. That's all I know." The woman started to shut the door.

"Wait, just a few more questions, please." The woman didn't respond, so Enid continued. "Does your family own this farm now?"

The woman shrugged. "I guess so."

"Who lives here with you?"

"I don't have to tell you." Although it was a statement, the girl's voice lifted at the end, making it sound more like a question.

"No, you don't, but would you ask whoever owns this place or lives with you to call me?" Enid handed her a business card. "I would appreciate it. By the way, what's your last name?"

But the young woman shut the door before replying.

"Oh, well. That wasn't much help."

Karla brushed a fly away from her face. "Everything is helpful, in some way."

As they walked back to the car, Enid saw a rusted metal sign lying on the ground by the driveway arch. She walked over to look at it. On the side facing up, there was nothing, so she flipped the sign over. After lying in the sun all day, the sign was warm to the touch, almost hot. After Enid read it, she stepped back from it.

"Are you alright?" Karla asked.

"The name . . ."

"What was it?" Karla asked.

"This place is the 7 Crows Farm."

CHAPTER 28

Josh missed Enid, sometimes so much that his heart literally ached. She deserved a better life than he could offer, but he couldn't bring himself to walk away. She had too much talent to stay at a small weekly newspaper, and though she tried to adapt to small-town life, she had also dropped hints that she missed living in a bigger city. He wanted to call her more often, but he had to stay focused on what he needed to do here. Thinking of Enid would only make things harder for him.

Since arriving in New Mexico, Josh had made a few contacts, mostly because he didn't want to surprise the local authorities. The captain of the undercover division was a nice enough guy, but he was understandably wary of Josh's return. However, being in law enforcement meant you were in a closed fraternity: men and women who had sworn allegiance to upholding the law—and to each other.

At least Josh had not been arrested when he showed up, so the evidence against him either wasn't strong enough or they were waiting for some other reason. For now at least, he was still one of them, but that could change quickly.

Josh pulled up to an abandoned gas station on one of the desert roads outside of town. He glanced around and pulled his gun from the glove compartment. A few minutes later, a whirl of dust announced a visitor. A black

Ramcharger pulled up beside Josh, and a man a little younger than Josh, but with his same features, got out.

The two men embraced. "Hey, bro, you always were better looking than me," the man said.

"Hello, Troy. Good to see you." Josh kicked at a rock with the toe of his dusty boot. "Wasn't sure you'd even come."

Troy took off his wide-brimmed hat and wiped his forehead with the back of his hand. "I know, man. I'm sorry about not returning your calls. It's just that . . ."

"I understand. How's your family?"

"Aw, you know I'm not the responsible kind. Eve left me and took off with the kids about a year ago." Troy grinned. "I miss the kids." He wiped his forehead again. "You still sheriff in that little Carolina town?"

"I'm the police chief, in Madden, South Carolina. It's a nice place. Quiet. Good people."

"Funny, I never could see you doing that kinda thing. But if it works, that's good."

Josh kicked the rock again. A small cloud of dust floated around it. "There's a newspaper guy investigating me. Said he got a tip about me. You know anything about that?"

"No, man. You know I wouldn't, I couldn't . . . No, man."

Josh put his hand on Troy's arm. "Calm down. I'm just asking. Guess you know what he's looking into."

"I suppose it's about the guy that killed Serena."

Josh backed up a step and leaned on his rental car. "You never really asked me what happened or if I killed him." He paused. "Why is that?"

Troy's arms were crossed against his chest, and he stared at the ground. "Dunno. Just didn't figure you wanted to talk about it."

Josh grabbed Troy by his arm. "I didn't do it. And you know that. But I'd be willing to bet you know who did."

Instead of pulling away from Josh, Troy slumped his shoulders. "I never thought you did it."

Josh released Troy. "If you know anything, you'd tell me. Right?"

Troy nodded, staring at the ground.

"I've got a good life now, but I've got to straighten out this mess before I can return to it." Josh poked his finger at Troy's chest. "Got that?"

CHAPTER 29

Enid held her finger over Madelyn's private phone number, hesitating as to whether to tap it. Finally, she called. Madelyn was in the flurry of campaign activity, so the odds of reaching her were slim.

"Hey, you. What's up?" Madelyn sounded happy.

"I'm sorry to bother you. You must be really busy these days."

"Don't be silly. What do you need?" Since Madelyn had gotten into state politics, she assumed everyone who called wanted something from her. Sadly, she was usually right, including now.

"You know Josh is still out of town."

"Yes, and how's he doing?"

"Okay, I guess. We really haven't talked much. Anyway, with him gone, Pete is acting police chief, but since the county is in charge of investigating the bones found at the inn, Pete's not in the loop."

"Ah, so that's what this call is about. What do you need?"

"Do you have a contact that can find out if they've made the identification yet?"

"Hold on a sec." Madelyn appeared to have covered the phone with her hand and was talking to someone else. "Okay, sorry about that. Now, what were you saying? Oh, wait, the bones. Let me see what I can find out. I'll get back to you."

"Thanks, I owe you a dinner."

Madelyn laughed. "You're not cooking, are you?"

"No, I wouldn't do that to a dear friend, but we'll get together soon. Good luck with everything. You're going to win, you know that, don't you?"

"Later, hon. I've got to run." The phone line went dead.

CHAPTER 30

Josh looked across the desert as he drove down New Mexico's Highway 14, otherwise known as the Turquoise Trail. This was home for him, in the traditional sense that he was born not too far from here. But was it really home now? When he moved to Madden to escape the memories of Serena's murder and all the issues surrounding it, he vowed never to return. But here he was again. The meeting with his brother Troy reminded him of what he had left behind and why. Family was important to Josh, but he viewed family in the broader sense now, just as he defined home as something more than a physical location.

Since he had arrived in New Mexico, he had only spoken to Enid twice. One of the things he loved about her was that she seemed to understand his need to be alone. Not once had she pressured him about what was going on, although he could tell it bothered her. For a reporter used to asking questions, she showed uncharacteristic restraint. Maybe she was afraid of what she might find.

He pulled into a gas station on the highway. Two eighteen wheelers were parked off to the side. He knew from past experience that cell phone reception was good here and the coffee was decent, so he parked and went inside.

The waitress brought him a cup without even asking what he wanted. He smiled to himself as he thought of Enid, if she were here, saying to the waitress, "I don't drink coffee." Everyone drank coffee in these parts. As the hot, acrid liquid warmed his throat, he pulled out his cell phone and found Enid's number. What would he say? Should he even call her?

Almost involuntarily, his finger tapped the number. "I'm going to take this outside," he said to the waitress. "Be back in a few minutes." Since there were only three people inside the restaurant and no noise for cover, having a private conversation would be impossible.

As he stepped into the bright sunshine, Enid answered. "Hey, babe, I miss you" he said, his voice sounding hollow and artificial. But he did miss her. "I'm sorry I haven't called you more often. You got a few minutes?"

"I miss you, too. Is everything okay?"

How much to tell her? And should he tell her by phone or in person? "Sure, everything's fine."

"When are you coming home?" she asked.

"Soon, I hope. How's the bones investigation going?"

"Getting information is tough. Boogie's department won't give me anything but a few tidbits here and there, and with you not here . . ." Her voice trailed off.

"I can call Boogie for you. You know how he is. Don't take it personally."

"No, don't do that." She paused. "How well do you really know him?"

"Well enough. I mean, it's not like we're close drinking buddies or anything. He was there for me when I needed to learn about small-town policing, and he's never given me any reason to doubt his integrity." He paused. "What's on your mind?"

Josh listened while Enid shared with him her concerns about Boogie and Reggie's trial. He looked at the coffee grounds in the bottom of his cup and wished for a refill. One of the truckers came out the door and tipped his cowboy hat in greeting as he walked toward his rig. "I'm not sure how to respond to all that. But it sounds like you've been busy."

The waitress walked out with a coffee pot in her hand. "Want a refill, hon?" Josh nodded and held out his cup. God bless attentive wait staff.

"Sorry, I'm back," he said to Enid as the waitress walked back inside. "Just remember, when you investigate a sitting sheriff, you're venturing into dangerous waters," Josh said. "Be careful."

"There's something else," Enid told him about going to the 7 Crows Farm with Karla. "Phyllis mentioned seven crows when she first came to see me, so I need to talk to her again."

As much as he respected Enid's instincts, he had some himself, a lawman's instincts—that little warning voice. He wished he was in Madden. She didn't like to be protected, but he worried about her.

"I've got to go," she said. "Come home soon."

After Josh ended the call with Enid, he went back inside and put his empty coffee cup on the counter, leaving a sizable tip.

"Want a to-go cup?" she asked.

"No, but thanks."

"Come on back here when you're not on the phone. Maybe we can talk."

Josh smiled. "Yeah, maybe so."

CHAPTER 31

"I need a feel-good piece for this week's edition," Jack said. "Mrs. Robertson came in to complain that all we write about is crime." He shuffled papers around on his desk at the newspaper office. "Where the heck did I put my glasses?"

"You left them in my office earlier." Enid handed them to him. "Do we have that much crime in the tri-county area? Maybe we need to report on the statistics. I'm doing this article on the impact of the super-store distribution center on the town's economy. I could expand it to discuss how crime is growing with the population. I'll include some stats."

"Good idea," Jack said.

"On the other hand, last time I checked, crime really hasn't increased much. The Madden folks were used to reading only news about their town. Now that we cover three counties, there's thrice the incidents, which probably makes them feel like there's more crime."

"Thrice. I like that word," he said.

Enid laughed. "My humble attempt at being literary. And, speaking of such things, remember that nursery rhyme, you know, the one about seven crows?"

"Something about a secret, never to be told." Jack shrugged.

"Karla and I went to the farm where Angel lived with her family. As we were leaving, I found an old metal sign, you know, like the ones you see around here hanging over the driveways to farms."

"And?"

"The name of the farm is 7 Crows."

Jack slapped his hands on the desk. "You're kidding me. Seriously?" He paused. "But did Phyllis know that?"

"Neither you nor I believe in coincidences. The odds are too staggering that she didn't know the connection to the farm when she came into my office spouting rhymes."

"Let me see if I've got all the pieces. Awhile back, Angel goes missing while she's involved with Phyllis' brother, Reggie, along with most of the Bowman County deputies. They find Angel's bloody underwear in Reggie's car. He's arrested, tried for murder, and later convicted on what you called 'dubious testimony and evidence' by the same sheriff's department. Then fast forward, and bones are found at the inn. A woman dressed in disguise comes to see you and quotes an ancient nursery rhyme about seven crows and a secret. The woman turns out to be Reggie's sister, and you discover that Angel lived on a farm named 7 Crows. Is that about it?"

Enid nodded. "Pretty much. It sounds bizarre when you describe it like that."

"They always say truth is stranger than fiction. If we tried to print that story, I can just see Mrs. Robertson walking in here accusing me of publishing fake news."

"Are you asking me to drop this story then?"

Jack laughed. "Hell, no. I can't wait to hear the ending."

"Good. I need to find out what else Phyllis knows that she's not telling me." Enid stood to leave.

"Can I get my feel-good article before you go off chasing nursery rhymes? We go to print this evening."

"How about if I interview Mrs. Robertson about her prized zucchini plants? Maybe she'll throw in a recipe or two."

"Brilliant, that ought to hold her for a while. Want me to go with you to check out this 7 Crows Farm? I'm starting to worry about where all this might lead you."

"I'll be careful." Despite her assurances, Enid made a mental note to keep her small handgun in her tote from now on. Just as a precaution.

. . .

Phyllis had agreed to meet Enid at a small restaurant near the school where Phyllis taught. The drive was about thirty minutes for Enid, but since moving to Madden, she had gotten used to everything being at least a half hour away. When she and Cade had lived in Charlotte, they spent just as much or more time in the car, but much of that time was sitting in traffic or inching along congested roads. Here in South Carolina, things were more spread out and there was far less traffic.

Enid had come to love the surrounding farms and fields on these commutes. But there were signs everywhere that this tranquility would end one day. Housing developments were popping up where wooded areas had once been. Piles of downed trees were distressing evidence of encroaching progress.

When Enid arrived at the restaurant, Phyllis was sitting at a table near the swinging door to the kitchen. "Thank you for seeing me," Enid said.

"You didn't say what this is about, but I wanted to see you anyway. I owe you an apology."

Enid refrained from lashing out at Phyllis by reminding herself that Phyllis' brother may have been convicted of a murder he didn't commit. "What do you want to apologize for?"

"Karla Burke came to see me after she had met with you."

"I wasn't aware you and Karla knew each other that well."

"We don't. But, Karla has a way of knowing everybody, if you know what I mean."

Enid nodded and waited for Phyllis to continue.

"Karla told me you were trying to help me clear Reggie's name, and that I needed to be more honest with you."

"Why didn't you tell me about the 7 Crows Farm? Maybe I can understand why you talked in riddles at first, just to get my attention. It worked. But when we met again, after I found out who you really are, you should have told me then."

Phyllis' eyes filled with tears.

"I'm sorry for your brother's situation," Enid said. "He may or may not have been wrongly convicted." Enid put her hand on Phyllis'. "And I'm very sorry Reggie didn't live to know that his sister believed in him and was trying to clear his name."

Phyllis started to speak, but Enid held up her hand to stop her. "Wait, I'm not finished. While I understand and sympathize with your plight, you have wasted a lot of my time and may have put me and Karla in danger by withholding information. So, here's the deal. If you want me to help you, you will be totally honest with me. Do not withhold information or play any more games. I'm on your side. Do you understand that?"

Phyllis tried to pull a napkin from the stainless dispenser on the table, but it was packed so tightly that she could only pull bits of napkin from it. Enid got a tissue from her tote and handed it to her.

Phyllis wiped her eyes then dabbed at her nose. "I'm sorry. You have every right to be upset with me. I'm not trying to make excuses, but I'd like to tell you my side."

Enid nodded for her go on.

"I appreciate everything you're doing, and I would never intentionally put you or anyone in danger." Phyllis wiped her eyes again.

"I'd like to understand this whole situation, and you, a little better."

Phyllis sat up straight. "I'm proud to be black. That might sound trite, confrontational, or even racist to you, but it's taken me years to be able to stand up for who I am unapologetically. And I still struggle with it at times. Being black can be scary as hell under certain circumstances. My family has been harassed for no reason. My brother used to get stopped by the county deputies all the time, even before he was involved with Angel. I know you're trying to find the truth, and I want you to." She reached across the table and put both hands on Enid's. "But I was afraid of the truth that might come of all this, even though I wanted to reveal it. I thought maybe if I gave you tidbits of information, you'd get intrigued, figure it out, and then I'd be off the hook. That sounds selfish and cowardly, and I apologize for my behavior."

Enid leaned back in her chair. "I'm not sure what to say about all that. But I appreciate your candor. Who exactly are you afraid of? The sheriff's department in general or is there someone specific?"

Phyllis sat back and appeared to be thinking. "I've been afraid so long that I'm not sure. I know that must sound silly. All I know is Reggie didn't kill Angel, if she's even dead. He was infatuated with her, with saving her from her situation. He was a dreamer, not a killer."

"I'm afraid we'll need more than your sisterly assurances if we try to clear his name."

Reaching down in her purse, Phyllis produced a folded piece of paper. "May I show this to you?" She handed the paper to Enid.

Enid smoothed the folds and read out loud.

> *My heart aches for you, my Angel.*
> *Surely you were misplaced at birth,*
> *as God would not send you*
> *to these men without souls.*
>
> *Escape with me. Run from evil.*
> *I will care for you. Somehow.*
> *And never again will you suffer*
> *at the place of 7 Crows.*

"Was this one of Reggie's poems?" Enid asked.

Phyllis wiped the tears from her cheeks and nodded. "I found it after you asked me if I had anything of his."

"It's lovely. But it's also sad. Make I take a photo of this to keep?"

"That's a copy. You can have it."

"May I show it to Sheriff Waters?"

Phyllis' eyes widened. "Oh, no. Please don't."

"If you want me to help you, then you've got to let me use this. Keep the original in one of those large plastic freezer bags, someplace safe, and make a note of when and where you found it."

Enid looked at the poem again, and her eyes kept going back to the last line: *at the place of 7 Crows.*

CHAPTER 32

Madelyn had insisted on meeting Enid at her house in Columbia instead of talking on the phone. The closer Madelyn got to the election date, the more paranoid she had become about phone records, texts, and emails—anything that might leave a trace. She admitted it was foolish, as she had nothing to hide.

Enid was excited about this meeting, because Madelyn had hinted that she had interesting information about the bones. Of course, Enid would have to corroborate whatever Madelyn told her with someone else before it could be printed. As they agreed, Madelyn would be kept out of the story at all costs.

The driveway from the road ended in front of Madelyn's garage apartment, where Enid had previously lived before moving to Madden. Madelyn had rented it to her for a fraction of what she normally charged, and Enid had been grateful for her friend's support. There was no way to repay Madelyn, nor would she expect payment.

The melodious chimes of the doorbell produced Madelyn's housekeeper, who invited Enid inside. "Miss Madelyn is expecting you. She's in her study on the phone, but she asked you to come in and have a seat. She'll be with you shortly."

Enid followed her down the hallway where the housekeeper opened a tall door and motioned for Enid to go in. "I'll be serving soup and sandwiches in a few moments."

Just as Enid sat down, Madelyn got off the phone. "Hey, girl." She walked over to Enid and hugged her. "I've missed you."

They shared information about their lives in bullet-point fashion. Madelyn just wanted the facts, with no embellishments. When the housekeeper brought lunch, Madelyn pushed her plate to the side of her desk. "While you eat, I'll fill you in on what I found out about the bones.

First of all, the DNA results haven't been matched to anyone. Not yet, anyway. So they don't know who it is. It is a woman, between twenty and thirty years old, and she's Caucasian." Madelyn stopped talking long enough to sip her iced tea.

"So that's it?"

Madelyn took a bite of sandwich and held up a finger for Enid to wait. "Sorry, I just love that woman's pimento cheese. Had to grab a bite." She dabbed at her mouth with a napkin. "Now, where was I? Oh, yes, the forensics report. According to the soil samples, a small amount of decomp was found there, but the body mostly decomposed somewhere else."

"That's odd. Why would someone move a partially decomposed body?"

"Fear of discovery? Second thoughts? Who knows," Madelyn said.

"Can they tell how she died?"

"They didn't find any poisons leached from her body into the soil. But, if she was moved, then there might be some traces in the original dump site. There also were no traces of embalming fluids found and no bullet or knife nicks on the bones."

"So we don't know anything more about her," Enid said. "Maybe if I tell them I think it's Angel, they might be able to find her family and do a DNA test. And what about dental records?"

"No luck so far on the dental. Apparently, she was one of those rare individuals who didn't see a dentist, at least not for any identifiable work. They've put out statewide alerts to dentists. Will your source, I forget her name, will she come forward?"

"I don't know if Phyllis wants to get involved, not with the police."

"Well, if she wants to clear her brother, she needs to get over herself." Madelyn paused. "Then again, this might prove her brother really did kill that woman." She glanced at her phone. "I've got a meeting in thirty minutes. Got to run." She took another bite of sandwich. "Stay here and finish your lunch." As she walked out of the room, she called over her shoulder. "And you got none of this from me."

. . .

On the drive to Sheriff Boogie Waters' office, Enid had thought about how to approach him. Finally, she decided just to be straightforward.

Boogie offered her a seat in his office. "Well, well, Ms. Blackwell. What a pleasure to see you again."

"I'd like to talk to you about the bones found at the inn."

Boogie leaned back and appeared to study Enid. "You're mighty interested in that case. But then, I guess your small-town paper doesn't get much real news. This is probably a big deal for you."

Enid resisted the urge to remind him that the paper now covered three counties. But he was right; it was big news. "I may have some information on the victim's identity."

Boogie slowly leaned forward and eased up to his desk. His face was as stern as her third-grade teacher's when Enid announced that she wanted to be a reporter. "Now, Enid. I'm sure you'll find something more practical to focus on. Won't you, dear?"

"And just who do you think she is?" he asked.

Enid wanted to smile but didn't. "So you are confirming it's a female."

"Yes, as a matter of fact. But I guess you knew that."

"It appears my confidential source may be right. The source informed me that the bones could be a woman who went by Angel."

Boogie shrugged.

"I understand she dated some of your deputies." Enid maintained direct eye contact with Boogie. His face registered no surprise.

Boogie leaned back in his chair again. "Of course, I know about Angel. As you know, I helped prosecute her boyfriend. But what makes you so sure it's her?"

"You had a missing woman, presumed murdered, and now you've got unidentified remains. Seems like a good assumption that it could be her. But since the DNA results haven't turned up in the database, I thought perhaps you could collect DNA from her family as a comparison. Also, I'd like to show you something that may give some insight into Angel's home life. That is, if you were not aware of it." She handed Boogie a copy of Reggie's poem.

Boogie put his half-frame reading glasses on and read it. When he finished, he took his glasses off again. "I'm not into poetry much. This sounds more like a young boy who has a vivid imagination, but I'll follow up on it." He underlined his note with a sweeping gesture for emphasis. "I always appreciate tips from our county's fine citizens. Now is there anything else I can do for you?"

"No. I'll follow up with you later."

Boogie chuckled. "I'm sure you will. Yes, ma'am, I'm sure of it."

CHAPTER 33

The young girl sat up in her hospital bed and ran her hand across her nearly bald, fuzzy head. "Will my hair ever grow back, Dr. Jean?"

The woman held the girl's hands. "Yes, honey, of course it will. And you'll be even more beautiful than ever."

"Promise?"

As much as Dr. Jean wanted to reassure her, the girl's cancer was not in remission and her journey ahead was uncertain at this point. "Only God can promise you that, but I ask Him every day to take care of you."

The girl leaned over and hugged her doctor. "Thank you, Dr. Jean. I love you." All the patients, and even the staff, referred to the pediatric oncologist by her first name.

No matter how many times these scenes played out with her patients, Dr. Jean had to fight back tears. "I love you, too, honey. Now you need to get some rest." She pulled the sheet and light blanket up to cover the girl. "Remember that angels visit you while you sleep. They'll protect you if you ask them to. Okay?"

The girl nodded and closed her eyes. Dr. Jean made notations on her iPad and uploaded them to the girl's medical file. Before leaving the room, she dimmed the lights and pulled the curtains shut.

As she walked toward the next room on her rounds, Dr. Jean stopped to check a text that had just come in. "I love you," was all it said. Most of the infrequent texts from her father contained only those three words. Sometimes he said, "I'm proud of you." Whatever the messages said, they always made Dr. Jean smile. Her world was mostly about suffering and loss. At one point, she had succumbed to alcohol to dull the pain of losing a young patient she had tried so hard to save. Had it not been for her father's intervention, she would have lost everything she had worked for. "Love U 2," she responded to the text.

"Can I call tonight?" her father texted.

"Call after 9. Working late."

Her father texted back the thumbs-up icon, followed by a red heart.

Dr. Jean put her phone in her pocket and entered the next patient's hospital room. "Hey, buddy, how you doing today?"

...

By nine o'clock that night, Jean had forgotten her father had planned to call her when she heard her cell phone ring. "Oh, hi. I dozed off for a minute. Had you called earlier?"

"No, I hadn't. I worry about you being so tired all the time. Can you take some time off and come home for a visit?"

Jean was caught off-guard by his invitation. She hadn't been home in many years. They had agreed it was best if he visited her instead. "You mean come there? You want me to come see you?" She paused. "We're short a couple doctors, so I'm not sure I can. One had her work visa revoked and another one is doing a tour with Doctors Without Borders. Is everyone okay?"

"I'm fine. When do you think you might be able to come visit? I think it's time, don't you?"

Thoughts swirled in Dr. Jean's mind. "I'm not sure my coming for a visit is a good idea."

"I hope you can. We need to talk."

Jean tried to push the fears from her mind and stopped herself from jumping to any conclusions. But her father's call concerned her. "Is anything wrong?"

"I just need to see you, that's all."

"Then I'll see if I can arrange for someone to cover for me a few days. I'll remind them I haven't taken time off in two years." She thought of her patients and how disruptive it would be for them if she didn't show up each day. But she pushed those thoughts aside. It was time to face the past head on. Besides, he needed her now, and she wasn't sure why. "Do you want me to get a room at the inn? Or stay in one of the nearby towns?"

"I'll make reservations at the inn for you. Just let me know when to expect you. Oh, and before I hang up, do you have those papers that belonged to your mother?"

"There are several boxes in storage. Why?"

"Can you ship them to me? Maybe we can go through them together, when you get here."

Jean ended the call and walked to the kitchen to put a pod of Colombian decaf in her coffee maker. A thousand thoughts were going through her mind, so no caffeine for her tonight.

CHAPTER 34

Glitter Lake Inn was not the kind of place Dr. Jean would have visited, at least not when she lived in the area as a small child. Back then, she didn't have the money or the right skin color. She had been nervous about checking in, but her father assured her it was safe and that she would be welcomed. She assured herself that things were different now.

Theo greeted her in the entry hallway and asked if she wanted any refreshments—coffee, tea, or wine, perhaps with a fresh baked scone.

"No, but thank you. I'd just like to rest a bit," Dr. Jean replied.

"I'll show you to your room then."

"I'm expecting a visitor. Is that permissible?"

Theo laughed. "Of course. Would you like for me to set something up for you in the library, overlooking the lake?"

Jean shook her head. "No, we'll just meet in my room. Perhaps you could bring some coffee and a couple of those scones?"

"Of course."

Jean heard the hinges on the inn's massive oak door squeak. Theo turned and smiled at the woman who walked in. "Enid, how nice to see you," he said.

Jean recognized the woman immediately from the articles she had read. Even though Jean lived hundreds of miles away, she subscribed to the *Tri-County Gazette*. Some of Enid's article series were in larger newspapers also. Jean started to hide her face but then realized how foolish she was being. Enid Blackwell had no way of knowing who Jean was. Pushing caution aside, Jean met Enid's gaze. "Hello, I'm a fan of your work, Ms. Blackwell."

"Thank you." Enid held out her hand to Jean. "Nice to meet you."

"Likewise. My name is Jean." Suddenly nervous, she turned to Theo. "I'm going to my room now."

As Jean walked up the stairs, she heard Theo and Enid laughing together. Was coming here a mistake?

. . .

Jean's father had texted her how to go through the kitchen to the rear entrance to open the back door for him. She wondered what she would say if Theo caught her sneaking her guest in through the kitchen at nearly nine o'clock at night.

She breathed a sigh of relief when she and her father were in her room. He was carrying the two boxes of papers she had shipped to him, so he wasn't able to take her hand or hug her. She was glad. She wasn't ready for a family reunion. While she wasn't one to hold onto resentment or anger, the wounds of their earlier years were always present, deep and painful, and even more acute now that she was with him.

The room had two chairs near the window, which overlooked Glitter Lake. She motioned for her father to sit down. "Please. Make yourself comfortable. May I get you some water? I'm afraid the coffee Theo brought up earlier is cold."

"I'm sorry I'm so late. I got tied up." He ran his hand through his hair. "I can't believe how beautiful you've grown up to be. You have your mother's eyes."

"Thanks." Jean looked at the boxes on the floor. "Have you been through those yet?"

Her father shook his head. "Thought I'd wait for you. Maybe we can do it together."

Jean looked at the man across from her. He was her blood father, but she had spent little time with him as a child. "Is there something specific you're looking for?"

"Maybe nothing." He looked around the room. "This is a nice place Theo's got here. Sometime I'll tell you about his daughter that went missing."

"I read that reporter's articles."

"Right. I forgot." He cleared his throat. "Can you ever forgive me?"

Jean looked down at her feet. "I'm not ready for this conversation. Maybe later. Before I go back." She looked up. "Okay?"

Her father nodded. "Let's see what's here." He cut the tape on the first box with his pocket knife and pulled back the top. The box was filled with papers, yellowed with age.

"Let's lay them out on the bed," Jean said. She reached in for a handful of papers and spread them out across the handmade quilt. After a few minutes, the papers had been organized: handwritten notes in one stack, photos in another, and newspaper clippings in the next. The fourth stack was for miscellaneous items. She surveyed the piles of paper. "It would help if I knew what we were looking for."

He picked up a handful of old photos. "This is a good one of your mother. I don't remember it." He handed it to Jean. "Why don't you keep it."

Jean took the photo and smiled when she saw her mother's face. "She was so pretty."

Her father nodded. "She still is."

Jean took her father's hands in hers. "I'd like to go see her."

"Are you sure?" He squeezed her hands.

Jean nodded.

"Then we'll go tomorrow. Now let's finish going through these."

After sifting through dozens of papers, Jean held one up. "Here's the plan mother drew for adding the storage room at the inn." She handed it to her father.

"They walled off one of the maid's rooms to build it. They plastered over the outside entrance and made a door to the kitchen. Or at least that was the plan."

"Why is this important to you now? What's going on?" The look of concern on her father's face worried her. It wasn't like him to fret over anything small.

"They found bones in that room. It was walled off after you went to live with your aunt."

"Bones? You mean, like, human bones?"

Her father nodded and lowered his head.

"But who?" A thousand questions ran through Jean's mind.

"We don't know for sure, but it may be Angel."

Jean's hands flew to her mouth. "I need to see Mother, tomorrow."

• • •

Jean's father left the inn by the front door. The time for secrets was over. With a heavy heart, he walked down the stairs, past the reception desk, and to the front door. The door squeaked as he pulled it open and he heard footsteps coming from the library.

Theo smiled. "I didn't know you were here."

"Just had a brief meeting with someone."

"Well, have a good evening, Sheriff Waters."

CHAPTER 35

The acrid smell of disinfectant burned Jean's nose as she walked down the hallway to her mother's room. The place was clean, and the staff seemed attentive enough. But it was still a hospital. Boogie walked by her side. When they approached the room, he knocked on the door. Lillian wouldn't answer, but one of the nurses would be with her. After no response, he slowly pushed the door open. Lillian sat in her favorite chair, staring at the window.

Jean turned to Boogie. "If you don't mind, I'd like to visit her alone."

Boogie nodded. "Just don't expect too much." He left and closed the door behind him.

Jean pulled up the rocking chair and sat down beside her mother. "Hello, Mother. Do you know who I am?"

No response.

"It's me, Jean." She took her mother's hand and caressed it gently as she talked. For the next ten minutes, the two women, mother and child, held hands and stared out the window.

Jean broke the silence. "I came to see you and to tell you I love you." Jean studied her mother's face. "And to ask your forgiveness for breaking a promise." Perhaps it was an involuntary muscle reflex, but Lillian's hand moved slightly.

Jean moved her chair slightly to face Lillian. "You asked me not to ever talk about Angel, but I was never sure why. And I promised you I wouldn't." Jean pushed a strand of hair from her mother's face. "But now I have to." Jean let go of her mother's hands to get a tissue from her pocket. Jean dabbed at Lillian's eyes. "Do you remember Angel? She was my best friend. You warned me to stay away from her, but I didn't understand why. She wasn't a bad girl at all. Just sad and lonely. You finally started letting her come to the inn where you were working. She loved to come there. I confess I got jealous for a while, because you began treating her like your own daughter, and I wanted you all to myself." Jean smiled at her childhood memories.

A knock at the door startled Jean. A nurse pushed the door open and peeped inside. "Everything alright in here? You need anything?"

"We're fine. Thanks."

The nurse studied Jean from head to toe in that protecting-my-patients way. "Let me know if you need anything."

Jean put some ice from the Styrofoam bucket into a plastic glass and filled it with water. She pulled a flexible straw from its paper casing and stuck it in the glass. "Are you thirsty?" She put the straw to Lillian's lips.

When Lillian puckered her lips around the straw, Jean was overcome with joy. Then she reminded herself that as humans, we share an animal instinct for survival. Jean watched her mother drink nearly half the glass of water. When she stopped drinking, she kept her lips around the straw, so Jean gently pulled it away and set the glass on the nightstand.

Jean patted her mother's arm. "I'm going to let you rest now. I'll send the nurse in, in case you need to go to the bathroom." She leaned over and hugged Lillian and then kissed her on the cheek. "I love you. Forgive me for breaking my promise."

Jean gathered her purse and walked to the door to leave, trying not to cry for the loss of the woman her mother once was.

. . .

As Jean walked out the door, Lillian turned her head slightly to watch. Her hand shaking, Lillian tried to wave goodbye but didn't have the strength. She laid her head back against the chair and closed her eyes.

CHAPTER 36

Boogie and Jean drove in silence as they left the nursing home. While Boogie focused on the road, Jean stared out the window, trying to recognize places she had not seen in decades and noting how much had changed.

Jean was the first to speak. "Well, you told me not to expect much, and you were right. She has no recollection of me at all." Her voice choked slightly, and she cleared her throat. "But I'm glad I saw her."

Boogie kept an eye on the large pickup that pulled alongside them to pass and felt his shoulders tense. As a law enforcement officer, he hated vehicles with windows shaded so dark you couldn't see inside. The occupants could have a shotgun aimed at you, and you'd never know it—until it was too late. Once the pickup had passed and sped ahead of them, he kept one hand on the wheel and reached out to Jean with his right. "I know it's a lot to ask. But can you ever forgive me and your mother for sending you away when you were a child?" He held onto her hand for fear she would pull away. Instead, she squeezed tightly in response.

"If you had asked me that a few years ago, I would have told you no. But I've thought a lot about how difficult it must have been for you and Mother to live apart and hide your relationship, much less trying to hide a child. I've convinced myself that in different times, both of you would have handled it differently."

Boogie kept his eyes on the road and pulled her hand up to kiss it. "That's why you're such a great doctor. You're smarter and wiser than me." They rode in silence for a few minutes before either spoke. "I'm going to drop you off at the inn, and then I need to check out something."

Jean pulled her hand away and turned slightly in her seat. "Is it somewhere I can tag along? I really don't feel like being alone right now."

"Why don't we just get something to eat? I can take care of the other thing later."

"No, I don't want you to change your plans. I can sit in the car. I've got to catch up on my emails anyway. That work?"

Boogie didn't feel good about taking Jean with him, but she rarely asked him for anything, and he wasn't about to deny her today. "Alright. But you'll have to stay in the car." A few miles later, Boogie pulled off the highway and traveled down the long, single lane road that led to a neglected farm.

Jean looked around the overgrown fields. "Is this . . ." She looked again. "Is this 7 Crows Farm? Why are we here?"

"I just want to see if I can find out where Angel's family is. I need to get a DNA swab. I don't think anyone is living here, at least not the Petersons, so this is probably a wasted trip. But then again, maybe the current occupants have some information that would help me find the Peterson family." He turned the key in the ignition and pushed the gear into park. "I won't be long."

As Boogie walked up the path to the house, he felt lighter than usual. Maybe it wasn't too late to make amends with Jean. Retirement had never seemed like an option.

What would he do with himself? But now he was having second thoughts. Maybe he could move closer to her, and they could spend more time together.

He knocked on the front door of the old house. After waiting briefly, he knocked again. When there was no response, he turned to leave. And then he heard the door open.

"What do you want?" a young woman asked.

Boogie pointed to the sheriff's badge on his shirt pocket. "I'm Sheriff Bernard Waters. Do you live here?"

The young woman stared in silence.

"Is there anyone else here I can talk to?"

She continued to stare.

"I'm trying to locate someone, any family member, related to a woman who lived here once. Her name was Angel."

A flash of recognition seemed to register on the young woman's face. Her eyes appeared to widen a bit.

"Are you related to her? Or did you know her?"

The woman seemed to be nodding toward Boogie's car, as if she were trying to signal something to him. It was probably nothing.

He held out a business card to her. "Here's my number. If there's anyone here I can talk to later, or if you want to talk, just call this direct number."

The woman didn't move to take the card.

Growing tired of this one-sided conversation, Boogie leaned down and put the card on the worn wooden porch. "I'll just leave it here." As he stood up, he noticed movement near the woman. He was expecting her to slam the door. Instead, a tall man in overalls pushed her aside and stood before Boogie.

"It's been a while, Boogie. Maybe you forgot me."

Boogie wished he could have forgotten that face, with its perpetual snarl. "Hey, Fred. Long time. Could you come out on the porch so we could talk a minute?"

Fred motioned for the woman to leave. "Sure thing."

Boogie glanced toward his car. Jean must have leaned against the window to take a nap. He could barely see the top of her head. "I don't have long but I was wondering if you had heard about the bones they found at the inn?"

Fred smiled. "I don't follow the news much."

Out of his peripheral vision, Boogie saw the young woman from the house approaching them. Her hands were behind her back, and her long, flowered skirt flared out in the breeze.

"Come on. Over here," Fred called out to her.

Boogie was ready to go. Seeing Fred again after all these years was unnerving. "I'm going to leave now, but if you're staying back here at the farm, I'll catch up with you later."

"You can't run from the past," Fred said.

Boogie watched uneasily as the young woman, moving as if in slow motion, handed Fred the shotgun she had concealed behind her.

"Go to hell, Boogie. Angel's there waiting on you."

• • •

The explosive shot jarred Jean from her nap. She bolted upright in her seat. Up the driveway near the house, a tall man and a younger woman were staring down at the porch floor, at Boogie's lifeless body, his crisp shirt now crimson red.

Jean's hand flew to her mouth. Had they seen her? She glanced at the ignition. The keys were still there. The man was dragging Boogie down the front steps by his arms toward the barn to the right of the house. The young woman kept her eyes on them.

Jean crouched lower in the seat and swung her left leg over the center console. Then she managed to get into the driver's seat and pull her other leg over. She slumped down as far as she could, while keeping an eye on the man and woman. When they dragged Boogie into the barn, Jean, raised by her Catholic aunt, crossed herself and turned the key. Please, please let it start.

As the engine roared to life, she sat up and slammed the gear into reverse to turn around. The man came running out and fired at the car. She heard buckshot hitting metal.

Dust, gravel, and tears flew everywhere as Jean gunned the accelerator. In the rear mirror, she could see the man still standing there, shotgun in hand. She managed to hit every pothole in the narrow road before she reached the main road. She turned so sharply, she almost lost control, but she held on with trembling hands.

She got up to nearly ninety miles per hour before she felt safe enough to look in the rearview mirror. So far, nothing behind her. Just ahead, she saw a BP gas station. She turned in and ran inside, leaving the car parked in the middle of the parking area, motor still running.

"Help me, please. Someone shot my father."

CHAPTER 37

News of Boogie's death traveled quickly throughout the county. Emotions ran high: shock, sadness, anger. Who would kill him and why?

Around Madden, everyone assumed the 7 Crows Farm had been abandoned years ago. Concerned citizens speculated that squatters had taken up residence and killed Boogie when he tried to run them off. Deputies swarmed the farm but found no one, other than Boogie's body in the barn. The state police were called in to help and set up roadblocks.

Enid quickly drafted a news article for a special edition of the *Tri-County Gazette*. With few facts at this point, she focused instead on Boogie's life, a third-generation sheriff who devoted his life to law and order. The *State* and the other South Carolina daily newspapers would be all over the killing of a county sheriff, so Jack agreed they should get something out quickly.

As speculation, fear, and rumors swirled around Madden, one bit of information caught Enid's attention: the biracial woman who reported the murder. The manager of the gas station said the woman had claimed to be Boogie's daughter. Theo had told Enid this morning that the woman had been a guest at the inn, and that Boogie had visited her. The woman had checked out, leaving a note for Theo and a check that included a generous tip. She included her cell number in case he needed to contact her. Her note stated she would be staying at a relative's house for the time being.

Boogie's murder was being handled by the Bowman County sheriff's office with assistance from SLED. In the middle of typing this information, Enid stopped suddenly. She needed to notify Josh in case Pete had not called him yet. She didn't want Josh to hear it on the news first.

She was relieved when Josh answered. She didn't want to leave this news in a message.

"It's good to hear your voice," Josh said.

"Same here." Enid's hand trembled. "Josh, there's some bad news here. Have you talked with Pete?"

"I was just about to call him. He left a message that he needed to tell me something. What's going on?"

There was no easy way to say it. "Sheriff Boogie Waters has been shot. He's dead."

Josh made a grunting noise, like someone had hit him. "Oh, God, no. When? Who? How?"

Those were the same questions everyone was asking. "We don't know all the details. Looks like he might have walked in on some squatters at the old 7 Crows Farm."

"I've heard of that place. It's a ways out from Madden, as I recall. Did they catch them?"

"Not yet, as least not that I've heard." Enid glanced at the half-written article on her screen. "Look, I've got to finish this story. I just wanted you to know, since you and Boogie were close."

"Thanks for calling. I'd much rather hear it from you, but I'll call Pete now." A brief pause, then, "I'm trying to wrap things up here. I'll be home in a few days." Another pause. "Enid, be careful until whoever did this is behind bars. Love you."

Enid held onto her cell phone, unwilling to let Josh go, even after he hung up. "Love you, too," she whispered to herself.

. . .

After uploading the article on Boogie's murder for Jack to edit, Enid turned her attention to finding the woman who reported the shooting. The *State* newspaper would have reporters looking, too, so she had to act fast. At first, Theo had been reluctant to give Enid the woman's cell number. But Enid assured him she would respect the woman's privacy and tread carefully.

As expected, she got the woman's voice mail when she called. What was unexpected was the recorded greeting: "You've reached Dr. Jean Waters. If this is an emergency, please call my office number, as I am out of town attending to family matters. Otherwise, leave a message and I'll return your call as soon as possible."

"Dr. Waters, this is Enid Blackwell. I'm with the *Tri-County Gazette*. I'd like to talk with you to confirm some information for an article I'm writing on Sheriff Bernard Waters' killing. Please call me back at this number."

In less than a minute, her phone rang. "Hello."

"This is Jean Waters. Meet me at the inn in an hour. Theo's set up a place for us to talk." The call ended abruptly.

CHAPTER 38

To protect their privacy, Theo set up Enid and Jean to meet in his personal quarters, a small cottage on a dirt road, about five hundred feet from the inn. He had the housekeeper prepare tea and muffins, which were placed on a small serving tray on the table in the living area. The sofa faced the window, so they could see if anyone approached the house.

Enid arrived first, and Jean drove up shortly afterward, a police car close behind her.

Jean extended her hand to Enid. "I'm Jean Waters, but obviously you know that." Jean sat in one of the chairs beside the sofa. "As you can tell, I'm a bit nervous. The sheriff's office insisted they provide protection until . . ." Her voice trailed off. "Until they catch the man who killed my father."

"I'm so sorry for your loss," Enid said. "I didn't know Sheriff Waters that well, but I must confess that while we were doing some research, my editor and I learned of your existence. No one seemed to be aware that he had a daughter."

"It's complicated." Jean glanced out the window. "I've been getting calls from reporters since this happened. I've ignored them, but I know your work, so I wanted to talk to you. Theo told me I could trust you."

"Thank you, I value your trust. Are you willing to do an interview, or do you want to talk off the record?"

"I know I can't contain this story, but if you write it first, then maybe we can manage the gossipy parts, at least."

"I have a good contact at the Associated Press. I'll see if we can get him to run this and get ahead of the pack."

Jean smiled slightly. "Thank you." She reached for the teapot. "Theo is a great innkeeper. He prepared my favorite." She poured a cup and handed it to Enid.

Enid pulled her notepad and pen from her leather tote. She also put her iPhone on the table. "May I record this? I can stop it at any time you feel uncomfortable. I just want to make sure the details are correct."

"Of course."

"Why don't you start by telling me about yourself and then what happened."

Jean took a sip of tea before speaking. Enid noticed Jean's hands were shaking slightly.

"I'm a pediatric oncologist at St. Jude's Hospital in Memphis. Until recent years, my father and I had barely spoken to each other. We weren't exactly mad at each other. We just weren't close." She paused to sip her tea.

"Is your mother still alive?"

"She's in a nursing home near here, an Alzheimer's patient."

Enid looked in her folder and pulled out the photo she had copied from the inn, showing Boogie and a black woman together. "Is that your mother?"

Jean took the photo and smiled as she ran her hand gently across the images. "Yes, that's her."

"I can imagine a mixed-race relationship around here must have been difficult at that time."

Jean nodded. "They tried to keep it a secret, my mother especially. She didn't want my father to lose his sheriff's position."

"Were you raised around here?"

"In my early years, yes. Then my parents sent me to be raised by an aunt who lived over in the next town. She'd drop me off at the inn sometimes, and I was able to visit with my mother. When that aunt died, Mother sent me to Philadelphia to stay with another aunt."

"During that time, did you have any contact with your father?"

"Gifts at Christmas and on my birthday. He usually left them with Mother, though. I saw him a couple of times." Jean smiled. "I thought he was a superhero in that uniform."

"It must have been hard for you, the fact that he didn't publicly acknowledge you."

"It was. A notary public married them when she got pregnant. She didn't have to keep working, but she loved the inn and stayed in the caretaker's cottage. Mostly, she was afraid that people, especially her close friends and family, would think she was a kept woman. She wanted to earn her own money."

"So the relationship wasn't really a secret."

"The black community was well aware of my mother and father's relationship. When her pregnancy became obvious to the inn's owner, he was supportive and allowed her to work until she delivered. But she never told him who the father was. During my freshman year of college in Philadelphia, my second aunt died." Jean smiled. "I thought she was barely making ends meet, but she left me a generous trust fund that paid for my college. I'm sure my father contributed to that fund also."

"Did you just recently reconnect with your father?"

"About ten years ago, we started talking on the phone once or twice a year. He always promised to come see me, and he did a couple of times. He didn't think it was wise for me to come down here."

"So why did you come this time?"

"He called me, out of the blue, and asked me to come down and send Mother's papers to him. He set up my reservation at the inn. While I was here, I told him I wanted to see my mother." Jean looked away and dabbed at her eyes with a tissue. "She had no idea who I was."

Enid patted Jean's arm. "I'm so sorry. Do you have any relatives left?"

"Just a few cousins, most of whom I haven't met. But I've got a large network of friends in Memphis. I'm not alone now, if that's what you're worried about."

Enid pushed thoughts of her own family, most of whom were now deceased, from her mind. "Do you know why your father wanted your mother's papers?"

Jean shook her head. "We went through two boxes of papers together. I don't know what he was looking for, or if he found it. Afterward, we went to that farm, and that's when he was . . . you know, when he was killed."

"Why did he go to 7 Crows Farm? And why would he risk taking you with him?"

"He said something about trying to find family members of someone who had been killed. He had a tip that the bones at the inn might be a woman named Angel. I honestly don't think he expected anyone to be at the farm. I sat in the car and waited for him and was going to check my emails, but I dozed off. Visiting my mother just took everything out of me. The shotgun blast woke me. The man looked toward the car, but I was a bit down the driveway and the glass is tinted. Besides, I was slumped down in the seat against the window, so he didn't see me, at least not until I drove off."

"You were lucky to get away. Was there only one person at the farm?"

"A young woman was there also. Long blonde hair. She was really thin."

"Do you think these people were squatters?"

Jean shrugged. "I have no idea." She paused. "You know, I remember that place, from when I was a child."

"How? Had you been to the farm before?"

"A couple of times when Mother took Angel home. I went with them."

"So you knew Angel?"

Jean nodded. "We were childhood friends. The first time I ever saw Angel, she ran into the kitchen at the inn and asked Mother to hide her."

"From whom?"

"I honestly don't recall. I was just a kid, but I recognized drama even then. Angel was always running from people, it seemed. She didn't want to go home, but Mother told her she couldn't stay at the inn."

"Was Angel afraid of her family?"

"Like I said, I didn't understand all that was going on. And I hate to admit it, but I was jealous of Angel, so I started trying to avoid her."

"Why is that?"

"Mother took her under her wing and tried to protect her, yet I was sent to live with relatives. I resented Mother for that." Jean dabbed at her eyes again. "I realize now she did what she thought was right for me. And for Angel."

"Were you aware of Angel's disappearance?"

"I had already moved away when she went missing. And my mother had been steadily slipping into dementia. She often forgot things and got confused. She may have mentioned it. If she did, I probably dismissed it."

"Do you know a woman named Phyllis Long? She's an English teacher."

"I don't think so. Why?"

"I'm the one who told Boogie that the bones at the inn might be Angel's."

Jean looked confused. "How could you know that?"

Enid told Jean about Phyllis' visit to her office and her claims about Angel's death. "She thinks her brother Reggie was wrongfully convicted of Angel's murder. And she thinks that the bones are Angel's."

Jean stood up and paced around the small living area a few times. "This is just so much to absorb." She sat down again. "So how is all of this related to my parents . . . and to me?"

"At this point, I'm not sure. But Boogie was trying to find a relative so that he could get a DNA swab. They've done tests on the bones, but they couldn't match it to anything in the NamUs or FBI data banks. They're still checking dental records. Without something to link those bones to the family, we may never know whose they are."

Jean held up her hand. "Wait. Let me think." Jean stood up and paced again. "I remember something about a storage room Mother was having built at the inn. Like I said, she was starting to ramble and forget things a lot. And to make things up. At times, she would confuse the past with the present, so it was hard to know if anything she said had merit." Jean paused. "You don't think my mother had anything to do with Angel's death, do you?"

"I have no idea. That's what we're trying to find out." Enid studied Jean's face and saw nothing but kindness in her eyes. "I'm so sorry you've had to endure all of this in your life. But you managed to overcome it."

"Thanks. It was tough at times."

"How long did your mother continue working at the inn?"

"The owner kept Mother on as long as he could, but she was eventually forced to leave. They gave her a generous retirement bonus. I remember something about her being upset that they wouldn't let her finish her remodeling project—something about a storage room behind the kitchen. It used to be a small maid's room, so she was going to shut it off and have it open to the kitchen. She hired someone to do the work, but the inn's owner wouldn't approve it." Jean rubbed her temples. "It was years ago. I just can't remember all the details."

"My editor, who inherited the inn from the last owner, looked for relatives but couldn't find anyone. They seemed to have all passed away, which is how he ended up with it." Enid saw another car drive up outside. The deputy went over to talk to the person. "I think we have visitors. Maybe we need to wrap this up for now. How long will you be in town?"

"Until sometime after the service, and then I need to get home to my patients. You've got my cell number. Just call me. I'll let you know if I think of anything else."

"The boxes belonging to your mother. Where are they now?"

"At my father's house, where I'm staying."

"Are you safe there with the killer still at large?" Enid asked.

"They've got deputies assigned to protect me. I imagine that man is long gone by now."

"May I get the boxes from you? I'll return them and even ship them back if you leave before I finish going through them. Maybe I'll see something that's helpful."

"Of course."

"Let's get out of here. Come on, we'll go out the back way."

. . .

After Enid picked up the two boxes from Jean, the ones that contained her mother's papers, Enid called Cade.

"Is everything okay?" he asked. "When you call, it's usually not good news. What's going on?"

"I'm fine, but I need something from you."

"Does this have anything to do with Josh?"

Enid caught herself before saying something she would likely regret. "No, it's not. It's about Sheriff Waters' murder."

"I saw something about that on the wire. Wasn't much info."

"If I give you the details, can you run a story on his daughter? She was there when Boogie was killed. I just met with her, and she wants a reputable reporter to cover it."

"What? How did you . . .? Never mind. I should know better by now than to question how you get this stuff. Where is she?"

"Here, staying at the sheriff's place. But she'll probably return to Memphis soon. She's a physician at St. Jude's. I've got a recorded interview and notes—enough for an initial story. And I can get more if needed. She trusts me, and I told her I'd talk to you about running it." Enid was prepared for Cade to refuse her, as this wasn't his kind of story.

"On one condition."

"What's that?" Enid held her breath.

"I'll write it with you."

"I . . ." She stopped to gather her thoughts. "I appreciate the offer, but I'll have to clear that with the paper, with Jack."

"Of course, but you know he'll support you. Talk to Jack and then send me what you've got. I gotta run."

CHAPTER 39

When Jack walked into the newspaper's conference room, Enid had papers spread out across the big table. "I'm sorry to interrupt, but you left me a message about working with Cade on an article, and I wanted to respond in person."

Enid put the papers in her hand on a stack and sat in one of the old metal chairs. "You don't want me to do it, do you?"

Jack sat down beside her. "I always want what's best for you, and for the paper. If you do this, the story will go national and be headlines for at least a news cycle. Is she prepared for all the attention this story will focus on her?"

"I've run all those questions and more through my mind. Jean, Dr. Waters, doesn't want to hide any longer. She regrets the years she didn't get to spend with her father, even though she doesn't blame him. She also thinks this story will get out anyway, so she wants to manage it, as much as she can. Besides she hopes the story will help catch her father's killer."

"Your motivations may be pure, but do you trust that Cade's are?"

Enid stiffened. "You've always told me what a great guy Cade is. Why would you question his motives? Besides, I'm the one who approached him about doing the story."

Jack rubbed the back of his neck. It was hard for him to manage Enid the same way he managed the other reporters and employees at the paper. As much as he tried, he couldn't deny it. "Look, you've always said I try too hard to fix things. And I know I'm overly protective of you at times." He laughed. "Why, I don't know, because you certainly don't need help from me."

"Forget it's me. If one of your other reporters were making this request, what would you say?"

Jack sat down and looked into Enid's eyes. "I'd say, 'It's a great opportunity. Go for it.' Jean deserves to have her story told by the best person—and that's you."

Unexpectedly, Enid leaned over and kissed Jack on the cheek.

"That was totally unprofessional, Ms. Blackwell." He grinned and walked out the door.

. . .

Cade and Enid's story about Sheriff Waters' murder ran on the wire and was picked up by many of the larger newspapers, including those in Tennessee, where Jean lived. In the AP article, Cade wanted to focus on the murder, because that was the bigger story. Enid insisted that they also tell the story of Dr. Jean, her dedication to treating pediatric cancer patients, and the loss of her father, whom she had not known due to years of racial prejudice. Dr. Jean also begged the public to come forward if they knew anything about who had killed her father.

Jean had called Enid immediately when the story ran, thanking her for the "raw honesty" of it. Cade had been forced to call in a few favors, as his editor wanted more about the murder and less about Jean. In the end, the editor admitted it was a good piece.

The *Tri-County Gazette* ran another article written by Enid. Boogie was one of their own citizens, and the county was still in mourning over his loss. Even those who didn't like him or his policing methods admitted he had been good for the area. Enid's article focused on finding the killer, or killers, who might still be in the area. The 7 Crows Farm was under 24-7 surveillance, but Enid withheld that and other information that might impede the investigation.

Now that the story was out, Enid could return her attention to the boxes of paperwork in the conference room. The hospital had offered Jean personal leave time to attend to her father's estate, for which she was the sole beneficiary. Jean had reluctantly accepted the offer and was readying the house for sale, under the watchful eyes of the deputies assigned to protect her.

When Enid had pressed Jean to describe the man who shot Boogie, Jean could give only a vague description: not too tall, but not short; light brown hair; not fat, but not thin either. Jean had only glanced at the man briefly. The woman who handed the gun to the killer was equally non-descript, based on Jean's recollection: tall, thin, blonde. The woman appeared to be younger than the man, but Jean wasn't sure how old the man was. He was muscular. She remembered that. Based on these vague descriptions, the killers weren't likely to worry about being identified from the article.

Around town, the squatter theory was now accepted as that's-what-happened. Squatters had become common, moving onto the farms when families moved on or put them up for sale. Getting the squatters out wasn't always easy.

Some were armed; most were belligerent and stood their ground. At Sarah's diner, the breakfast crowd, mostly older men, talked of arming themselves and forming a militia to protect the farms from squatters. Enid was pleasantly surprised that these men were sympathetic to Boogie's daughter, Jean. A few grumbled about the problems caused by interracial marriages, but those who had met Jean at the diner seemed to be impressed with her warmth, as well as her credentials. Many of the county's citizens felt betrayed by Boogie's decades of deception about his marriage and daughter, while others said the sheriff's personal life was of no concern to them.

Enid walked into the diner to get a cup of tea to go, as the electric tea kettle at the newspaper office had shorted out with a display of fireworks. When she walked in, most of the men turned to look at her. A few greeted Enid with a smile or a head nod before they returned to their conversations.

"Good article, Ms. Blackwell," someone called out from the rear booth. She couldn't see his face, so she walked toward him.

"Thank you, sir."

When the man in the back booth swung his legs out to stand up, she nearly fainted. "Josh, oh my, it's you." She ran to him. Applause broke out in the diner when Josh held her in his arms.

"Hello, Enid. I've missed you."

CHAPTER 40

With everything that was going on, Enid had almost forgotten about the papers in the conference room. Ginger, the office manager, stopped Enid in the hallway. "I need that table. When are you planning on getting those papers out of there?"

"Sorry. I'll get them out today. It's just been—"

Ginger interrupted her. "Yeah, I know, you're a famous reporter now and your man is back in town." Ginger looked at Enid. "But I really do need that space." Enid took no offense, as Ginger was just being Ginger.

"I'm going now." Enid headed toward the conference room, but her mind wasn't on her work. It was on Josh. He was only in town for a few days before he had to return to New Mexico.

When Enid opened the door to the conference room, she was taken aback by the stacks of paper. A few days ago, they seemed fewer and shorter. She pulled out a chair and methodically began going through Lillian Waters' papers. The problem was that Enid wasn't sure what she was looking for.

Two hours later, Enid was ready to give up. She needed to pack all this stuff away and return it to Jean. She had no idea what Boogie could have been looking for.

Enid sat back and closed her eyes, both to rest them and to think about what Jean had told her. The storage room had been closed off when the inn's owner ended Lillian's project, so the only people who knew about the "secret" room were the owner, Lillian, and the construction person or crew who worked on it. Of course, they may have also told others.

Enid looked for the stack of receipts. Lillian had apparently been fond of paying in cash. Most of the purchases were food; a few were prescription drugs. Near the bottom of the stack of receipts was a handwritten note where she had paid Tom's Construction Company to do work on the inn's kitchen. Surely the inn's owner didn't make Lillian pay for it herself. Or maybe they reimbursed her. Enid straightened the folds in the paper and took a photo of the receipt with her phone.

As she arranged the paperwork back into the two boxes, Enid thought about Lillian Waters sitting in the nursing home, her life reduced to several boxes of old papers and a few photographs.

• • •

Finding Tom's Construction Company in a nearby town was easy. Small companies like his depended on word-of-mouth advertising to keep them going, so they were well known to locals. As is the case with most small-town businesses, they are family owned and passed down through generations. Tom's grandfather started the business doing custom carpentry work, and then his son, Tom's father, continued the business. By the time Tom inherited the small company, custom carpentry had given way to installing mass-produced cabinets and thermoplastic moldings. Few locals wanted, or could afford, custom woodworking these days, but Tom's business was seeing an increase in construction and remodeling activity due to the influx of new people in the area.

The door to Tom's workshop was open when Enid arrived, so she peeped inside. "Hello, Tom?"

From the back of the shop, she heard a man's voice. "Be there in a minute."

While waiting for Tom, she glanced around the work area. Everything was meticulously arranged, and the floor was spotless: the signs of someone who took pride in their work.

A large man in overalls emerged from the back of the shop. "Sorry to keep you waiting. I'm Tom." He held out his hand, which was worn and calloused from years of handling wood and tools.

"I'm Enid Blackwell. It's a pleasure to meet you." Enid waived her arm as she gestured around the shop. "Nice setup here. I'm impressed."

Tom shrugged. "It's what I do. Been at it my whole life, although the work is a bit different these days." He pointed to what looked like a large bench against the wall. "This guy moved into the area and wants to build a tiny house. I guess that's a thing nowadays." He pointed toward a large piece of furniture being built. "That there is going to be a sofa, bed, and storage cabinet." He ran his hand through his mostly silver hair. "Actually, it's pretty clever. At least it's more creative than some of my work." He motioned to a small office at the back of the shop. "Let's go sit down in there. You said you had some questions about a past job."

Unlike the rest of the shop, Tom's office area was a jumble of falling stacks of paper, fat loose-leaf notebooks crammed with paper, and the obligatory coffee maker on a metal table.

"I'd offer you some coffee, but I'm out. Got to make a run to the IGA today."

"I'm fine, thanks." Enid pulled a printout from her tote that showed Lillian's payment for work on the inn's kitchen. She handed it to Tom. "Do you remember doing this work at the Glitter Lake Inn?"

Tom glanced briefly at the paper. "Where did you get this?"

"I'm sure you know Sheriff Waters was shot dead. These papers belonged to his wife, Lillian. I think you did some work for her. Do you remember it?"

Tom put his hands to his face, covering his eyes. He seemed to be deep in thought. When he lowered his hands, his smile was gone. "Miss Lillian was a good woman. I had some hard times back then. Some days, the only meal I got was from her kitchen. She tried to send work my way as often as she could." He paused and looked up at the ceiling, as if looking for a script to guide him. "When she started getting sick, she'd forget what day it was. Some days she was perfectly normal. Other days, she got confused a lot."

"When you did this work on the storage area for her, did she seem to know what she was doing? Did you find anything odd about this particular job?"

Tom put his face in his hands again. This time he sobbed. "I knew it was wrong, but I couldn't say no to her."

Enid wanted to let Tom tell the story at his own pace, so she tried not to rush him. His emotional pain was palpable.

He pulled a big, white cotton handkerchief from his overall pocket and blew his nose. He sounded like an angry goose. "I'm sorry. It's just that . . . I knew this day would come. And when they found them bones, I prayed it would all go away."

"Why don't you start from the beginning. I can't promise you anything, but I'll help you talk to the authorities."

Tom nodded and gasped, as if breathing air for the first time after being nearly suffocated. "Okay. I need to talk about it anyway. My late wife tried to get me to go to the police, but I was afraid they might arrest me, and then what would happen to her? She was frail and couldn't have made it on her own."

"What did you do?" Enid paused. "Did you kill someone and hide the person in that secret room?"

Tom's eyes widened. "Oh, no, ma'am. I didn't hurt nobody. I swear." Sweat popped out on his forehead.

"It's alright. Just take your time and tell me what you and Lillian did."

He wiped his forehead with the back of his hand. "When I got to the inn that day to do some work, Miss Lillian was agitated. She kept saying, 'I got to protect her.'"

"Who was she talking about?"

"I asked her that, but she just kept saying the same thing over and over again."

"Who did you think she was talking about?"

"Honestly, I figured she was just ranting about something in her memory—or what was left of it. But then she asked me to drive her to Pinewood."

"You mean the old cemetery?" The memory of Enid's past encounter there a couple years ago with a biker gang made her hand tremble as she took notes.

Tom nodded. "So I took her there, to Pinewood, late one afternoon." He paused to look up at the ceiling again. "Oh, Lord, this is tough."

"Take your time."

He sighed. "She told me I had to bring her back to the inn. I didn't know who or what she was talking about, but it was creepy being in that old cemetery that late, with her talking about bringing somebody back." A brief pause. "Then she pointed to a fresh grave that was on the edge of the property. There wasn't no headstone or marker, just a patch of dirt."

"Did she mention the person's name at all while you were there?"

Tom shook his head. "I didn't want to know. Honestly, I was hoping someone had buried a dog or some kind of animal there. Like I said, she was confused about a lot of things."

Enid waited for Tom to collect his thoughts and continue.

"I had brought a shovel, like Miss Lillian asked me to. She pointed at the patch of dirt and said, 'I need to take her to the inn where I can protect her.'" Tom shook his head, as if trying to rid his memory of the past. "I dug. It wasn't too deep. I hit something and threw the shovel aside, finished uncovering the thing with my hands. I didn't know what it was, so I didn't want to damage it." Tom stood up. "I got to get some water. Would you like some?"

"No, thanks." Enid waited for Tom to get a small bottle of water from the mini fridge.

Tom took several gulps and then continued. "Turned out to be a body. I could tell from the long hair it was a woman. I turned to Miss Lillian and asked her who it was. She just asked me to wrap the body back up and put it in the truck." He paused to take another sip of water. "It was dark by the time we got back to the inn. We went in the back door. I had already started walling up the hole in the room off the kitchen because Miss Lillian said the inn's owner didn't want her to build a storage room. She wasn't happy about that. She pointed toward the room and said, 'In there.'"

"Why didn't you tell her what you were doing was illegal?"

"I wanted to, but like I said, Miss Lillian fed me when I was hungry, and she never asked anything in return. I just couldn't say no. And it wouldn't have mattered, at least not that day. She just wasn't herself."

"Do you recall any clothing or wrapping being found with the remains?"

Tom nodded. "After I put the body in the room, I removed the clothes and tarp when she wasn't looking. I didn't want to leave any more evidence than I had to." Tom wiped his forehead again.

"Did you keep any of it?"

Tom shook his head. "Oh, no. I burned it all right when I got back home. It was heavy canvas and had paint drippings on it. The clothes looked like a dress, but it was torn and falling apart."

"How did she know where to find the body at the cemetery?" Enid asked.

"I asked her that myself. All she said was it was supposed to be a secret, but she found out."

"How? Whose secret?" Enid asked.

"She said she overheard a conversation."

"At the inn?" Enid asked.

"I guess so. Miss Lillian said they didn't know she could hear them."

"Who was she talking about?" Enid asked.

"I'm not sure, but she was really upset about it. She said, 'You can't trust anybody.' She repeated that several times until I agreed with her. Like I said, she wasn't herself, so it was hard to know what was real and what she imagined."

"And she never told you whose remains you dug up or why she wanted the bones at the inn?"

"All she kept saying was, 'I need to protect her.' So that night, I finished the wall and put drywall on it. The next day, I went back and skim coated it with plaster to match the rest of the old walls in the inn."

Enid glanced at her notes. "If you were trying to destroy evidence, why did you give her a receipt for the work you did? I thought you said you did it as a favor to her."

Tom smiled slightly. "I did, but the next day, when I went to the inn to finish the work, she acted like nothing had happened. She gave me coffee and cookies and thanked me for finishing the room. She insisted that I give her a bill for the work. So I gave her one, but I told her she had already paid me. She said, 'Oh, alright' and it was never mentioned again." Tom pointed to the old cash receipt. "I can't believe she kept that."

"It must have had some emotional significance to her." Enid recalled finding a receipt in her mother's papers after she died for a dress purchased twenty years prior to her mother's passing. Enid often wondered why her mother had kept that memento.

"Not long after that, Miss Lillian left the inn and went to the nursing home."

"Did you ever see her again?"

"No." Tom wiped his eyes with the back of his hand. "I guess I was foolish enough to think that if I forgot it and went on about my life, everyone else would, too."

Enid put her notepad in her tote. "I'll talk to my friend in law enforcement. He'll know what to do about all this."

Tom walked Enid back to her car. "Thank you."

Enid turned to look at Tom. "For what? I'm sure you were not happy to see me."

"Deep inside, I knew somebody would show up one day. Secrets don't stay buried forever. At least it was a nice lady like you." Tom put his baseball cap on. "'Bye, Miss Enid. Guess I'd better get back to work and finish up a few things before they come for me."

CHAPTER 41

While Josh had been gone, Pete continued to work from the front desk, so nothing had been disturbed in the police chief's office. A layer of fine dust on the old desk was proof no one had disturbed it. Josh was nervous about seeing Enid again. He wanted to hold her and tell her he was home for good and that everything had been handled in New Mexico. But neither was true. He would likely have at least one more conversation with his brother Troy. His thoughts were interrupted by Pete.

"Hey, Chief. It's good to have you back. I mean it was fun being boss for a little while, but I'm not ready for your job."

Josh grinned. "Good to know you're not ready to take over just yet. But you will be. Soon." He looked down at his clutter-free desk. "What? No phone messages or emergencies to handle?"

Pete blushed slightly. "No, I've handled everything. You back for good now?"

Josh sat down at his desk and sighed. "I'm not sure just yet. I'm trying to wrap up everything back home." But New Mexico wasn't home any longer. His life and heart were here, in Madden.

. . .

Enid walked into the police station as Pete was walking back to the front desk. "Hi, Pete. So our wandering police chief has returned, I see."

"Yes, ma'am. He's in his office. You can go on back. I'm sure he's anxious to see you." Pete focused on his computer screen. "I'm just out here doing some searches, so don't mind me, if you know what I mean."

Enid smiled. "Thanks."

When she walked into Josh's office and saw him sitting at his desk, her first impulse was to rush in and hold him tight. But despite Pete's thinly veiled assurance of privacy, she and Josh had a firm rule about not touching in either of their workplaces. Josh appeared thinner, and he looked tired. "Hey, you. I missed you."

Josh stood up and glanced toward Pete at the front before planting a kiss on her lips. "Rules are made to be broken, right?" He held Enid tightly for a few seconds before releasing her.

"I'm glad you're home. You are home now, right?"

"I need to go back in a day or so and finish up, but I wanted to come back for Boogie's memorial service, so I could say a few words. He was good to me, helped me understand this job."

Enid couldn't help but notice the dark circles under Josh's eyes. He looked like he had not been sleeping well. "There's so much I have to tell you. Do you have time?"

Josh made a sweeping gesture across his desk. "Pete took care of everything. No messages to return, no lonely widows calling about imaginary stalkers. So, I'm good."

For the next thirty minutes, Enid filled Josh in on all that had happened while he was gone. She stopped short of telling him about Tom and the bones he moved to the inn.

"Wow. That's quite a story. So the bones belong to Angel, after all?"

"Well, the DNA hasn't been matched to anyone yet, and they haven't turned up any dental records to compare. But the circumstantial evidence points to it being her."

"I sure didn't know Boogie had a daughter. She sounds like an amazing woman."

"She is. I really like her. Did you know about Lillian?"

"Boogie hinted at a relationship with a woman who was in a nursing home, but I had no idea who it was or that they had married. It's amazing how much I didn't know about him."

Enid took a deep breath. "There's more I have to tell you. And I need your help."

Josh ran his fingers through his dark hair. "Okay. Shoot."

"There's a man named Tom that runs a small construction company, actually more like a remodeling company."

"I know him, he's over in the next town. He's as good a finish carpenter as I've ever seen. How's he involved in all this?"

"He put those bones in the walled-up room at the inn."

Josh sat up straight. "What?"

"Lillian asked him to dig up a body at the Pinewood Cemetery and put it at the inn. She kept saying she was protecting her."

"But why would Tom go along with that? Doesn't he know grave robbing is a crime?"

"From the way he described it, the body was stashed there, not exactly buried in a grave."

"Well, I guess there's no better place to dump a body than in a cemetery. But even so, why would Tom go along with Lillian's request?"

Enid explained Tom's rationale and his relationship with Lillian. "I told him I'd help him talk to the authorities."

"I assume you mean me, but you know this is out of my jurisdiction. I can talk to the new sheriff, though. I'm sure he, or perhaps she, will bring Tom in for questioning."

"He knows that. In fact, he's anxious to talk about it. This secret has been festering in him a long time."

Josh crossed his arms across his chest and looked around the room. "I can't help but wonder how much of this Boogie knew about. I hate to see his memory sullied. On the other hand, if he's involved in all this, it needs to come out. Have you told Jean about what Tom and her mother did?"

Enid shook her head. "No, Jean is the one who gave me the receipt that led me to Tom, but I haven't told her about my conversation with him. I wanted to talk to you first."

"Aside from all this, don't forget there's a killer or two out there somewhere. Whoever killed Boogie hasn't been apprehended. You've got to be careful."

"I will."

"I won't lecture you, but please don't take any chances." The frown disappeared. "Dinner tomorrow after the memorial service? I'll cook. And pack your toothbrush."

CHAPTER 42

The small Baptist church was packed for Sheriff Bernard Waters' memorial service. Jean had no idea what her father might have wanted, but she chose to cremate him and inter his urn in the church cemetery. She had talked to the minister first to be sure Lillian's urn could be added to the grave when she passed. At first the minister hesitated, saying the church "rules" would require a second plot for Lillian when she passed. Jean explained that Bernard and Lillian Waters had been denied a life together, and Jean wanted them to be together eventually. She also offered a generous donation to the church, so the minister granted permission.

Jean had been raised Catholic by her aunt, and the long, emotional service at the country church was more than Jean had envisioned when she asked for a simple service. But her father would have been pleased with the outpouring of well wishes from the attendees, especially the law enforcement officers, and with Josh's eulogy. Mountains of flowers covered the front of the church.

When the choir sang, "The Old Rugged Cross," Jean wept softly. A dozen or more of Bernard Waters' cousins, nieces, nephews, and other distant relatives sat with her in the family pews, but none of them put a comforting arm around Jean.

. . .

After the memorial service, Jean politely declined an invitation from Enid, as she wanted to return to Boogie's house and to spend some time alone. She went to the kitchen to get a glass of water. It was mid-afternoon, so she didn't turn the lights on. Since the kitchen was on the east side of the house, it got a full dose of morning light through its only window, the one over the sink. But in the afternoon, it was dark.

When she first heard the noise, she was getting a pitcher of water from the refrigerator. She assumed it was the raccoon that routinely knocked over and raided the trash can outside the kitchen door. Being raised mostly in the city, Jean assumed raccoons came out to forage for food only at night, but one of the farmers at the diner told her they'd come out anytime they were hungry. She always put the cover on the metal trash can, but the clever raccoon figured out if he knocked it over, the lid usually came off. She smiled to herself at the instinctive resourcefulness of animals.

When she heard the noise again, she wasn't as sure this time that it was her four-legged intruder. She set the glass of water on the counter and instinctively reached for a butcher knife in the drawer beside the sink. Her phone was in the bedroom, so she held onto the knife as she turned to go retrieve it.

At the sound of splintering wood, Jean put both hands on the knife handle and pointed it toward the kitchen door. Her heart was pounding, as she heard another loud thud and more splintering. Then the door lock gave way. A man in a baseball cap and sunglasses pushed the door open and stepped inside.

In a split second, Jean had to decide between fight or flight, the most primal of human instincts. If she ran, could she get to the phone in time? Or would she simply trap herself further inside the house? If she tried to run past the man and out the kitchen door, he would surely grab her. In her flash vision of him, she had not seen a gun or knife, but he could have either. She secured the butcher knife in her right hand. With all her might, she rammed her body weight against the man and tried to push past him. When he tried to grab her arm, she slashed out at him, drawing blood. Jean the doctor wanted to be sure the man was okay, but Jean the victim took another swipe at his shoulder. She couldn't bring herself to aim for his heart. She just wanted to slow him down and run out that door. Again, she put her full body weight against the bleeding man. She dropped the knife and ran out the back door, down the side of the house to the road. "Help! Please!"

Jean ran toward the county police car parked in front of her house, but there didn't appear to be anyone in it. She ran to the driver's side and saw the deputy on the ground in a pool of blood. As much as her instincts told her to stop and check on him, she didn't. Right now, she had to find help.

The closest houses weren't close at all. People out here valued their land—and their privacy. She had not met any of the neighbors, other than the lonely man down the road who had offered his sympathy and asked her out to dinner. He worked, so she knew he wouldn't be home.

The intruder staggered from the house and jogged toward her, holding a dish towel on his shoulder wound, blood dripping from his arm. Jean kept running, while glancing over her shoulder.

Suddenly, a pickup truck appeared on the street, headed toward Jean. She waved her arms and stood in its path. The driver slammed on the brakes and got out. "Lady, are you crazy? I could have hit you."

"Please, help me. A man broke into my house, and a deputy has been wounded."

The driver appeared to be wrestling with whether to believe her story. "Get in the truck and lock the door." He pulled his cell phone from his pocket.

Jean got in the passenger side and locked the door. She watched the driver talking to someone and then walk back toward her. He unlocked the driver's side door and reached under the seat, grabbing a metal lug wrench. "The police are on the way." The driver walked to the front of the truck after making sure all the doors were locked.

Jean shook all over. The adrenalin that had gotten her past the man and out of the kitchen was now raw fear. The intruder walked toward them. When the driver raised the lug wrench, the intruder turned away and walked toward the woods near the house. Although she wanted to bury her face in her hands and hide, Jean studied the intruder's gait and every detail that she could.

The driver stood in front of the truck until the county deputy arrived a few minutes later.

"Ma'am, are you alright?" the deputy asked. "Do you need medical care?"

"No, I'm fine. Just check on the deputy over by his car." Jean clasped her hands to quell the shaking.

"My partner is checking on him now. Can you tell me what happened?"

"The man that killed my father just tried to kill me, too."

. . .

Enid was nervous as she watched Josh finish preparing dinner. There was something between them that had not been there before. Secrets that separated them. Until now, she had been willing to wait, assuring herself that he would eventually open up and tell her what was going on in New Mexico.

"Almost ready," Josh said. "I hope you're hungry."

"Famished. That smells delicious."

"My mother's recipe for bison chili. I've had some meat in the freezer waiting on a special occasion."

"You never talk about your parents much. I know they're both dead, but how old were you when they passed?"

Josh stirred the pot with a long wooden spoon and then put the cover back on it. "My dad died when I was five. I really didn't know him that well."

"What about your mother?"

"She died right after my wife, Serena, was killed. My mother did an amazing job raising us kids." He paused. "Well, except for Troy. He was the baby, never listened to anyone. I had a sister, Kimi. She left home when she was fifteen. No one has heard from her."

"Do you stay in touch with Troy?"

"Some."

"What about your sister? Has anyone tried to find her?"

"They looked some, a few years back, but I don't think she wanted to be found." He motioned toward the table on the porch. "Grab those bowls. We're ready to eat."

Enid wanted to pull out her phone and take a picture of the setting, but she didn't want Josh to make fun of her. He had set up a small table on the screened porch. A bottle of wine was ready to pour, and candles were everywhere, flickering in the evening. "This looks great. So romantic."

Josh came up behind her and grabbed her around the waist. "Not bad for a small-town cop, huh?"

Enid turned to face him, and they kissed until Josh pulled away.

"Let's eat. We've got the whole night to catch up."

Josh poured the wine and proposed a toast. "To the best damn reporter I know."

"And to the best police chief I know." Enid sipped her wine. "This is delicious. What is it?"

"It's Rioja, a Spanish wine. Glad you like it."

Over dinner they keep the conversation light, talking about the weather and Madden gossip. Afterward, when they were clearing the dishes, Enid asked, "Have you talked to Cade recently?"

Josh kept working, without looking up. "Not since I've been back. Is he still in Madden?"

"No, he left. I'll call him about the article, to see if he's still planning on writing it."

Josh wiped his hands on the dishtowel and took her hands in his. "Come on. I'll get all this later. Let's sit on the porch a while."

They settled into a metal daybed that served as an outdoor sofa. A dozen or more pillows created a snuggle-worthy nest. Josh spoke first. "I know you want to know about what's going on. I wasn't intentionally keeping you in the dark. I just had to figure some things out first."

Enid laid her head on his shoulder. "Can you tell me now?"

Josh kissed the top of Enid's head and caressed her arm. "Cade had good reason to believe I killed Serena's killer. I had motive, opportunity, and means. Believe me, I contemplated it many times. I was angry with the legal system that allowed a killer to go free. But I didn't kill him. I swear."

"But why didn't you tell Cade that? He says you never denied it."

"That would have been too easy."

Enid put her hand on Josh's. "I don't understand."

"I didn't do it, but I know who did. Or at least, I'm pretty sure I do."

Enid pulled away and turned to face Josh. "Who, then?"

"I think Troy did."

Enid sat up to face Josh. "Your brother? But why?"

"Serena was the big sister Troy needed, a replacement for Kimi. Troy took her leaving harder than anyone."

"Why would Kimi run away?"

"Life was brutal. We were poor, and my sister wanted a better life. She began dating older men and asking them to take her away. Apparently, someone took her up on it."

"I'm so sorry. I never realized how difficult things were for you as a child."

Josh shrugged. "My mom did the best she could. I was the oldest and the most responsible. Troy was always getting into mischief, mostly harmless stuff. But when Serena got killed, he never got over it. And then when her killer got off on a legal technicality, Troy lost it. I tried to get him to see someone to get over his anger, but he refused, kept saying he'd handle everything himself."

"But you don't know for sure that he killed that man, do you? Have you confronted Troy?"

"That's why I went back home. I didn't ask him directly, but I told him I was being investigated." Josh pulled Enid back toward him. "Funny thing is that before I met you, I would have taken the fall for him. Troy is still a kid at heart. He won't last in prison. But now I want my life." He took Enid's hand. "I want a life with you."

Enid fought back tears and was debating how to respond, when her cell phone rang. "Okay," she said. "I'll be there as quick as I can. I'm bringing Josh with me."

Enid stood up. "We've got to go. Now. That was Jack. The EMT driver, a friend of Jack's, called and told him someone just tried to kill Jean Waters. Jack's going to Boogie's house now."

· · ·

Jack was sitting in the deputy's car with Jean when Enid and Josh arrived at Boogie's house. Even though it was early fall and the air had only a slight chill, Jean was bundled in a blanket and shivering.

"May I talk with her?" Enid asked the deputy standing outside the patrol car.

The deputy nodded.

Enid got into the back seat. Jack was on one side, with Jean in the middle. "Jean, are you okay? What happened?"

Jean sniffled and dabbed at her nose with a tissue as she told Enid about the intruder.

Enid glanced out the car window and saw Josh talking with one of the deputies. "I thought they had a protective detail assigned to you."

"They did," Jack said, "but he was attacked. They took him to the emergency room. He was lying near his police car with a stab wound when help arrived."

Enid squeezed Jean's hand. "You're lucky. Thank God you're safe."

Jean nodded.

Enid said to Jack, "If you're going to stay here with Jean, I'll go see what I can find out."

"Go ahead," Jack said.

Enid walked over to where Josh was standing. "What did you find out?"

"Not much. As you can see, there aren't any close neighbors and plenty of woods to hide in. They followed the blood trail over there to those trees by the road, but then it stopped. He may have been picked up by someone. And the guy Jean flagged down, the one who called for help, could only give a vague description of the man."

Enid glanced at the thick pine forest surrounding the house and shivered. "Do you think it was the same guy that killed Boogie?"

"That's the most likely explanation. Didn't you say there was a woman involved, too?"

Enid nodded. "But Jean said it was a man who grabbed her in the kitchen." She looked at all the blue lights on the cars, flashing in the darkness. "What about the deputy? Will he be okay?"

"The knife nicked his heart. He's in critical condition, but with any luck he'll make it." He paused. "You're shaking. Put this on." Josh took off his jacket and put it around Enid. "You told me you and Karla went to the 7 Crows Farm, and you talked to a young woman there. I need for you to come in and give me as many details about her as you can."

"At the time, I had no idea she might be involved, so I wasn't studying her features. I can give you a general description, but I'll bet Karla remembers more than I do. I like her a lot, but she can be creepy at times."

"You stay here. I'm going to talk to the ranking deputy who's filling in for Boogie and see if he needs help. While they're focusing on finding Boogie's killer, maybe we can find the woman who was his accomplice."

CHAPTER 43

Karla Burke arrived at the police station promptly at 9 a.m., as agreed. Josh accepted Enid's suggestion that they also invite Lindy, the artist Enid had used to create a drawing of her then-unidentified visitor, who later turned out to be Phyllis in disguise.

"Lindy, thank you for volunteering to help us with this sketch." Josh then turned to Enid. "Remember, you're here as a witness, not as a reporter."

"I understand," Enid said.

Josh then turned to Karla. "You look familiar. Do I know you?"

"It's likely our paths have crossed." She gestured with her arms. "Look around. Not too many Indians here."

"How long have you lived in the area?"

Karla shrugged. "A while."

Josh nodded to Lindy. "If you're ready, we'll get started on that sketch."

Lindy asked Enid and Karla about the facial features and other characteristics of the woman they had seen only once. As Enid had predicted to Josh, Karla had far more details in her memory than Enid. When Lindy had the information she needed, she made a few flourishes across the big sketch pad and then turned it around for Enid and Karla to see. "Is that the woman you saw?"

Josh could tell from their expressions, even before they replied, that Lindy had captured the essence of the woman who might be an accomplice to murdering Boogie. "You're a good artist," He said to Lindy. "Ever think of working for the police?"

Lindy smiled. "Thanks. I toyed with the idea once, but it's not my thing." She looked at Karla. "Is that the woman?"

Karla stared at the sketch, appearing to take in all the details. "Yes, that's her."

"I agree," Enid said.

Josh reached out for the sketch. "Good. I'll take that and get some copies made to distribute. Hopefully, we'll get lucky and find this woman, and she'll lead us to the man." He thanked Lindy again and offered to pay her a stipend, which she refused.

After Lindy left, Josh said to Enid. "Thanks for your help on the sketch and for getting Lindy involved. If you don't mind, I'd like to talk to Karla alone." The formality of his tone didn't sit well with Enid, he could tell. That line they had drawn in the sand was hard to find sometimes and even harder to manage. Enid said goodbye to them and left Josh and Karla alone in his office.

Before Josh could speak, Karla began. "It's clear how much you and Enid care for each other, but I'm sure it's difficult for both of you."

"We manage, but, yes, it can be a challenge." Josh stood up. "Coffee? I'm going to get some."

Karla shook her head. "No, thanks."

Josh stood at the metal table in the back of the police station and stirred the powdered creamer into his coffee longer than necessary. Something was also stirring in his memory, but he couldn't nail it. Something about Karla.

He walked back slowly to his office, contemplating what questions he should ask her. She was still sitting in the chair across from his desk, but she had lowered her head and her eyes were closed. She appeared to be napping. When he sat at his desk, she spoke without moving or opening her eyes.

"I knew her."

Josh dropped the pitted stainless-steel spoon on the floor and leaned to pick it up. "I thought you were asleep."

"Isn't it strange that we live in a world where if you're not talking or moving, everyone assumes you're asleep or something is wrong?"

Josh tried to regain his composure. "I used to say that very thing, to my sister."

Karla opened her eyes and looked up at Josh. "I know. She told me."

Josh held his coffee cup midway to his mouth. His hand trembled as he placed the cup on his desk. "You knew Kimi?"

"She was Heather by the time I knew her."

Josh leaned forward. "But how? Where?"

Before she could respond, Pete knocked on the door and came in. "I'm sorry to bother you, Chief, but you've got a call you need to take."

"Can't you handle it?"

Pete looked pale. "Not this one. It's the governor."

Karla stood to leave. "We can talk later. I'm not going anywhere."

Irritated, Josh watched the only connection to his sister walk out of his office. Was his sister alive? If so, where was she?

Pete pointed to the phone on Josh's desk. "I'll transfer him to your phone." The antiquated phone system was overdue for an update.

Josh picked up the phone, wondering if the call could be a hoax. "Governor?" Josh listened for several minutes without saying anything. Not only was he speechless, but the governor didn't give him a chance to say much. "Yes, two o'clock this afternoon at your office will be fine."

Josh's head was spinning. Karla said she knew his sister. And now he was being summoned to the governor's office.

. . .

Josh sat across from Governor Larkin in his office at the South Carolina state capitol in Columbia. "Thank you for meeting with me this afternoon, Chief Hart, and for making the drive to Columbia. I hope I didn't inconvenience you."

"No, sir." Josh looked around the office. Even in its elegant, historical setting, the office itself seemed spartan. A huge mahogany desk and leather chair took center stage, otherwise, there were few other decorations.

"I've never really made this office my own. The former governor displayed a number of items, including a shovel, from a ground-breaking, I assume. I've just never made an effort to add my own décor. My personal office in the governor's mansion is much more to my taste."

"I'm sorry to say I've never seen the mansion."

"It's more than a residence. It houses a repository of treasures, silver, china, furniture, paintings and documents that are part of the rich history and heritage of our great state. Sometimes you feel like you're in a fish bowl when they're conducting public tours." Governor Larkin smiled. "Being head of this great state is both a challenge and an extreme privilege." He rolled his desk chair closer to the desk. "But I asked you here for a specific reason, so I'll get right down to business."

Josh tried to maintain a poker face, but he was nervous. Was he being fired? Had the attorney general in New Mexico contacted him? As he mentally ran through his list of "what if" scenarios, the governor continued.

"You are well respected in Madden, especially for an outsider, so to speak. Your current position is, I'm sure, beneath your abilities. I hate to see any man, or woman, work beneath their capabilities, which is why I'm appointing you as sheriff in Bowman County to take Bernard Waters' place."

Josh wasn't sure he had heard correctly. This whole meeting was surreal to him, and now he thought he had heard the governor make him sheriff.

"That is, Chief Hart, assuming you're interested." The governor wasn't smiling now.

Josh cleared his throat. "I'm sorry, Governor, it's just that I wasn't expecting this. I'm a little surprised, that's all."

"You shouldn't be. Your work in New Mexico was exemplary. You were responsible for putting a number of bad people behind bars. My staff and I looked at several possible replacements for Sheriff Waters. His second in command is ready to retire and the next person down is a young man with little experience. In fact, most of his deputies and staff are quite young. I understand the Bowman County sheriff's office has had a number of retirements in recent years."

Josh gripped his own hand until it was white. "Thank you, sir, but there's something I should tell you."

The governor sat quietly.

"I'm currently under investigation by the media for an incident in New Mexico—"

The governor interrupted. "I'm aware of those allegations. Surely you realize I vetted you before I made this decision."

"Well, sir, I—"

"Did you kill that man who shot your wife? If you did, based on what I know, I could probably understand why you did." He shook his head. "Terrible tragedy all around, just terrible."

"No, sir, I did not kill him." *But I wanted to, and would have, given the opportunity.*

"I got a phone message about ten minutes before you arrived. Perhaps you'd be interested in hearing it."

Josh nodded, but he wasn't sure where this conversation was going.

The governor hit a button on his desk phone. "Governor Larkin, this is Al Montero in New Mexico. We spoke a few days ago about Police Chief Joshua Hart from Madden, South Carolina. I just wanted to let you know that we are closing that case. The shooter has stepped forward and admitted guilt. We are continuing the investigation to wrap up the loose ends, but I wanted to let you know right away, as you said you wanted to meet with Hart. You have my number if you have any more questions."

The governor had his fingertips together, like children do when they're making a church steeple, as he looked at Josh. "I take it from the look on your face you were not aware of this development."

Josh shook his head. "No, sir, I was not." He wanted to run from the room, to run from the man who was turning his life upside down. What was going on?

"Unless there's something else about that matter you think I need to know, then the New Mexico matter is closed." He tapped his fingers together lightly.

"No, there's nothing else."

The governor smiled. "Well, good then. Your appointment will run until the next general election, a little more than a year from now. At that time, should you wish to continue in that role, you will run, along with any other candidates. Of course, if you do the great work I'm assuming you will, you'll have my full backing." He stood and held out his hand. "Congratulations, Sheriff Hart."

CHAPTER 44

Lindy's sketch of the female suspect was circulated to law enforcement agencies across South Carolina, North Carolina, and Georgia. A BOLO alert was issued, describing her as armed and dangerous.

Since his meeting with Governor Larkin yesterday, Josh tried to stay focused on the task at hand: finding Boogie's killers. SLED was assisting but the bulk of that responsibility fell on Josh's shoulders now. The governor had agreed to withhold the announcement of his appointment for twenty-four hours. He didn't have much time left. If Enid heard about it on the news first, there would be hell to pay. Josh had not talked to anyone at the sheriff's office, as he didn't want to arouse suspicions. He looked at the clock on the wall and then picked up his cell phone.

Enid's voice message said she wasn't available, so he grabbed his hat and gun. "Pete, I'm going out for a bit."

"No problem, Chief. I got it."

Josh planned to talk to the mayor about appointing Pete as Madden's interim police chief. She would likely say Pete was young and inexperienced, and he was. But he had done a good job while Josh had been in New Mexico, and Josh would mentor Pete, just as Boogie had mentored Josh. More importantly, the ladies of Madden loved Pete. He listened to their concerns and gossip and ate their pies. He was perfect for the job. But for now, Josh had to focus on his own situation.

"Good morning, Chief Hart," Ginger said when he walked into the newspaper office.

"Morning, Ginger. Is Ms. Blackwell in?"

Ginger winked at him. "For you, I'm sure she is. She's locked in her office trying to finish an article before deadline."

Josh tapped on the closed door to Enid's office.

No response.

"Enid, it's Josh. I'm sorry to bother you."

The door swung open. "Josh. What on earth are you doing here?" She motioned for him to come in and then shut the door behind him.

"Ginger says you're on deadline, so maybe we can meet for lunch when you finish."

"Sure. Is everything OK?"

"I need to run something past you."

"You look tired."

"I didn't sleep much last night, but I'm fine."

Suddenly, Josh's police radio crackled with Pete's voice, "Chief, the governor's office said because of Dr. Waters' home invasion, he's going ahead with the announcement and for you to assume responsibility ASAP." Pete paused. "Do you know what's he's talking about?"

Josh closed his eyes and sighed. So much for the twenty-four-hour delay.

"What was that all about?" Then the color drained from Enid's face and her hand went to her mouth. "You've been appointed county sheriff."

"I'm sorry you found out this way. That's why I've been trying to get in touch with you. Can we talk about this tonight? I've got to get going."

Enid nodded. "Of course. May I at least get something in tomorrow's paper? If the *State* runs it then too, at least we won't be behind them."

Josh knew Enid was only doing her job, just as he was. She was in reporter mode, and he had to accept that about her. Unfortunately, tonight would not be a celebration of his promotion, but rather a reconciliation of two lives struggling to find their individual and their combined paths. Had he done the right thing accepting the sheriff's position?

. . .

Josh walked into the Madden police station. "Pete, I need to talk to you," he said, walking straight to the chief's office, which would soon belong to Pete or someone else. "Bring some coffee, please."

Pete put the cup of coffee on Josh's desk. "What's going on?" he said, as he sat down in the metal chair across from Josh.

"I wish I more time to say this the right way, but I've got to get going in a minute. Governor Larkin has appointed me to fill Sheriff Waters' vacancy until the general election. Apparently, I start now."

Pete's shoulders slumped, and he looked like a small child who had been abandoned. "What about your job here?"

"I can't make any promises. You know our mayor as well as I do, but I'm going to recommend that she put you in charge. Assuming that's what you want."

"I'm not ready to fill your shoes. You know she'll say that."

"You're right. But you are ready to fill your own shoes and make this role your own. You did a great job while I was gone, and I'll work with you on the things you need to know and do."

Pete sat up straight. "If you think I can do it, then I'm ready, Chief. I mean, Sheriff. Wow."

CHAPTER 45

Somehow, Enid managed to finish her article and upload it for editing. Josh's announcement had left her reeling. Once again, her world was in turmoil. Now, with him as county sheriff, his involvement with a reporter would be scrutinized even more closely.

She walked down the hall to Jack's office. He wasn't there. She walked to the front lobby. "Ginger, do you know where Jack is?"

"Sarah's. Getting coffee." Ginger shrugged. "Guess he doesn't like mine."

"I need to talk to him, so I'm going to get an early lunch."

As Enid walked away, Ginger called out to her. "Sure, leave me here alone with only my bad coffee and a stale sandwich. And, no thanks, I didn't want anything. But thanks for asking."

. . .

The crowd in Sarah's Tea Shoppe was thin. It was too late for the older crowd that came in for coffee or breakfast, and it was too early for the nouveau riche lunch crowd who had moved into the area. Things were changing in Madden. In fact, things were changing all around Enid.

Jack was sitting in a booth near the back, reading yesterday's Wall Street Journal. His half-lens reading glasses were perched on the end of his nose. "Hey, what a surprise." He motioned for Enid to join him. "You want some lunch?" He glanced at his watch. "It's about that time. At least we'll be ahead of the rush."

Enid laughed. "I never thought of Madden having a rush of anything." She sat across from him. "I'm in the mood for a BLT with lots of mayo."

"Uh, oh. What's wrong? You avoid extra calories like the plague, until you get stressed."

"And I'll have sweet tea," Enid said.

"Now I know you're losing it. Tell me what's happened."

They ordered lunch, and then Enid told Jack about Josh's appointment to county sheriff. Their food came before she finished talking, but neither touched it. After a few minutes, she sipped her tea. "Ugh, this is awful. How do you drink this stuff?"

Jack motioned for their server. "Can we get a glass of unsweetened tea? The lady changed her mind." He looked at Enid. "How do you feel about all this?"

"I'm not sure. Lost. And a bit angry."

"You mean because he didn't tell you before he accepted?"

"Would that be awful if I felt that way?"

"Would you have wanted Josh to turn down the governor?"

Enid shook her head. "No, of course not. I just wish I had some time to adjust."

"Imagine how Josh must feel," Jack said. "He's probably adjusting as well. And now he's suddenly in charge of finding his friend's killers."

"He'll also inherit the investigation of the bones found at the inn."

Enid and Jack ate in silence for a few minutes. "Anyway, I need some space for a short article about Josh's appointment. I don't have many details. Maybe I need to call the governor's office."

"That's not a bad idea. We don't have an exclusive on Josh, even though we'd like to claim it. Maybe we can beat the other papers to it."

"I hope Pete gets to take his place. He deserves it, although I know he doesn't have much experience." Enid took another bite of her sandwich.

"Let's be sure to include a few comments recognizing Pete for stepping in while Josh was gone. Might help." Jack handed a napkin to Enid. "Speaking of experience, or lack thereof, you've got mayo on your face. You obviously have no experience eating messy sandwiches."

CHAPTER 46

When Josh arrived at Boogie's house to take a statement from Jean, he talked briefly to the deputy who had been assigned to guard her. Given the attempt on Jean's life, they were not taking any chances.

Jean was sitting in Boogie's old easy chair, the fabric on the arms worn from years of use. She was sipping bourbon. "I don't normally drink the hard stuff, but today seems like a good time to make an exception." She took another sip. "May I offer you some coffee or tea? I assume you're on duty."

"I'm fine, but thanks." Josh sat at an angle on the sofa so he could face Jean.

"I'm glad you're here. That makes me feel better."

"The deputy that responded to your call gave me the basics, but I wanted to follow up and see if you had remembered anything else, any other details."

Jean took another sip of bourbon and then set the glass on the small table beside her. "I've relived those few minutes a hundred times, but what I told the deputy is all I can remember." She paused. "It's funny how life is. There I was, tending patients and living a normal life when my father called and asked me to come home. Then he's killed, and someone tried to kill me." She sighed. "It's almost too much for me to take in."

"Are you sure the man who attacked you is the same man who killed Boogie?"

Jean nodded. "I can't tell you the details of his features, but I'd recognize his posture and movements anywhere." She paused briefly. "And he had on that same dark red baseball cap. It was him. I'm sure."

"Did you make contact with him when you lashed out?"

Jean nodded. "As a doctor, I can't believe I intentionally hurt another human being, but I shoved that knife in his shoulder." She hugged her arms around herself and rocked back and forth in her chair. "I cut his arm too, but that was just a slash. The county investigators took the knife." She rocked back and forth again. "It was covered in blood." In Madden, Josh was the only investigator. Having a county crime scene investigation team was a luxury.

Josh stood up. "I'm going to check out the kitchen. We'll keep the deputy assigned to you until we catch this guy. There's an APB out for him, although we don't have a good description of him or a vehicle. We'll just have to hope he does something suspicious and we'll get a call on him. All the clinics and hospitals within one hundred miles have been alerted. If he stays in the area, we'll get him."

"Thanks. I hope it's sooner rather than later. By the way, Enid invited me to stay with her. Unless you have objections, I'm going to take her up on the offer."

Josh wanted to object but wasn't sure why he should. "That was kind of her. I'll ask my deputy to drop you off at her house."

"Your deputy? Does that mean you're sheriff now?"

Josh ran his hand through his hair. "Yes, ma'am. I guess I am."

. . .

After the deputy dropped Jean off at Enid's house, he assured them both he would be in his car, guarding the house until his relief arrived. Enid took Jean to the guest room and put fresh towels out for her. "Please make yourself at home. I don't have many overnight guests, but I think you've got all the essentials here."

Jean hugged Enid. "Thank you so much. Everything is lovely. I won't stay long. It's just that . . ."

"Stay as long as you'd like. I appreciate the company." She hooked her arm in Jean's. "I've got to get to work, but there are books, TV, stereo. Just do whatever you like. I'll check on you later."

Jean sat on the edge of the bed. "Can I ask you one thing before you go?"

"Sure." Enid sat down beside her.

"Chief Hart told me he's sheriff now. That's a nice promotion for him, but how do you feel about it?"

Enid stood up and walked toward the door. "Honestly, I don't know. As you might imagine, I have conflicting emotions. Of course, I'm happy for him. He'll be a wonderful sheriff."

"But what about you? Can you two juggle your respective jobs and maintain a relationship?"

Enid shrugged. "We'll just have to see where all this goes."

Jean stood up and put her hands on Enid's shoulders. "Would you give up your career for his?"

A flood of emotions washed over Enid. She wanted to shout, kick, or cry. That was the question she had been avoiding. She had been down this road before, giving up her own dreams for someone else. Would she do it again? "I've got to run. But before I go, I have a proposal for you. It's about those bones at the inn."

CHAPTER 47

Jack sat across from Enid in the newspaper office conference room. He took off his glasses and rubbed his eyes. "You know I have to assign Dr. Jean's story to another reporter."

Enid wanted to lash out at Jack but reminded herself that he wasn't the problem. "I don't think that's necessary."

Jack perched his reading glasses back on his nose. "She's staying with you, and your boyfriend is investigating an attack on her. How can you possibly stay objective?"

"First of all, Jean's staying with me is a non-issue. She's not a suspect or under investigation herself, unless there's something I'm not aware of. And, as for Josh, Sheriff Hart, we don't discuss this or any other case. Not anymore."

Jack leaned back in his chair and shut his eyes. "Life used to be much simpler, you know." He sat up again and looked at Enid. "I hate this, all of this, for you. It can't be easy to juggle your personal and professional lives under the circumstances."

"Women have been doing it for years."

"Meaning that men haven't?"

"I didn't mean that, but women have taken the brunt of it. No one would ask Josh if he'd give up his career for me." Enid smiled faintly. "Of course, even if he would, we'd have a hard time living on a small-town newspaper reporter's salary."

Jack feigned a frown. "What? Are you asking for a raise? It that what this is all about?"

Enid slapped at his arm. "Stop making fun of me. This is my life."

Jack's face softened. "I know." He closed his notepad. "I'll leave you on this story for now, but if there's the hint of a problem or conflict of interest, I'll have to reassign it. Agreed?"

"Yes." She watched Jack as he was leaving. "Jack?"

He turned back to face her.

"Thanks. You're the best bossy friend and friendly boss all rolled into one that I've ever had."

Jack winked at her. "I love you, too. Now get back to work."

. . .

Enid walked into the police station. Pete, as usual, was staring at his computer screen. "Is Sheriff Hart in, or has he already moved out?"

Pete looked up. "Hello, Ms. Blackwell. The chief, I mean Sheriff Hart, is in his office. Or at least his old office. It's all a bit confusing right now. Anyway, I'll tell him you're here."

As Enid watched Pete walk to Josh's office, she remembered how it used to be when Pete told her to go on back herself.

Pete walked out of Josh's office. "He says to come on in."

Josh was staring at his computer screen when she walked in. She tried to remember if the previous police chief, Dick Jensen, had ever even used a computer. "Thank you for seeing me." She wasn't sure whether to call him Sheriff Hart or Josh, so she just left it alone.

"I'm going to get some coffee, and I'll bring you a tea if you'd like."

"I can get it."

"What? You think I'm too highfalutin' now to fetch coffee?"

Josh returned shortly with a cup of coffee and a Lady Grey tea. He put the cups on the table and sat behind his desk. "I assume you want to interview me about developments in the case, and I'm happy to answer whatever questions I can." He paused. "But first, let's get something clear. As far as I'm concerned, nothing has changed between us. Yes, I admit, we're going to have to make sure we maintain our boundaries, but we were doing that before I, you know, before I became sheriff."

"I don't even know what to call you."

"Sheriff Joshua Hart, at your service, ma'am." Josh laughed. "Don't look so serious. I'm kidding. I'm still Josh. That's what I'm trying to tell you."

Enid pulled her notepad and pen from her tote. "Okay, Josh. I have some questions for you. And, just to let you know, I'm doing two articles I need to get information on. The first is about you. The citizens of Madden would like to know more about your new role and how all of this will affect them, like who will be their new police chief? And I'm also doing a follow-up on the bones at the inn. Has any progress been made on the case?"

Josh put his hand on his heart. "Ouch, that hurts. You're asking if we're doing anything, anything at all, to solve that case."

Enid tried not to smile. "Well, yeah, something like that."

After a series of questions about his appointment by the governor and the process for appointing a new police chief, Enid flipped to a new page in her notepad. "Now, let's talk about the bones found at the inn. What progress has been made?"

"Madame Reporter, can we go off the record? Just for a minute?"

Enid put her notepad on the desk and picked up her teacup. "Sure."

"You know as well as I do that identifying old bones isn't a top priority. SLED is assisting, but the sheriff's office has the lead on this. If nothing else was going on, then perhaps the case would get more resources or attention."

"But those 'old bones,' as you put it, were once someone's sister, wife, or mother."

"I know, and I want to find out who they belong to. But we've got no DNA match, we can't find a family member, and no dental records have been located, not yet anyway."

"Have you considered facial reconstruction?"

"Actually, Boogie had put in a request."

"And?"

"It's being considered. But, you know, lack of funds. We don't have the population or resources Richland, Greenville, and Charleston have."

"What if there was a private citizen who would pay for it?"

Josh tilted his head. "Did Jack give you a big raise?"

"Not me, silly. But I know someone who might."

Pete came in to remind Josh of a meeting with the mayor in fifteen minutes. "Thanks, I'll be there." Josh turned his attention back to Enid. "Would this 'someone' be a pediatric oncologist, by any chance?"

"Maybe."

"Have you already discussed this with her?"

"Maybe."

Josh unlocked his desk drawer and got his pistol. "I've got to go to my meeting. If Dr. Jean is willing, then so am I. I'm not sure what the procedure is for this kind of thing, but for a while at least, I can get away with claiming not to know any better." His hand brushed her shoulder as he walked out of the office. "Take your time and finish your tea. I'll see you later." He called over his shoulder, "But don't report that we've hired a forensic sculptor. Not yet, at least."

. . .

Enid was sitting at her desk at the newspaper office when her cell phone rang. She didn't recognize the number, but it was local. "Hello."

"Ms. Blackwell, this is Pete." He giggled like a teenager. "I mean, this is the acting police chief of Madden."

"Pete, that's great! I'm so happy for you."

"Yeah, thanks. But that's not why I called. Chief Hart, I mean, Sheriff Hart wants you to meet with him and Dr. Jean." He gave her the address in West Columbia. "That's where this facial reconstruction guy lives. He said you'd know what it was all about. That address is his art studio, but he lives upstairs. Can you bring Dr. Jean with you?"

"Of course." She jotted down the time and details of the meeting. "We'll be there."

. . .

Art by Alex was in a studio filled with watercolor paintings, as well as clay sculptures. A few wood carvings were in the corner, which Jean admired. "These are exquisite." She waved her arm, gesturing around the room. "Did you do all this?"

Alex smiled broadly. "Yes, ma'am. I did. Thank you."

"Your work is beautiful," Enid said. "Sheriff Hart will be here shortly. He asked me to apologize for being late. As you may know, he's just been appointed as the Bowman County sheriff, so his plate is rather full."

"No apologies necessary. I totally understand. I sleep late and work until the wee hours, so I'm in no hurry. If you'd like, I'll tell you about some of my work while we're waiting."

"That would be great, thanks," Enid said. "I had no idea that forensic sculptors were artists, as well, but I guess that makes sense."

"I imagine our days are numbered. Much of the reconstruction work is now done digitally using reconstruction software programs."

Alex was telling them about his technique for painting eyes when Josh walked in carrying a big cardboard box.

"Sorry I'm late." He put the box on the floor and held out his hand to Alex. "Thanks for seeing us this afternoon."

"My pleasure."

"You were recommended to us by several people in the state. I understand you worked for the FBI and even taught forensic facial reconstruction at the academy."

"Yes, that's right. I have a folder of my credentials and past work that I'll give you before you leave. You may need it later."

"Thanks. This project is being funded by a private citizen, Dr. Jean Waters." He nodded toward Jean. "She has generously agreed to pay your fee, and I understand you two have worked out an amount."

"We have," Jean said, "and Alex was kind enough to give me a civilian discount."

Alex turned to Josh. "Do you have permission and access to the skull found at the inn?"

"I'm going to ask forgiveness rather than wait for permission. For now, I have full access. You'll need to preserve the chain of evidence, but, of course, you know all about that."

"Yes, of course."

Josh knelt down and cut the evidence tape on the box. He pulled the skull out and removed the protective wrapping before handing it to Alex. "Here she is."

"Are you sure it's a female?"

"The DNA says so." Josh studied the skull in Alex's hands. "But that's about all we know for sure."

CHAPTER 48

Josh drove back to Madden with a lot on his mind. He wished Boogie was around to help him learn the new job, but instead, Josh would have to rely on his own instincts and experience. He hoped the county deputies would accept him. If they branded him as an outsider, the job would be twice as hard. If one of those deputies had hoped to be appointed, Josh would face some tough resentment.

But it was Josh's personal life, not his new role as sheriff, that kept invading his thoughts. How did Karla know his sister Kimi? And who confessed to killing his wife's murderer? He wanted to push the pause button on his life and catch up, but he would have to figure it all out on the fly. And then there was Enid. What would happen to them as a couple? Their relationship was strained, but with all the changes, maybe that was to be expected.

His police radio crackled. "Hey, Sheriff, this is Pete. Are you headed back? There's been a sighting of that intruder who broke into Dr. Jean's house. Oh, and I forgot to tell you, Sheriff Waters had a camera on a tree near the road. It was one of those wildlife cams and camouflaged pretty good. One of your deputies has a video of the guy. It was grainy, but your office put out a BOLO on him. Just a little while ago, an out-of-town, off-duty cop on vacation spotted the intruder at a convenience store and called it in. The cop had his family with him and was out of his jurisdiction, so he didn't try to stop the guy."

"That was a good decision. Do they know which direction he went in?"

"The guy and a blonde girl headed north. I'll send all the details to your phone."

• • •

After checking in with the sheriff's office, Josh made arrangements through Miss Murray, the Madden town historian, to meet with Karla. He was uncomfortable that Karla only interacted with the townsfolk through an intermediary. Perhaps Karla just wanted her privacy protected. Otherwise, she had given him no reason to question her or her motives.

At first, he suggested they meet at the Madden police station, but then he realized it wasn't his office any longer. It was Pete's. Besides, he didn't want Karla to feel like she was being interrogated. Karla suggested they meet at Glitter Lake Inn, so Josh called ahead to alert Theo they were coming.

As Josh pulled into the inn, he looked around the parking area. He saw a couple of cars he didn't recognize, but they could have been guests. Rather than alarming folks by having a uniformed policeman show up, Josh decided to go to the back door.

"Hey, Chief Hart," Theo said as he greeted Josh, dishrag in hand. "Oh, sorry. Sheriff Hart. It's going to take me a while to get used to that. Congratulations on the new job. Although, I really hate to see you leave Madden."

With all that had been going on, Josh had not thought of moving, although he did need to be closer to the sheriff's office. Relocating was just another issue he'd have to address later. "Is Karla here yet?"

"Oh, yes. She's out on the library balcony. There's a bit of chill in the air today, so if you'd like to move inside, I'm happy to take care of it. Miss Karla said she was fine."

"Then I'm sure I can handle it. Thanks."

Josh walked down the hall to the library and then through the French doors onto the balcony. Karla was sitting at the small round table covered with a crisp, white linen tablecloth. "Sheriff Hart, how nice to see you again."

"Likewise." Josh sat at the table. "I don't usually take my coffee in real china in such fancy settings. I'm more of a chipped mug kind of guy."

Karla laughed. "This place is good for the spirit, even with what happened here. Whatever negative energy that might have lingered is gone now. Theo brought peace and serenity with him. He's a good soul." She paused. "But you're here because you want to know about your sister Kimi."

Josh nodded. "You said she changed her name to Heather." He smiled. "She had a picture of an English countryside from a magazine taped to her wall. She loved the purple English heather, said she wanted to go there one day to see it herself." He paused. "Is she alive?"

"Very much so."

"Why hasn't she contacted me or anyone else in the family? Is she ashamed of us?"

"On the contrary, she's afraid of the family's reaction to her running away."

"I don't understand."

"Heather left because she couldn't handle life on the reservation. Even at her young age, she knew that many Native American women suffer some kind of physical or sexual assault, especially on the reservations. Four out of five women are victims. One of her best friends was raped, and Heather vowed to leave and find a safer life. But she thought the family would consider her disrespectful for abandoning them."

Josh pushed his chair back. "I remember when her friend was assaulted, but I had no idea it had such an impact on her." He poured another cup of coffee to buy some time before responding. "I'm disappointed she didn't trust me enough to confide in me. I must have been a crappy big brother to her."

Karla put her hand on Josh's. "Don't judge yourself or her harshly. That's exactly what she was afraid the family would do." She reached into her pocket and gave him a slip of paper. "Here's her cell phone number. She's willing to talk to you if you want to contact her."

"Does Kimi, rather Heather, know about my wife's murder and the killing of the suspect?"

Karla nodded. "She does."

Josh's head was spinning as he tried to process all that Karla had said. "You've been in the area for years. When did you make the connection that I was Kimi's brother?" Josh didn't believe in coincidences.

"I met Heather when I was doing a spiritual healing workshop in New Mexico. We started talking, and she asked me if I knew you since I lived near Madden. As I've said, the Native American population isn't that large. She might have been out of touch, but she's kept up with all the family members. At the time I didn't know you, but I told her I'd look you up. She asked me not to tell you she and I had met. I honored that commitment until I began having dreams about you and Enid. At that point, I contacted Heather and told her I needed to reach out to both of you. She understood."

"Enid mentioned your dreams. I must admit, that's a bit weird for me."

Karla smiled. "You've lost your connection to the old ways. Your ancestors wouldn't think it was so strange." Karla rose from her seat as graceful as a dancer and someone half her age. "I've enjoyed my years in Bowman County, but I will be leaving soon, as I have work to do elsewhere. Please give Heather my regards if you connect with her. If you ever need me, Miss Murray will know how to reach me." She took Josh's hands in hers. "You'll find your way, Joshua Hart. Trust your instincts."

CHAPTER 49

Nothing made sense any more. That's all Josh could think about after he left his meeting with Karla. He wanted to run to Enid, bury his face in her copper hair, and never leave her side. But he had to face this situation, and there was no need to drag her into his chaos.

Josh had been avoiding his new office, because it still felt like Boogie's. But Josh had to face it. He needed to meet with the deputies and begin building relationships with them. He also needed to follow up on the bombshell the governor had dropped on him. Someone had confessed to the killing of his wife's murderer. Had there really been an arrest? Or were they conveniently dropping the case against him so he could be sheriff? He had no reason to question the governor's integrity, so Josh pushed those thoughts aside.

Still, Josh needed to get to the bottom of it. He pulled into a small roadside diner on the state highway. The only vehicle was a rusted red pickup near the back, probably the owner's. Josh went inside and stood near the cash register until an elderly man appeared.

"Whatcha need, son?"

"Coffee to go." Josh looked around. "I need to make some calls. Am I the only one here?"

The man chuckled. "Yeah, unless you see something I don't. I'll put it in a go cup in case someone comes in. I'll be in the back. Just holler if you want a refill." He poured coffee into a large paper cup and set it in front of Josh. "On the house. You know, support the local police."

"Thanks." Josh put a couple dollars on the counter after the man left and then settled into one of the back tables. The coffee was dark and bitter, but it helped clear Josh's head. After drinking several swallows, he pulled out his cell phone and called one of the numbers in his contact list. After a few rings a familiar voice answered.

"I figured you'd call soon," Troy said.

"What the hell is going on?" Josh tried to keep his voice low.

"Good to talk to you too, big brother."

"Let's not play games," Josh said.

Silence.

"Troy, who was arrested for the killing? And why didn't you let me know?"

After another brief silence, a painful sob filled the airspace. "I'm sorry. I'm so sorry."

"You did it, didn't you?" Josh asked.

"I loved Serena. She was like a sister to me, and I couldn't stand that the man who killed her was laughing and walking free."

"Did you kill him?"

No reply.

"Did you kill that man, Troy? Answer me. Now."

Another loud sob. "I'm sorry. I didn't think they'd come after you. After all, you're a lawman. Why would they suspect you?"

Josh didn't bother to explain that the spouse is always the first suspect, and a spouse with a need for revenge was a slam dunk. "But someone thought I did, and called in an anonymous tip, didn't they?" He regretted the bitter tone in his voice. "Do you know who did that? Was that you too?"

"No, man, I swear, I don't know anything about that tip."

"If you confessed, why aren't you in jail?"

"I'm out on bail."

"You don't have anything. Who posted for you?"

No reply.

"Dammit, Troy. I'm so tired of your games and lies. Tell me how you got out."

"Look, I don't know, okay. They told me some woman named Heather posted bail for me. I don't even know who she is."

Josh's hand starting shaking. He took a deep breath to steady his nerves. "Everything will be fine. I can't come out there now. I've been appointed sheriff here, but when things settle, I'll come see you. Text me your lawyer's name, and I'll do what I can to help."

"I got a court-appointed lady, but she's real nice."

"That's good Troy, that's good." Josh's limbs felt heavy. He wanted to curl up and sleep. "I gotta go. Call me if you need anything or something changes." Josh recalled Karla's final words to him. "We'll find our way through all this."

CHAPTER 50

Josh's head throbbed as he drove to the sheriff's office. How could Troy have done such a thing and then kept quiet? Troy had always been emotional and irresponsible—a bad combination.

And, why had their sister Kimi re-emerged as Heather and bailed Troy out? Where was she? Where did she get the money? Who had called in the tip that alerted Cade that Josh was the killer? Did someone in Madden want Josh out of the way? Or was it someone from his past life out West? All the questions were pressing against his throbbing temples, as Josh pulled the piece of paper Karla had given him from his shirt pocket.

"Sheriff Hart, come in. This is dispatch."

Josh put the paper back in his pocket and pressed the button on his police radio. "Go ahead."

"They got a blonde woman in custody. She's in holding, waiting on you."

"I'm on the way." Josh turned on his blue light and sped toward the sheriff's office.

. . .

The blonde in the interrogation room looked younger than the nineteen years indicated on her arrest sheet. Josh turned to the deputy. "You can wait outside."

The woman glared at Josh. "I don't know why I'm here."

"Have you been read your rights?"

"I suppose so."

"Yes or no?"

She shook her blonde hair back from her face. "Yeah, okay. I know my rights."

"Do you want an attorney?"

She shook her head.

"Answer me, please."

"No, I don't need no attorney."

Josh looked at her arrest sheet again. "Darla. You got a last name, Darla?"

She just stared at Josh.

"It says here you were with an older man when they apprehended you. Where is he?"

She shrugged. "Dunno."

"He your father? Your pimp?"

She sat upright in the chair. "I ain't no whore."

Josh pointed to the paper on the table between them. "Says here he got away. Not much of a guy to run off and leave you."

"He'll be back."

"Why did you and your friend kill Sheriff Waters?"

"I didn't shoot nobody."

"But you handed your friend the shotgun. That's the same as killing him."

She shrugged.

"Are you related to a woman named Angel?"

Darla's eyes widened. "No. I don't know anybody named that."

"Then why were you at the 7 Crows Farm? Were you and your friend squatting there?"

Darla looked down at the floor.

Josh put her arrest sheet back in the folder and stood to leave. "When you're ready to talk, let us know. You're going to a lineup shortly. If the witness picks you as the killer, you're going to jail. I'd suggest you think about what kind of life that will be for a pretty blonde like you."

Darla's hands were in handcuffs, so she curled her head down toward her shoulder to wipe away the tears streaming down her face.

CHAPTER 51

Enid's drive to the Bowman County sheriff's office was short—less than thirty minutes. She avoided the highways and took the back roads instead. She had not grown up around farms and open land, but over the past couple of years she had learned to appreciate the beauty and serenity of the area. The new distribution center, though it provided needed jobs, had spawned housing developments that were encroaching on the farms. Piles of cut trees by the road, now brown and dying, were a reminder that progress would soon change much of the landscape.

Her mother used to say that change is inevitable. To a small child, change sounded like an adventure—a new place to explore, new ideas, new things to do. But later, she learned that change can also be scary. Sometimes change means loss and heartache.

Enid switched the radio station from easy listening to a rock station. She needed to energize herself and shake off this feeling of impending doom. There was no reason to assume she and Josh would have to change their relationship. But if she were honest with herself, it had already changed. Ever since Cade had told her about investigating Josh, she had been uneasy. As a reporter, she wanted to know all the facts, but she had resisted doing her own research into Josh's life. Maybe she just didn't want to know. She pushed those thoughts aside.

She pulled into the parking lot beside a red brick building several times larger than the Madden police station. She gathered her tote and took a deep breath. Everything is okay.

Inside, she was greeted by a female deputy. "Can I help you?"

"I'm looking for Sheriff Josh Hart." It sounded funny to even say that.

"His office is upstairs. Just take a right off the elevator and someone will help you."

As instructed, Enid walked off the elevator and turned right. People were scurrying around with far more activity than she was used to seeing in Josh's old office. "Excuse me, I need to see Sheriff Hart."

The deputy pointed to the next doorway. "You can see the desk clerk in there."

Enid walked through the door and saw a dozen people sitting in chairs against the wall and others waiting in a long line. She should have made an appointment, especially since she didn't even know if he was in. Looking around again, she decided to leave.

Back in her car, she called Josh on her cell phone. Several rings later, his voice message responded.

"Josh, I need to talk to you. I just left your office, you know, the new office. I don't even know if you're there. Just call me. I miss you, and I need an update on the bones story." She then added, "I miss us."

. . .

Enid called Jack from the car and told him she had been unable to talk to Josh to get an update on the bones. She promised to keep digging and to have an update for the next news edition. She tapped on Jean's cell number, and Jean answered quickly.

"Hi, Enid, I was just getting ready to call you and then your call popped up."

"What's going on? Everything okay? You sound . . ."

"Nervous is probably what you're hearing. I've got to go to a lineup. They've arrested a woman they think was one of my father's killers. They want me to identify her. And I was wondering, could you go with me?"

"Sure, where do you have to go?"

Jean gave her the address of the sheriff's department, where Enid had just left.

"I'll meet you there," Enid said. "I'm not far away."

• • •

Enid had been waiting about twenty minutes when Jean Waters arrived at the Bowman County sheriff's office. Jean approached Enid and hugged her. "Thank you so much for coming. I'm so scared."

"What are you afraid of?" Enid asked.

"I don't want to make a mistake." Jean glanced at her watch. "I guess I'd better check in and let them know I'm here."

Enid waited while Jean talked to the front desk. She checked her phone. No text or call from Josh.

Jean walked back and sat down in the chair next to Enid. Unlike the metal chairs in the Madden police station, these had upholstered seats and padded arms. "They said they'll come get me in a few minutes."

"Have you heard anything from the facial reconstruction artist?"

Jean pulled her phone from her purse. "Actually, I saw a message from him, but I haven't listened to it yet." She held the phone between them so Enid could hear the recording also. "This is Alex. I've got some preliminary results and have notified Sheriff Hart. Give me a call when you get a chance."

Jean put the phone back in her purse. "We can call him after we leave here. I hope they let you go back with me."

"I'm sure they won't, but you'll be fine. The people in the lineup can't see you."

"I've watched enough TV shows to know that, it's just that . . . What if I can't remember her face? Or what if I pick the wrong person?"

Enid put her arm around Jean's shoulders. "Stop worrying. You'll do fine. I know you're used to having people's lives in your hands, but you're not alone in this." She squeezed her shoulders again. "Josh and I are right beside you."

A deputy approached them. "Dr. Waters. They're ready for you."

"Can my friend come with me?"

The deputy turned to Enid. "I'm sorry but you'll have to wait here. It shouldn't take long.

• • •

It was nearly an hour later when Jean joined Enid. "I'm finished. We can leave now."

Enid put her files and papers back in her tote and stood. "Well, what happened?"

"I'll tell you outside. Let's get out of here."

A gust of wind tugged at Enid's hair as they walked to their cars in silence. "There's a cold front coming through tonight. How about we stop by the inn and get some of Theo's soup du jour to have tonight?"

Jean stopped walking and turned to look at Enid.

Enid put her arms around Jean and held her. "What's wrong? You're shaking like a leaf."

Jean held onto Enid and sobbed.

"Come on, let's sit in the car and wait until you feel better. We can even leave your car if you want to and pick it up later."

Jean nodded and followed Enid to her car. "I'm sorry, I didn't mean to fall apart on you."

"You've been through a lot. No need to apologize. Come on, I'll take you home."

"No, just give me a minute, and then I can drive." Jean shifted in the seat to face Enid. "I know you want to know what happened."

"Only when you're ready to tell me. Maybe later tonight you'll feel more like it."

Jean leaned back in the seat and closed her eyes. "I can still see her. In my memory, she was a monster, the woman who handed the shotgun to the man who shot my father. But that wasn't the same woman I saw in the lineup."

Enid stiffened. "You mean you couldn't identify her as the killer?"

Jean opened her eyes. "Oh, it was her alright, the same person. No question. But instead of a monster, today I saw a scared young woman. I saw it in her eyes. She's a victim, too."

CHAPTER 52

Outside, the wind howled, and rain pelted the windows. Enid and Jean sat at the small dining table enjoying Theo's chicken enchilada soup when the doorbell rang. "It's nearly eight o'clock," Enid said. "Who could that be this late?"

"Don't go to the door," Jean said, her eyes wide. "Maybe we should call someone."

Ignoring the warning, Enid walked to the door and looked through the peephole Jack had installed for her. "It's okay," she said to Jean as she unbolted the door. "Josh, what a nice surprise."

Josh walked in and greeted Jean. "I hope I'm not intruding."

"No, let me get you a bowl of soup," Jean said. "Theo gave us more than we needed."

Josh sat down at the table. "Best offer I've had all day."

While Jean was getting Josh's bowl from the cabinet, Josh kissed Enid lightly on the lips. "Sorry I didn't get to call you back. One of those days."

"I understand."

Jean put the steaming bowl in front of Josh. "Here's some bread Enid baked to go with it. It's great with this honey butter."

Josh looked at Enid and grinned. "Wait, Enid made bread? This Enid?" he said, pointing to her.

"Stop it. I can cook . . . sort of." She made a face at Josh. "Okay, it was frozen dough, are you happy now?"

"She did make it, and it's good, so you two behave and let's eat," Jean said. She put her hands over her face. "Oh, God, I just realized I don't have any makeup on. I must look a fright."

"You're beautiful," Josh said.

"Puffy eyes and all?" Jean asked.

"Well, now that you mention it, you do look a little puffy. Is everything okay? I know today must have been hard on you," Josh said.

"I wasn't prepared to see the helplessness on that child's face."

"First of all, she's not a child," Josh said. "According to our records, she's nineteen. And she's far from being a helpless victim. She knows how to get sympathy and work the system. Don't let her play with your head."

"Josh is right," Enid said. "You can't forget what she did, even if she's not the one who pulled the trigger."

"I'm sure you're both right," Jean said.

Enid looked at Josh. "The facial reconstruction artist called Jean today, and he said he had left a message for you about some preliminary results."

"Ah, yes," Josh said. "With everything that's going on, I almost forgot about it. I have an appointment to see him tomorrow."

"Can Jean and I go with you?" Enid asked.

"Of course Jean can go. After all, she's footing the bill for this. But would you be going as a reporter or as Jean's friend?"

Enid stood up and collected the empty soup bowls. "I'm both."

CHAPTER 53

Josh was waiting for Enid and Jean when they arrived at the art studio in West Columbia. He looked at Enid. "I wasn't sure if you were coming." Looking down at his feet, he added, "I'm sorry for that crack I made last night. I was just tired."

"You had every right to ask," Enid said. "I won't use anything without your permission."

"I asked Enid to come today," Jean said.

Alex came from the back of the studio, wiping his hands on a towel. "So good to see all of you again. Coffee? Tea?"

Josh spoke first. "I've got a bit of a tight schedule, so if you don't mind, let's see what you've got."

"Of course," Alex said. "Come this way."

Josh, Enid, and Jean followed Alex down a dark hallway to a back room. It was locked with a huge padlock. Alex fished the keys from his pocket and opened the door.

A large circular table sat in the center of the room. An object sat on it, draped by a cloth. "There she is," Alex announced as he pulled the cover off the object.

Jean gasped. "Oh, my."

Enid leaned forward. "I've seen reconstruction work before, but it's always shocking to see how you can transform a skull into a person again."

"How do you know her skin color and hair color?" Jean asked.

"I don't, actually. Her markers indicate she's of European descent, so I assumed she had Caucasian skin. The dark brown hair color is an educated guess, based on overall hair color statistics and her origin. Most Europeans have either dark brown or black hair. Unless she was Scandinavian, blonde would be rare." He nodded to Enid. "And only two percent of the population are natural redheads like you. Of course, some women are prone to dye their hair, but the forensic report you gave me didn't mention any trace of hair coloring in the recovered strands."

"Do you recognize her?" Josh asked Jean.

Jean looked at the sculpture again. "I was a small child when Angel used to come to the inn. It could be her, but honestly, I'm not sure."

"Are you finished with the reconstruction?" Enid asked.

"I'd like to do a little more work, but I know you wanted something quickly."

Enid looked at Josh. "May I take a photo? She frowned. "Don't worry, I'm not going to put it in the paper. Not yet, anyway."

Josh nodded, so Enid took the photo from several angles.

"I'll include all my marker information in the accompanying report. It will explain how I determined the facial features and all the other technical information."

"Thank you so much for doing this. I hope all this eventually leads to justice for my father," Jean said.

"I hope so, too," Alex said.

Enid and Jean said goodbye, and Josh stayed behind to talk to Alex. As Enid and Jean were leaving the studio, Jean leaned into Enid and whispered, "What are you up to?"

Enid smiled. "Got time to come with me? I want to show this to Phyllis."

. . .

Enid and Jean sat in Enid's living room with Phyllis. "Thank you both for meeting here with me. I know you haven't actually met, but you're both part of this case," Enid said. "Phyllis is Reggie's sister. He was convicted of murdering Angel and later died in prison. Let's just say the case against him is open to debate."

Jean looked at Phyllis. "I'm pleased to meet you."

"Jean is Dr. Jean Waters, daughter of the late Sheriff Bernard Waters," Enid explained.

"Please don't be hesitant to talk freely about my father's involvement in this case," Jean said. "I'm not here to defend him. On the other hand, no matter what, he didn't deserve to be killed in cold blood."

Phyllis nodded. "Thanks. I understand."

"Now, for the reason I invited you both here," Enid said. "These two cases seem to be connected. Reggie may have been framed by the sheriff," Enid said, looking at Phyllis, "Or Reggie may have actually killed Angel. And then Sheriff Waters was killed by someone living at or squatting on the property where Angel once lived, 7 Crows Farm." Enid looked at Phyllis. "You suspected some connection with Angel and the farm when those bones were found at the inn. That's why you came to see me with that riddle about seven crows."

Phyllis lowered her head. "Again, I'm so sorry for that whole incident. I should have been straight with you."

Jean moved over to the sofa and sat beside Phyllis, putting her arm around her shoulders. "We're all just trying to figure this out. You wanted to get Enid's attention, and you did."

Phyllis nodded. "Thanks."

Enid continued, "To further complicate this story, Jean's mother, Lillian, is in a nursing home with dementia. Unfortunately, she holds many of the answers but can't communicate. Whoever those bones are, Lillian had them moved to a walled-off storage area behind the kitchen at the inn when she was working there. During that time, she befriended Angel and wanted to protect her, but from what or whom, we're not sure."

"I had no idea how complex this situation is," Phyllis said. She turned to Jean, still beside her on the sofa. "I'm sorry for your family troubles. First your mother gets dementia, and then your father is killed."

"Thanks," said Jean. "Both of us have suffered losses."

"We've got several questions to answer," Enid said. "Are those bones from the inn actually Angel? If so, then why was she killed and who did it? And why were her bones moved to the inn?" Enid turned to Jean. "And then, who killed Sheriff Waters and why? Did he simply startle whoever was staying at the farm? Or was he targeted? And why did the killer come after you?"

"What do the police think?" Jean asked Enid.

"Even though Josh and I are seeing each other, we don't share everything we know. We have 'boundaries,'" Enid smiled making air quotes with her fingers. "What I'm trying to say is, Josh and I haven't talked about this level of detail."

"Uh, oh," Phyllis said. "I think there might be some complications on the home front." All three women laughed, easing the tension.

Enid pulled her phone from her tote. "Jean, you knew Angel and can identify her, right?"

"I hope so. I've tried to pull her face into my memory, but it's been years."

Enid asked Jean, "You knew Angel when she was a young child, before you left the area?"

"That's right."

Enid opened the photos of the facial reconstruction and handed her phone to Phyllis. "Jean has seen this, but I'd like for you to look at it."

Phyllis looked at the photos. She closed her eyes, and then opened them and looked again. "That's her. That's Angel."

"Are you sure?" Enid asked.

Phyllis nodded and then buried her face in her hands and sobbed. "I'm sorry. This is all just too much for me." Jean reached in her purse and handed a tissue to Phyllis. "We'll all get through this . . . together."

Jean turned to Enid. "Can you send me a copy of that reconstruction? I'd like to show it to someone."

. . .

At the newspaper office, Ginger followed Jack down the hallway. "But he wants to talk to you now," she said.

Jack stopped and turned to face her. "I said, I'll call him later." He began walking again. "Where is Enid?"

"I imagine she's in her office. You know, like where she belongs."

Jack walked into Enid's office and shut the door. "That woman is driving me crazy."

"Who are you talking about?"

"Ginger."

Enid laughed. "She says the same thing about you. Is that all you wanted to tell me? Or to what do I owe this visit?"

Jack rubbed his neck. "I think we need to sit down with Josh, Sheriff Hart, and fill him in on Phyllis' identification of the reconstruction." Jack waived a piece of paper in the air. "I read your report. This is damn good stuff, but we can't sit on it, and we sure can't report on it."

"I was going to tell him. His focus has been on finding Boogie's killer, which should be his priority. I'm not sure he accepts yet that somehow the bones are connected." Enid shrugged. "Or maybe they aren't. I think Phyllis really wants those bones to be Angel. She needs closure, although if it is Angel, that won't exonerate Reggie."

"What about the girl they arrested? Is she talking?" Jack asked.

"I don't know." Enid tapped her pencil eraser on the desk. "You know, I think I'll do an article on squatters. It's apparently become a real problem, not just here but across the country."

Jack stood up. "Yeah, alright. That's fine. But let's set something up with Josh. The sooner the better."

CHAPTER 54

Jean waited in the lobby of her mother's nursing home. According to the nurse, Lillian had been agitated all night and had not slept well. The nurse wasn't sure Lillian was up to having visitors. Jean was flipping through a two-year-old copy of *Reader's Digest* when the nurse approached her.

"I'll let you see Miss Lillian, but if she becomes agitated again, we'll have to sedate her."

Jean stood to follow the nurse. "I understand."

Lillian was sitting in her favorite chair staring out the window. The nurse pointed to the red button on the side of Lillian's bed. "Just push that button if you need me. I'll check on her later."

After the nurse left, Jean sat in the rocking chair near her and pulled an enlarged photo from a folder. She put it in Lillian's lap, without a word. Lillian's gaze never changed, as she continued to stare out the window.

After a few minutes, Jean picked up the photo and held it in front of Lillian. "Momma, I don't know if you can hear me, but I need for you to look at this photo. We think this is Angel. You tried to protect her."

Lillian continued to stare out the window with a blank expression.

"Is that her? Is that Angel?" Jean leaned back in the rocker, rocking gently, and closed her eyes. She was tired and soon drifted into a light sleep. She didn't know how long she had been napping when she became aware of a noise, or a hum of some kind. And then she felt someone touch her hand. Remembering where she was, Jean opened her eyes slightly and saw Lillian's hand resting on hers. Her mother was humming a nursery rhyme Jean had not heard in a very long time.

"Hush little baby, don't say a word. Papa's gonna buy you a mockingbird."

Jean put her hand on her mother's and squeezed it slightly. The humming continued.

"And if that mockingbird won't sing, Papa's gonna buy you a diamond ring," Jean sang softly. She turned her head slightly toward Lillian. "Momma, do you remember singing that to me when I was a little girl?"

The slight smile on Lillian's face lit up her face, but she remained silent. Jean noticed that Lillian was holding the photo in her other hand. "Is that Angel, Momma? Who was trying to hurt her?"

The smile faded from Lillian's face, and she slipped back into the in-between world where she lived. In that place, she was not quite dead, but not quite alive either.

Jean kissed her mother on the cheek. "I'll see about getting you moved closer to me in Memphis. Would you like that?" She didn't expect a response. "I'm going now, but I'll be back in a couple days." Jean squeezed Lillian's hand gently. "I love you, Momma."

Slowly, Lillian turned her head and looked directly at Jean. Her mouth moved slightly, but no sound came out.

"It's okay. I know you're trying to say you love me, too."

CHAPTER 55

Jack was right. Enid needed to let Josh know Phyllis had identified the reconstruction as Angel. Enid had left several messages for Josh, saying that she wanted to meet with him and had new information. While waiting on Josh to call back, she did some research on squatters. In South Carolina, a squatter can claim property after openly being on the land and treating it as his own for ten years. Enid made a note to check the tax records on the 7 Crows Farm. If no one had been living there, perhaps the man who shot Boogie and his blonde companion had decided just to take up residence.

On her laptop screen, a news announcement popped up. "Male suspect in Bowman sheriff's murder shot during a traffic stop." When she clicked on the news link, a photo of the suspect appeared. The man appeared to be in his mid-thirties. Somehow, she had assumed he would be older. She clicked on the local news' website to look for additional information and found the man's identity. His name was Fred Peterson, and he had a long history of legal troubles. The next line caught her attention. Peterson lived on his family's farm in Bowman County.

So, perhaps Peterson wasn't a squatter. Enid flipped through her notes. She didn't have the blonde woman's last name anywhere. She called Ginger and left a message. "I need for you to check something for me stat. What's the last name of the blonde that was arrested in Sheriff Waters' murder? Her first name is Darla. I need it right now."

Enid continued to check other stations for news of Peterson's shooting, when Ginger burst into her office. "I got it," she announced. "I got her name."

After a few seconds, Enid asked, "Well? What is it?"

"Darla Smith, that's her name," Ginger said.

"Good work. Thanks."

Ginger turned on her heels and walked out of the office. Enid stared at the names she had written on her notepad. Fred Peterson and Darla Smith.

Enid called Jean. "Hi, sorry to bother you . . ." She could hear Jean sniffling. "Are you okay?"

"I'm fine, just thinking about my mother."

"This is probably not a good time to bother you, but the guy suspected of shooting your father has been shot. I don't know if he's alive. His name is Fred Peterson. Does that sound familiar?"

There were a few seconds of silence before Jean responded. "I'm not sure, honestly."

"What about Darla Smith?"

"Darla. Darla." Jean repeated the name. "I remember something about that name." She sighed. "I'm sorry, I just can't remember."

"That's okay. Why don't you come here to the newspaper office? I don't want you to be alone right now, and I need to stay here."

"That's kind of you to offer, but I'm okay. I'm just going to check in with my office at St. Jude's. I've got to get back soon, and I need to find a place near me where I can transfer my mother."

"Alright, but if you change your mind, I'll be here. And I'll let you know if I find out anything else."

Enid held the phone in her hand, wishing she could make Jean's troubles go away. But Enid knew all too well Jean would have to work her way through most of these things on her own. She was searching the online Bowman County tax records when her cell rang. It was Jean again. "Hey, did you change your mind? Maybe I can get free for lunch."

"I just got a call from the nursing home. My mother died."

CHAPTER 56

Unlike Sheriff Bernard Waters' memorial service that was attended by hundreds of mourners, Lillian Waters' funeral was a small, simple affair. Other than Jean, Enid, Theo, Phyllis, and Jack, the only other attendees were Lillian's nurse and a nursing assistant from the center where Lillian had lived out her final days.

The minister who had performed Boogie's memorial service had agreed to say a few words and read a couple verses of scripture. Jean managed to find a photo of Lillian and had it enlarged. But the photo had been taken years ago and it was grainy. It was a poor likeness of the woman Jean had visited just prior to her death.

Lillian's photo stood on a small easel on a table next to a hand-blown glass urn. Jean had frantically searched online for something befitting, but it was Phyllis who found the perfect vessel, made by an artist she found on Facebook. In the Chihuly-glass style, the urn was colorful but elegant. Purple and royal blue, punctuated by red and deep yellow, encircled a single, black swirl of glass. When Jean saw it, she immediately thought it looked like Lillian reaching for the heavens, surrounded by a field of flowers. It was perfect. Jean contacted the artist, who agreed to ship it overnight.

After the minister's brief comments, Jean stood at the front of the church sanctuary to speak. "Today, my mother will lie down with her husband, my father, in their final resting place. Being together was a luxury they were denied in life." Her words echoed in the nearly empty space, and Jean stopped to dab a tissue at her eyes. "For years, I resented my parents for sending me away. Now, I know they did what they thought was best for me, their only child. I longed for memories of family picnics and carols around the Christmas tree, but a Hallmark life wasn't in the stars for me or for them. But what I did get was two loving, devoted parents, who put their own personal desires aside to ensure that I had the best life possible. My father was a good man who knew that love is not defined by skin color. Until he was taken away from us, he was devoted to my amazing mother. She may have had dementia, but she knew when he had left this earth and that it was time to join him. They are together now, inseparable forever."

When the service ended, Jack carried the urn out the church and down the path that led to the cemetery behind the white-sided building. The church bells tolled four times, the specific number requested to symbolize the four directions of the earth and the four seasons. At least that's what Jean told the minister. The real significance of the number came from Karla, who had identified Jean's four friends—Enid, Jack, Cade, and Josh—as warriors who sought the truth so that her parents' spirits could be at peace. One bell toll for each warrior.

Jean linked her arm through Theo's, as the small procession followed Jack and the minister to Lillian's grave. A slight movement caught Jean's eye, and she looked toward a large oak tree at the edge of the cemetery. Jean smiled at the woman dressed in a long, colorful skirt standing beside the tree. Before she turned and walked away, Karla smiled back and nodded to Jean.

CHAPTER 57

For the next few days, all the news stations carried the story of Fred Peterson's shooting. He was alive, but in critical condition. The next edition of the *Tri-County Gazette* would be coming out in a few days, so Enid gathered facts for her story. But after an hour of phone calls, she still had scant information. The shooting had occurred in Anderson County, not far from the Georgia state line. Peterson was likely trying to get out of the state when he was stopped for an expired license plate. Fred was weak and suffering from the wound Jean had inflicted on him, but he tried to pull a knife on the highway patrolman and was shot.

According to the tax records, the 7 Crows Farm was owned by an out-of-state developer who had purchased it from the bank after foreclosure. Plans to develop the land had been put on hold, so the property had been vacant for years. The previous owner had been Clyde Randolph Peterson. Enid also found that Peterson had two children: Fred and Angelina.

And who was Darla? Enid made several phone calls but was unable to find out anything other than what had already been reported. Josh probably had more information, but she didn't want to put him in an awkward situation, so she would find the information another way. Enid eyed her cell phone and hesitated before hitting a familiar number in her favorites. The phone rang only once before a male voice answered.

"Enid, is that you?"

"Hi, Cade. How are you?"

"Speechless, mostly. I'm surprised you called. Are you alright?"

"Everything is fine, but I do need your help. Can you use your contacts to get some information on a shooting down here? By the way, where are you?" Enid asked.

"I'm at LAX, trying to get out of here. I hate this place. Give me what you have and what you need. I'll see what I can do."

Enid filled Cade in on the shooting but left out the possible connection to the bones at the inn. "I appreciate anything you can find for me."

"Feels like old times. You and me, side by side, trying to find the truth."

"We're on opposite coasts."

"True, but that's a small point. I'll be back in touch."

・・・

Jean was watching the news, and each time Fred Peterson's image filled the TV screen, she stared at it. Not out of hatred, but out of curiosity. The anger would come later. For now, she just wanted to know why this man had killed her father. If he died, she might never know.

The phone rang, and a woman spoke. "Dr. Waters, I'm sorry to bother you in these troubling times. We were all very fond of Miss Lillian here at the EverLife Center, and we're so sorry for your loss."

"Thank you," Jean said.

"Being a doctor, you probably know there's a serious shortage of memory care beds available in the state. We have a long waiting list." The woman paused. "We can put your mother's belonging in storage until you can pick them up, but we need to clear her room right away."

"I had planned on coming tomorrow, but I can come later today."

Jean then called Enid. "I hate to ask, but do you think Jack can help me with Lillian's belongings? I know the rocker is hers, but I don't know what else. I'm going to need his pickup."

"If he can't go, I'll borrow his truck. We can get someone there to help with the heavy items. When do you want to go?"

"I have to get there this afternoon. They said they'd put her stuff in storage, but . . ." She paused. "I'd rather not have strangers going through her things."

Enid glanced at the stack of notes, phone messages, and files on her desk. "Either Jack or I will be over soon."

· · ·

About two hours later, Jean and Enid arrived at the nursing home in Jack's pickup. Enid pulled into a parking space near the loading area.

They walked inside, and Jean located Lillian's nurse. "I talked to you earlier. We're here to get Lillian Waters' things."

"I apologize again for rushing you. It's just that—"

"Don't worry," Jean interrupted. "It's fine."

"Follow me." The nurse began walking down the hallway. "There are some items, you know, clothing and things, in her room. But we also have several boxes of things in our storage area. The facility provides a small storage space for each patient, in case the family wants to keep certain things nearby. It's a nice benefit that other nursing homes don't often provide."

Jean looked around the room Lillian had died in. The bed linens had been stripped and the drapes pushed completely open. Harsh sunlight filled the room, revealing a few worn spots in the carpet and a thin layer of dust on the dresser.

"I know it looks so empty now. That's what everyone says. Humans have a spirit, you know, and when they go, it goes. That's why the room feels that way." The nurse opened the closet door and pointed to a large shelf at the top. "She's got some things up there. I can get you a step stool so you can reach it. And she's got clothes here and in the drawers."

"I know the rocker is hers. What about the rest of the furniture?"

"The bed, nightstand, and dresser belong to the facility. When you're ready, I'll take you to the storage area."

"What about her favorite chair over there?" Jean asked, pointing.

"That must be hers, too. As I recall, her husband brought that for her. Go ahead and take it if you want it. It's too worn to use anyway."

Jean went back to the waiting area and got Enid. For the next half hour, they packed clothes in plastic bags and got everything from the closet shelf. Two of the men who worked at the facility loaded the rocker and chair on the pickup and then all the boxes and bags.

"Oh, I almost forgot. There are some other items in a storage area." Jean turned to one of the workers. "Do you know where that is?"

"Yeah, I can take you there." He looked at the ring of keys on his belt and patted it with his hand. "Got the keys right here." The man pointed out the window to a small road. "If you want to drive down there just a bit, you'll see a building. That's where we store everything. I'll meet you there."

Enid pulled the pickup truck in front of a big steel building that looked like a barn. The man from the facility drove up in a golf cart and got out. "Go on in. They said at the desk her space is number 40. It should be near the back on the first level."

Enid and Jean walked into the building. There were wire cages everywhere with padlocks on them. Each storage space was about five feet square. Jean walked ahead, as Enid looked at the belongings inside those cages. Just as the owners of these items were locked inside their own mental prisons, so were the things so dear to them. She saw boxes, silver chests, and other containers that held their past lives and memories.

"I found it. Here's number 40," Jean called out from the rear of the building. "There're a lot of plastic containers in here."

The facility worker pointed to a dolly on wheels at the back wall. "We can put everything on there and wheel it out to your truck." He unlocked the cage, and the three of them started stacking plastic boxes. Most of them were fairly small, not much bigger than banker boxes used to store files.

When they had all the boxes loaded, Jean tried to tip the worker who had helped them. "Oh, no, ma'am. But thanks. I'm sorry for your loss. Miss Lillian was one of the good ones."

"Did she ever talk to you?" Jean asked.

"Yes, ma'am. She said a lot with her face and eyes. We communicated regularly, just not in the normal way. You have a safe trip home now. Have a blessed day."

. . .

When they were on the road, Enid called Jack to let him know they were on the way to Boogie's house. He agreed to meet them there and help unload.

A little more than an hour later, Enid pulled into the driveway. Jack was sitting on Boogie's porch reading articles for the next edition. "You two look like trouble. Although, I have to say there's something appealing about two beautiful women in a truck."

Jean smiled. "That sounds like something my father would have said."

Jack put down the tailgate and started carrying the storage boxes. "Where you want me to put these?"

"Just put them in the dining room. I'll go through each box at the table. Most of it is probably old papers, but I'll go through each one to be sure I don't throw away anything we might need to settle the estate."

By the time the three of them finished, there were eleven containers stacked up beside the dining room table.

"What do you want to do with the rocker and chair?" Enid asked.

"They're both junk, but would it be foolishly sentimental of me to keep them?" Jean asked.

"Not at all," Jack said. "Although, getting them to Memphis might be a challenge. Tell you what. Unless you want them right away, I can put them in my storage building behind the house. In a few months, if you still feel the same way, we'll have them shipped to you."

"That's very kind of you, but I don't want to impose."

"Jack's a fixer. He likes to solve everybody's problems." Enid laughed. "So indulge him. It'll make him happy."

"Well, alright then, I will," Jean said. She hugged Jack, apparently catching him by surprise. "You're the best."

"Do you need for me to stay here and help you?" Enid asked Jean. "I'll be glad to."

"No, thanks. I've taken enough of your time. I'll just pour myself a glass of wine and sip my way through all this stuff." Jean took Enid's hands in hers. "I will never forget what you've done to help me."

Before Enid could reply, her cell phone signaled an incoming text. She looked at the screen. "Call me ASAP." Enid looked at Jack. "I need to make a call, but I can do it on the way home. It's Cade."

. . .

After riding several minutes in silence, Jack asked Enid, "Do you want me to pull over somewhere so you can call Cade in private?"

Enid stared out the window.

"Enid?"

"Sorry. I was lost in thought. What?"

"Do you want to call Cade in private?"

"I don't have any secrets from you. In fact, I was just thinking about Cade. Maybe I shouldn't have called him."

"You called him because you wanted to. Seems pretty simple."

Enid frowned at Jack and tapped on Cade's cell number.

When Cade answered, he said, "I'm in Chicago getting ready to board a connecting flight."

"You couldn't get a direct flight back to Charlotte?"

"Flight got canceled in L.A., had to be rerouted. When I get to the airport, I'm going to rent a car and drive to Madden. I'll be there later tonight."

"You're coming here?" Enid looked at Jack, who was staring straight ahead at the road.

"I'll explain later. See you in a few hours."

Enid put her cell phone back in her tote and stared out the window again. "Please don't say anything right now. I really don't want to hear whatever is on your mind."

"What would I say to you? Oh, you mean something like, 'I think you're still in love with Cade.' Is that what I might say?"

Enid closed her eyes and leaned her head back against the headrest. "Yeah, you'd probably say something like that."

They rode in silence the rest of the way, and by the time Jack dropped Enid off at his house so she could get her car, the tension between them was palpable. "I'll see you tomorrow," Enid said as she got out of the pickup.

"If you need some personal time, I can divvy out your small assignments so you can focus on the bones and Boogie's story."

"Why would you think I need time off?"

"Just offering, that's all."

"'Bye, Jack. I'll see you tomorrow." She slammed the door and walked to her car.

CHAPTER 58

Jean went through about half of the boxes and filled several big plastic trash bags full of papers to be either trashed or shredded. She took off her reading glasses and massaged the bridge between her eyes to relieve the tension. While taking a break, she opened her laptop and checked flights to Memphis. There was little left here that she needed to do right now, and the hospital was shorthanded. It was time to step back into the life she had before her father had called her. In some ways it seemed long ago, but in other ways, the shooting still seemed fresh and raw. She had tried repeatedly to wipe the image from her memory of her father's bloody body lying on the ground at 7 Crows Farm, but it would likely be a long time before the pain eased.

As she resumed going through her mother's boxes, Jean was overcome with a sense of loss, not so much from Lillian's passing, but from the years spent apart from her, from both of her parents. Jean's sorrow felt like a weight pulling her down into a deep, emotional abyss.

She pulled one of the few remaining boxes across the floor to the side of her chair and took off the cover. Most of the boxes had contained loose papers that appeared to have been hurriedly packed. With more time to sort through them, most of those papers would likely have been discarded. She could imagine her father having someone put all the papers in the boxes and stored when he had to put

Lillian in the nursing home, with intentions of going through them later. But later never came, and now decades of papers filled the trash bags in his dining room. But this box was different. It was full of books that appeared to be journals. Blank pages had been filled with handwritten notes, some dated, some not. All of the pages were yellowed with age, and a few had water damage.

Jean put the cover back on the box of journals and set it aside to go through later. Part of her was anxious to read what her mother had to say, but part of her was afraid.

CHAPTER 59

After waking up the next morning, it took a few minutes for Enid to remember that Cade was in her guest room. He had arrived late, nearly midnight. They had spoken only briefly before he crashed on the futon sofa bed in the multipurpose room that served as guest room and office. Before getting up, she tried to assess her feelings. Was she glad he was here? Or had she made a mistake in inviting him back into her life? The smell of bacon and coffee aroused primal responses of hunger and pushed all other thoughts aside.

When she walked into the small kitchen, Cade was standing there in jeans and an old tee shirt she had bought him at an Aerosmith concert years ago. The printing had faded and the back had a large tear in it.

"I can't believe you're still wearing that old thing," Enid said.

"Good morning." Cade looked down at his shirt. "Lots of good memories with this shirt. Remember how we—"

"It's a bit early for reminiscing, don't you think?" Enid took a cup from the cabinet. "Thanks for heating water for my tea."

"You still like bacon, or have you gone healthy on me?"

"I don't eat it often, but I still love it. Nothing else smells like bacon cooking."

Cade pointed to the small dining table. "Drink your tea. Breakfast will be ready in a few minutes."

Enid sat at the table and watched Cade cook. He never used to do that. When they were married, he drank a couple cups of coffee and bolted out the door each morning. Living alone had made him self-sufficient. Or was he living alone? "I see you've taken up cooking. But then I guess you'd have to unless you eat out every meal."

"I do alright. What about you, did you learn to cook?"

Enid laughed. "I do alright."

Cade put a plate of scrambled eggs and bacon in front of her. "Good thing I stopped by the store before I got here. Your cupboard was bare."

Enid took a bite of eggs and munched on a piece of crisp bacon. "Why are you here?"

"You mean instead of staying at the inn? I can do that, if you'd prefer."

"No, I mean why are you in Madden at all?"

"I wanted to talk to you about a couple of things, and I'm also doing an article on Madelyn Jensen's campaign."

"So you came to stay with your ex-wife so you could visit Madelyn?"

Cade wiped the bacon grease from his fingers with his napkin. "I thought you and Madelyn were friends."

"We are." Enid pushed the plate of uneaten food away from her. "It's just that, well, having you back here, the memories, the pain. I feel unsettled, that's all."

"I get it. But let's not complicate things. Fair enough?"

"Sure. So what else is going on?"

"I know you were concerned about the article I was doing that involved Chief Hart."

"He's Sheriff Hart now."

"Oh, right. I forgot. Anyway, I wanted you to know he'd been cleared."

Enid sat up straight. She had pushed Josh's personal problems out of her mind lately. So many times, she had wanted to ask him, but he was a private person and needed to work through whatever was going on. She trusted that in time, he would tell her everything she wanted to know. "You mean, you're not doing the article on him?"

"I'm doing it, but the focus has changed. His younger brother confessed to the killing. He apparently idolized Josh's wife and was determined to avenge her death."

A flood of emotions washed over Enid. She was relieved that her faith in Josh had been affirmed. Yet, she was hurt he had not told her what was going on. Maybe Josh wanted to protect her from getting involved. "I knew Josh wasn't the killer. He's a good man."

"As you've reminded me." Cade sipped his coffee. "You also asked me to check on Boogie's killing and the suspect they shot and apprehended."

"Is he still alive?"

"Yes, but barely. He probably won't make it. His name is—"

"Fred Peterson," Enid said, interrupting.

"That's right. He was staying on the farm his family used to own. Boogie must have stumbled onto them, and they panicked."

"Fred's sister was Angelina. Phyllis thinks those bones found at the inn are her." Enid explained to Cade how Lillian had asked the contractor to move Angel's bones to the inn and then instructed him to seal off the storage room.

"I hope you're going to write about that, otherwise I might steal that story from you."

"We're waiting to positively identify the bones. There was no DNA match or dental records. I've got a photo of the facial reconstruction." She got her phone from the bedroom and brought it back to the table. "Phyllis says this is Angel. She's sure. But I'm going to push Josh to get a DNA sample from Fred to compare with the bones."

"When we talked earlier, you said something about Phyllis' brother, I can't remember his name, being convicted for killing Angel."

"His name was Reggie. He was convicted on flimsy evidence and died in prison. I'm going to help Phyllis see if we can get the courts to vacate the conviction against him."

Cade threw back his head and laughed. "You don't play small, do you? That's a tall order."

"I know, but it's worth trying. Maybe if we got a national news story and built some public support it would help."

Cade put his hand on Enid's. "Are you using me? If so, I'm loving it."

Enid eased her hand away. "But even if it is Angel, we still don't know who killed her."

CHAPTER 60

Instead of calling ahead for an appointment, Enid drove to Josh's office, hoping to catch him. When she walked into the sheriff's office, the desk officer told her Josh was out. Disappointed, Enid scribbled a note for Josh and left it.

As she was walking to her car, she heard her name called by a familiar voice. "Enid, wait."

Looking across the parking lot, she saw Josh walking toward her. She wanted to run to him, put her arms around his neck, and turn back the clock to the time before Cade's investigation, before this feeling that they were slipping away from each other. "Josh, I'm glad you're here. Can we talk?"

Josh's gaze held hers until they were both uncomfortable. "I miss you. Forgive me for not calling you back. It's just that—"

"It's okay."

"Let's go to the coffee shop down the road. If I go inside, we'll never get to talk."

Enid followed Josh in her car until he pulled into a small diner near the interstate. When they walked inside, Josh looked around to check out the lay of the land, as he called it. He sat with his back to the kitchen so he could see who was coming and going. He looked tired.

"How are you adjusting, to the new job, I mean?" Enid asked.

"It's fun in some ways, but I miss Madden. And I really miss seeing you."

"Are you going to move here?"

"I haven't decided. I love my home in Madden, but I do need to be closer to my office. If I rent out my house instead of selling it, why don't you move in? I'll give you a great deal."

Enid picked at her napkin. "I don't know if I could do that. It just wouldn't be the same without you there. And it would stir up even more gossip."

"I want to spend more time with you, it's just that—"

"You don't have to apologize for being dedicated to your work. That's something I understand."

He glanced around the diner. An elderly couple, the only occupants, sat across the room. Josh took Enid's hands in his. "But I want a life, too, not just a job."

"I keep thinking about Boogie and Lillian. I can't imagine how hard and painful it must have been to keep their marriage and child a secret all those years. We can't live our lives trying to hide our relationship, not if we want to be happy. As for your job, it will get easier. You're still learning the ropes."

"I sure miss Boogie. If he were here, he could help me a lot."

"Cade is in town."

Josh let go of Enid's hands. "Oh? What's going on?"

"He's doing an article on Madelyn's campaign. And he's helping me do some of the legwork on the suspect's shooting."

"I'm so sorry I haven't been able to share anything with you," Josh said. "We don't know much at this point."

"I hope you plan to get Fred Peterson's DNA."

Josh massaged his neck, much in the same way Jack did when he was stressed. "Of course. I'll order the test as soon as I get back. I admit I haven't worried too much about the bones, what with Boogie's murder, and then the suspect's shooting."

"I'm convinced it's all connected. What about the girl you took into custody? What's her story?" Enid paused. "Or can you tell me?"

"She's not in the system, so no prior run-ins with the law. I suspect she's related to Fred Peterson, though."

"Why is that?" Enid asked.

"More of a gut feeling than anything else, and there's a slight family resemblance." Josh's police radio crackled. "I've got to take this." He went outside.

When Josh returned a few minutes later, he motioned for the wait person so he could pay the bill. "I'm sorry, but I've got to go. Can we do dinner tonight? I'll cook." He paused. "And there's something I need to tell you."

"I hope you're going to tell me about Troy's arrest and why you haven't mentioned it."

CHAPTER 61

Jean had ignored that one storage box as long as she could. It sat in the dining room, beckoning her to return to its contents. "Alright, you win," she said, kicking gently at the box. She sat down and pulled the journals out, spreading them across the table. Some were small, but several were crammed with photos and papers. The same dates sometimes appeared in two or more journals, so Lillian had apparently forgotten which journal she was using.

Jean picked up the largest volume and opened it. She felt like she was invading her mother's sanctity, but Lillian was gone. Whatever privacy she once had was now in the urn with her ashes.

One of the first photos Jean found tucked in a journal was her own baby picture. The resemblance was unmistakable, and Lillian had penciled Jean's full name and the date on the backside. Jean had no pictures of her younger self. Putting the photo back in the journal, she looked at the next one. A picture of her mother and Boogie had been taken a few years later, after Jean had been sent to live with her aunt. They looked like any other couple, except that Lillian was dark skinned and Boogie was white, an anomaly then and even now in some parts of the rural South. In the photo, Boogie had his arm around Lillian, holding her close. The affection between them was apparent.

Jean looked at several other photographs of family members on her mother's side. Thankfully, Lillian had noted their names and the dates. Jean put those in a separate stack so she could track them down, assuming any were still alive.

The notes in the next journal she picked up were about everyday life. Lillian talked about a "secret date" with Boogie, even though they were a married couple by then. She talked about life at the inn and the pride she took in running it. This owner seemed to be merely holding onto the inn for posterity's sake and as a placeholder for the next person who inherited it. In the owner's stead, Lillian assumed the responsibility for maintaining the inn's culture and history.

Jean put that journal aside and picked up another one that had a few photos stashed in it. The names on the back didn't mean anything to her. She didn't know if they were relatives, friends, or just guests at the inn her mother had befriended. Jean replaced the photos in the journal, and as she did, she found another picture crammed into the binding near the back.

Staring back at Jean was a young woman with light brown hair. She looked familiar. A wave of anticipation and dread washed through Jean, as she recognized the image. The young woman looked very much like the facial reconstruction photo. Jean flipped the photo over and read Lillian's inscription on the back: "Angelina." Jean dropped the photo to the table and pushed back. No one had been able to find anything on Angel. Was this an image of the young woman whose bones may have been found at the inn?

Jean put the photo to one side and began looking for dates in the journals that coincided with Angel's disappearance. The journal that was the smallest with the least number of pages turned out to be the one Jean was looking for. She read her mother's entry out loud.

"Angelina came to the inn again today. She is terrified and can't go to the police. I've talked to Bernard, but he doesn't believe her father would offer his daughter to the deputies in exchange for favors. Bernard also refuses to believe any of his deputies were involved. But, he did promise me he'd look into it. I wish I had somewhere I could send Angelina to keep her safe."

Jean flipped through several pages about a party at the inn until she found an entry two weeks later.

"My heart is broken. Angelina has disappeared, and Bernard arrested her boyfriend Reggie. This is wrong. Why is Bernard not seeing that? I fear Angelina has been killed at the farm, because that's where she was most afraid. I must find her."

Jean pushed the journal aside and put her head in her hands. Part of her wanted to burn these journals, so she could return to Memphis and resume her old life. But this was too important. Although her father's reputation was at stake, so was Reggie's. Jean wept and prayed for guidance through this mess.

The doorbell rang and startled Jean. She wiped the tears from her face and walked to the front door. "Who is it?"

"It's me, Enid. Is this a bad time?"

Jean flung the door open and almost knocked Enid over as she wrapped her arms around her. "No. This is perfect. Come in."

• • •

Enid finally had to pull away from Jean. "What's wrong. Are you okay?"

Jean smiled slightly. "I'm sorry. You must think I'm crazy. And I probably am, at least right now."

Enid went to the kitchen and made them a cup of tea. She put Jean's cup in front of her. "Would you rather have coffee?"

"What?" Jean looked at the cup. "Oh, no. This is fine. Thanks."

"So tell me what's going on. You look like you've seen a ghost."

"What would you do if you found out your father may have covered up a murder? Or at least covered up the real murderer."

Enid glanced into the dining room and saw the box on the floor and papers and small books all over the table. "Is all of that Lillian's?"

Jean nodded. "I found a photo of Angel and some journal entries about my father. And about Reggie." Jean walked into the dining room and brought back the photo and the small journal. "Here, you can see for yourself."

Enid looked at the photo and then pulled out her cell phone. She opened the picture of the facial reconstruction and held it beside the old photograph of Angel. "I admit, there's a close resemblance." She then read Lillian's journal while Jean sat in silence, sipping her tea.

After a few minutes, Enid closed the journal. "Well, I can see why you were upset. But, wasn't this about the same time Lillian was slipping into dementia? She might have been mistaken. We only know one side of this story." Enid picked up her cell phone again.

"Who are you calling?" Jean asked.

"Pete, the acting police chief in Madden. He may know . . . oh, hi, Pete, it's Enid Blackwell. Yes, I've missed seeing you, too. Maybe we can do lunch soon at the diner, and you can tell me how the new job is going. But right now, I have a question. Do you know the names of any of the older county deputies? Josh said most of the deputies there now are fairly new, but I need to talk to someone who worked for Sheriff Waters earlier. Maybe they're retired and still living around here." Enid scribbled in her notepad. "Thanks, Pete. I'll call you later about lunch."

"Did he know anyone?"

Enid held up her notepad and waved it in the air. "Yes, and he should be easy to find."

"Maybe I should go with you?"

Enid put her phone and notepad in her tote. "No, I'll be fine. You don't need to put yourself through the wringer."

Driving away from Boogie's house, Enid called the office and had Ginger find the address for Walter, the retired deputy Pete told her about. "Tell Jack where I'm going."

CHAPTER 62

Enid had no trouble finding Walter's house. It was less than a mile away from 7 Crows Farm. The yard was littered with two old pickups and a rusted boat trailer. Enid looked around before getting out of her car. She thought of the empty can of dog repellant sitting on her kitchen counter that she had left there as a reminder to buy more.

She opened the car door and stood nearby for a few seconds. So far, no dog. But when she looked toward the house, an elderly man was standing on the porch, shotgun in hand.

"You can turn that car around now and get out of here," he said.

"Are you Walter?"

The man lowered the gun slightly. "What if I am?"

"My name is Enid Blackwell. I'm from the *Tri-County Gazette*. Pete, you know, the acting Madden police chief, said you might be able to help me with an article I'm writing."

"You can come up on the porch." He laid the gun on the floor.

Enid walked toward him and held out her hand. "It's nice to meet you." The man took her hand in the way men do when they're not used to dealing with women. "I won't take much of your time."

Walter laughed. "Got plenty of time. In fact, that's about all I got." He sat down in one of the rockers and pointed to the other one, which appeared to be a little sturdier. "You can sit here."

Enid took out her notepad. "Do you mind if I take a few notes?"

Walter looked concerned but didn't protest. He made a grunting noise that Enid took for approval.

"I'm doing an article on Sheriff Bernard Waters. I understand you worked for him."

Walter nodded again. "Good man. Worked for him near 'bout thirty years."

"Goodness, that's a long time. I bet you saw a lot and have a few stories to tell."

Walter shifted slightly, and the rocker groaned under his weight. "Been meaning to fix this rocker. Just keep putting it off. Don't sit out here much. Not like I used to. Too many mosquitoes in warm weather, and the cold freezes my joints in the winter."

"What kind of sheriff was Bernard Waters?"

"Not sure what you mean."

"Anything about him that bothered you?"

Walter stared at Enid briefly before responding. "Well, he was a bit too rigid at times, if that's what you're getting at. He was a stickler for certain things. Expected all of us to be loyal to the uniform and to him."

"Do you think he was a fair man?"

"Oh, yeah. Definitely."

"I'm wondering if you heard any of the talk about the sheriff helping to convict a young man for the alleged murder of Angelina Peterson. Would you like to comment on that?"

Walter cracked his knuckles, making a loud popping noise that made Enid's skin crawl. "That black man killed her. No question. And you don't need to be diggin' up shit. You hear me?"

"I didn't mean to upset you." Enid looked at her car and wondered if she could outrun Walter if needed. Even so, she couldn't outrun a shotgun. "But I have information that Waters may have rushed to judgment, and that others may have been involved in her disappearance."

Walter glared at Enid and remained silent.

"Did you know Angel's father?"

Walter moved so quickly that Enid didn't have time to react. He was standing over her pulling her up by her arm. "You can get the hell out of here now, missy." He shoved her down the porch steps, and she landed on the ground. Walter picked up her notepad and slung it into the bushes beside the house. He then picked up her tote and threw it at her. Enid raised her arm to keep from getting hit in the face.

As Enid got up and brushed the dirt off her clothes, Walter picked up the shotgun and pointed it at her. "You got mere seconds to get in your car and get off my property."

Enid picked up her tote and limped to her car, her ankle throbbing and her arm in pain. A cut on her arm was bleeding. As she got in the car, she glanced back at Walter, still aiming at her.

CHAPTER 63

Enid winced as Jack put ointment on the cut on her arm. "Ouch." Ginger had left for the day, so she and Jack were the only ones in the newspaper office.

"Hold still. You're behaving like a three-year old with a boo-boo on her arm. Good thing we keep this first aid kit around." He finished dressing the cut. "There. You're good to go."

Enid sat in silence, knowing a lecture was coming. She and Jack had become best friends, the kind who knew in advance what the other would do or say in certain situations.

"You need to file an assault charge against that Walter guy. I'm going to call Josh."

"No, don't do that. Josh has enough to deal with now."

"Well, if he can't deal with more than one thing at a time, he needs to step aside."

Enid brushed dirt off her pants leg. "That's not fair, and you know it."

Jack took Enid's hands in his. "I know, and I'm sorry. It just that it makes me crazy when you get yourself in these situations. I worry about you."

Enid squeezed his hands and then pulled away. "We've got to find Angel's father. Is he still alive?"

Jack rubbed the back of his neck. "I don't know, but you're right."

"You know, I feel really sorry for Jean. What if we find out her father was involved in something illegal or covered up for someone else? Or something even worse."

"We're in a tough business. Of all people, we have to stay above personal feelings. It's hard at times, and we may end up hurting people we care about. But it's what we do. It's who we are."

Enid stood up. "Thanks for the lecture on journalist ethics. I'm going to my office to get started with the search. Can you help me?"

Jack smiled. "Of course."

Half an hour later, Enid was tracing the whereabouts of the Peterson patriarch, Clyde. She couldn't find an obituary, but neither could she find anything that might prove he was still alive. The county records showed his last address as the 7 Crows Farm, but that was more than ten years ago. She was deep in thought when her cell rang, startling her. It was Josh.

"Hey, are we still on for tonight?"

"Yes, I guess so," Enid said.

"You sound . . . Are you alright?"

"Just having a bad day. I'll see you around seven o'clock, if that's okay."

"Sure. Oh, I forgot to tell you. Fred Peterson regained consciousness. I'm going to take a statement from him."

"If there's anything you can tell me, you know, anything you would ordinarily tell the press, I'd appreciate a head start on the bigger papers."

Josh sighed. "Of course. I'll fill you in on what I can tonight."

As soon as she hung up, Jack ran into her office. "I found him."

"Who?" Enid asked.

"Clyde Peterson. He's living not far from here."

"How did you find him? Wait, did you find him or did Rachel?"

Jack's face reddened slightly. "She might have helped a bit. But legally." He waved his notepad in the air. "She just knows how to search better than we do and has access to, let's just say, different resources. She found an old county document filed online. Anyway, here's what we've got."

Enid listened to Jack's newly discovered information. "I wish we could hire her as a research assistant. I'm sure SLED or the county investigators will find this information also, if they haven't already." She reached for her tote.

"Where do you think you're going?" Jack asked. "I hope you're not even thinking about going out there."

"I was thinking maybe we could go see him. Come on."

"Only if you tell Josh first."

Enid turned around to face Jack. "So now you think Josh is a savior. Which way do you want it?"

Jack took a step back. "Whoa. Sorry."

Enid sighed. "No, I'm the one who's sorry. I didn't mean to snap at you. But if I wasn't in a relationship with Josh, you wouldn't ask me to call him."

Jack pulled out his cell phone. "Fair enough. Just checking to make sure I've got enough charge left to call 911 if we need help."

CHAPTER 64

While Jack and Enid rode in silence, he kept his attention on the road and all the potholes. Enid stared out the window, catching the occasional glance of rural life in the poorest part of the county. Rusted car shells and mobile homes reflected the economic reality for these residents, many of whom were once farmers.

"According to the GPS coordinates Rachel gave me, we're getting close."

Enid checked her cell phone. She had one bar on the signal strength. Maybe she should have called Josh. Dinner! She nearly forgot she was soon due at Josh's. He would be worried if she didn't call or show up.

Jack pulled off the side of the road. "I'm not going up that driveway, or we might get trapped. I wish there was room to turn around here so we'd be headed back out in case we need to leave quickly."

"The road ahead looks okay. I'm sure there's a place not too far ahead where we can turn if we need to." Enid looked at her phone again. No signal.

"Come on, let's go before it starts getting dark. I don't want to be here too long."

Jack parked on the shoulder of the road, and they walked up the dirt drive for about a hundred yards. The drive was just two ruts with tall grass growing in the middle and on each side. There were fresh tire tracks in the dirt.

"There's the house." Jack pointed to a small, one-story house with peeling white siding. "There's a pickup beside it. I think someone's home."

"But there're no lights." Enid checked her phone. At least she had one bar of signal again. She held her phone up toward a clearing in the surrounding woods. "I've got two bars. I'm going to call Josh like you suggested, so he won't worry. I'm supposed to meet him tonight."

"Good. I'd feel much better if he knows where we are." Jack walked to the side of the woods to look at what appeared to be a rotted carcass of something dead.

When she got Josh's voice message, she spoke as quietly as she could. "Josh, I may be late tonight. Jack and I found Clyde Peterson's address and we're here to interview him. The coordinates are . . ." The sound from behind her silenced her.

An elderly man held Jack by the arm. He had a shotgun in the other hand. Shotguns seemed to be the weapon of choice in these parts.

"You lookin' for anything in particular?" the man asked. He shoved Jack to the ground and stepped back, raising his shotgun toward Enid.

"Wait, we're just here to interview Clyde Peterson," she said. "Is that you?"

"Interview? About what?" The man looked down at Jack. "You just stay right there, mister. Don't move."

"We're doing a follow-up on the murder trial involving your daughter, Angelina."

Peterson raised his shotgun so that it was leveled right at Enid's chest. She was having a hard time breathing. Despite her fear, she maintained eye contact with the old man.

The look in his eyes revealed a lot. "You really loved her, didn't you?"

At first, Enid thought Peterson was having a convulsion of some kind. His shoulders shook, and the shotgun wavered up and down a bit.

"Mr. Peterson, just take it easy," Jack said, looking up at him. "Can you put that gun down and let's talk? We're not here to hurt you. We're just small-town newspaper reporters who want to do a story about your daughter."

He lowered the shotgun and let it fall to the ground. Sobbing, he buried his face in his hands, shoulders slumped. "I loved her so." His words were muffled, as his hands still covered his face. "She was my Angel."

Enid looked at Jack, and they both looked at the shotgun on the ground. "Mr. Peterson," Enid said, "I'm going to pick up this gun and put it aside, so no one gets hurt. Is that okay with you?"

Peterson continued to sob as Enid slowly reached down and picked up the shotgun. Josh had taken her on a turkey shoot, so she knew how to break the barrel open to remove the shells, but there was nothing in the chambers. "It's not loaded," she said to Jack.

Jack stood up and put his arm around Peterson. "Let's go to the house. We'll talk up there." As Peterson followed Jack up the path, a basset hound wandered from the back yard and trotted beside the old man.

There were two metal chairs, both nearly rusted through, so Enid sat on the top step of the porch. After a few minutes, Peterson regained his composure. "You must think I'm an old fool," he said.

"Not at all," Enid said. "A father's love for his daughter is very powerful." She glanced at Jack, and he pulled out his cell phone and tapped the red recording icon. "We're going to record your comments to make sure we get it right."

Peterson glanced at the phone in Jack's hand but said nothing.

"May we ask you a few questions?" Enid asked. "Do you feel up to it?"

Peterson nodded. "I've had a lot of time to think about what I'd say when somebody showed up. Knew somebody would. Some day."

Enid and Jack exchanged glances again.

"If you want to tell us what's bothering you, we'll listen," Jack said. "Might be good to get it off your chest."

Peterson leaned his head back and briefly closed his eyes, and then he sat up again and looked at Enid. "I tried to do good by both my children. Raised them the same, didn't favor either of them whatsoever." He paused. "But Fred always had it in his mind that Angel was the favorite. He resented it."

Enid didn't want to push Peterson too fast, but she didn't know how long he would keep talking. "Do you think Angelina's boyfriend, Reggie, killed her?"

Peterson stared ahead without talking for so long, Enid assumed he must not have heard her. "Mr. Peterson, do you think—"

"I tried to tell Bernard that Reggie boy didn't do it," Peterson said. "To be honest, I didn't like Angel dating a black fella, but he was decent, as far as I could tell. And I could see he loved Angelina."

Jack grabbed his cell phone to keep it from sliding off his leg. He glanced down to be sure it was still recording. "Are you saying you told Sheriff Waters that Reggie didn't kill Angel?"

Peterson nodded.

"But how would you know that for sure?" Jack asked.

"'Cause I know who did."

Enid pointed to Jack's phone. "Mr. Peterson, I'd like to remind you that we're recording this interview. Are you aware of that?"

Peterson shrugged like a man with nothing left to lose. Jack held the phone up closer to Peterson.

"If Reggie didn't do it, then who killed your daughter?" Enid asked.

Peterson put his hand on his chest. "I got a bad heart, had it for years. That's why I had to give up the farm. This whole thing with Angelina nearly killed me. Especially when I found out what Fred was doing."

"What did he do?" Jack asked. "Did your son, did Fred kill Angel?"

Peterson sobbed again and pulled a blue bandana from the pocket of his overalls. Enid realized she was holding her breath and exhaled deeply. "Tell us what happened."

Peterson blew his nose into the bandana again and stuffed it back in his overalls. "Fred was always in trouble with the law. Bernard, Sheriff Waters, he did what he could to protect him. Bernard did it for me, though, not Fred. Me and Bernard, we was kids together. One day, Fred got busted for growing pot on our farm, the 7 Crows. The deputy made an offer to Fred, I found out later, that he'd drop the charges for a night with Angel."

"You mean Fred pimped out his sister?" Jack asked.

Enid frowned at Jack. "Is that what happened?" she asked Peterson, who nodded in reply. "Was this just once or how long did it go on?"

"Over a year, I found out. But Fred had been physically abusing Angelina since she was a little girl. He just had a mean streak in him, slapped her around a lot. When she was about fifteen, Angel disappeared once, was gone for months. I thought she was dead, but she showed up about seven months later. Never would tell me where she had been." He paused. "I think she was afraid to tell me."

"Why didn't you stop Fred or at least tell Sheriff Waters?" Jack asked.

"I was nearly an invalid after my heart attack. Fred started pushing me first, that was all. Then he struck me a few times. I hate to admit I was afraid of my own blood, but I was. And I tried to tell Bernard what Fred and the deputies were doing to my Angelina. He said his men would never do such a thing, but he'd ask around."

"So when Angelina disappeared the second time, why did Sheriff Waters assume she was dead and then go after Reggie?" Enid asked.

Peterson dropped his head. "I don't know. But Bernard stopped coming to see me after Reggie was arrested. I called the county prosecutor's office and told them I needed to talk to them. Somebody called me back and took the information, but that's the last I heard of it."

"Was there more than one deputy involved?" Enid asked.

"There were at least two. One of 'em left town after Reggie was arrested. The other one, Walter, retired. Don't know where he is now."

Enid looked at Jack and then glanced at the sky. It would be dark in an hour, and they needed to get out of there. "Mr. Peterson, why do you think Sheriff Waters and the prosecutor pushed for Reggie's conviction?"

Peterson looked at Jack. "Turn that thing off, will you."

Jack tapped the record icon on his phone. "It's off."

"Much as I hate to say it, I think it was purely a race thing," Peterson said.

"Are you aware that Sheriff Waters was married to an African American woman?" Enid asked.

Peterson paused before replying. "I heard some talk, but I figured it was just that. You know, mean gossip." He shook his head. "That was for real, huh?"

Jack leaned forward. "Are you suggesting that Sheriff Waters intentionally railroaded an innocent man into prison because he was black?"

Peterson looked out toward the field by the house. "I'm just a simple, country fella. I don't read the papers no more and my TV is busted. Don't even have a phone. But that don't mean I don't know what's going on. Racism isn't always something you choose. When I found out Angelina was dating a black man, I wanted to go after him. My daddy would have killed him on the spot. That's how I was raised. But when I saw Angel's eyes light up when she talked about him, you know, Reggie, I knew he must be treating her good. I wasn't happy, but for Angel's sake, if he could give her a better life than she had, then I wasn't going to stop them. I gave 'em my blessing, so to speak. Angel wanted to leave here and go to West Virginia with Reggie. We still got some relatives there."

"Did you ever discuss Reggie with Fred?" Enid asked.

Peterson nodded. "I asked Fred to let Angelina alone, to let her have a decent life for once. But he liked having control over people. She was terrified of him, had been all her life, and there weren't nothing I could do to stop him. Nothing short of killing him, and sometimes I wish I had." He pulled the bandana from his pocket and blew his nose.

"Do you know that Fred was shot and is in hospital?" Jack asked.

"One of the boys down the road told me. This here is their property I'm staying on. Them two grew up with Fred and know he's got the devil in him, so they keep my whereabouts to themselves. They said Fred came back and was looking for me. He told them he wanted to see if I had any money he could get." He laughed. "Do I look like I got money squirrelled away?"

"We'd like to give your interview to the new sheriff, Joshua Hart," Enid said. "He's an honest man. If Fred killed your daughter, or was in any way involved, the sheriff needs to know. In any event, Fred will go away for killing Bernard Waters, so he can't hurt you anymore."

Peterson rocked back and forth slowly, tears streaming down his face.

"Will you be alright?" Enid asked. "Is there anyone we can call to stay with you?"

Peterson shook his head and then looked at Enid. "I'm free now. Free from the secrets and the burden of this guilt."

CHAPTER 65

When Jack and Enid got back to the car, she called Josh to let him know they were safe.

"I've been worried sick. Where are you?" Josh asked.

"We're headed back to Madden. Jack and I need to talk to you, so we may have to postpone our dinner. Can you meet us at the newspaper office? It might be better than having two reporters show up at the sheriff's office at this hour." They agreed to meet in thirty minutes.

"I feel sorry for Clyde Peterson," Jack said. "He's a broken man."

When they parked beside the newspaper office, Josh was sitting in his patrol car. Enid braced herself for the lecture he was sure to deliver. Jack walked ahead to unlock the side door. As soon as Jack had his back to them, Josh embraced Enid and held her so tight, she was having trouble breathing. Josh whispered in her ear, "I kept thinking, is this the time? Is this the one time she can't get out of a jam?" He stepped back and held her by her shoulders so he could look directly at her. "It's going to happen at some point if you keep this up."

"We're fine. Really." Enid put her hand on Josh's arm. "I'm sorry I make you worry so much. Let's go inside. Jack's waiting on us."

For the next hour, Josh listened to the interview and asked Enid and Jack to fill in some details. Josh pushed back from the table and rubbed his eyes. "Good work, guys. Actually, it's excellent, even if it was foolhardy. From what you learned, Fred or one of Boogie's deputies must have killed Angel. I'll contact this Walter guy you went to see and then confront Fred with this information."

"I just hate tarnishing Jean's memory of her father," Enid said. "But why would he have an innocent man convicted?"

"It hurts me to think Boogie would do something like that. But I have to push that aside and find out what his involvement was."

Jack cleared his throat. "I guess this is the point where we need to assure you we won't print any of this. Not yet, anyway."

Josh laughed. "When we're ready to make this public, I'll let you interview me before the press conference. That should give you a little jump on the *State* and the other daily newspapers."

"That's good. We can do a special edition," Jack said. He turned to Enid. "I'll see if we can get the *State* to pick up your story. Of course, they'll probably want to assign their own reporter."

"I'll get started on the series of articles tonight, at least on what we know so far," Enid said. "I can't wait to write the ending to this story." She looked at Jack and then Josh. They both looked sad, or maybe they were just tired.

CHAPTER 66

Ginger brought extra chairs to the newspaper's conference room in anticipation of Enid's interview with Sheriff Hart. There was a buzz of anticipation in the office, and several *Tri-County Gazette* reporters from the other two counties had asked to attend. Enid had initially protested their coming. "This is not a side show," she told Jack. But some of these reporters were young and ambitious, and if watching this interview would help them, then Enid was willing to go along with it. It was hard for her to see herself as seasoned reporter and a role model to those with less experience.

But something else was in the air. Jack seemed a bit distant, and so did Josh. He had a press conference scheduled at the sheriff's office later in the day, but this morning, it was Enid's exclusive interview. The other papers were sure to complain, but Josh did not seem concerned. Jack had arranged to print a special afternoon edition rather than holding the story for their usual Thursday schedule.

Two chairs had been placed at the front of the room for Enid and Josh. The other chairs were around the big conference table and at the back of the room.

Enid and Josh took their places. "Go easy on me, okay?" Josh whispered to Enid. "But show 'em how it's done. I'm proud of you."

Jack stood at the front of the room. "Ladies and gentlemen, thanks for joining us. As we've discussed, no notes or recordings. This is Enid's interview, and she has graciously allowed all of you to observe. It's her story, and if I find out any of you leaked any of this before we get it out, you're toast. Got it?"

All the reporters nodded.

"We'll do what we can to get this story into wider circulation with Enid's byline," Jack said.

"I'll make sure that happens," a man said as he walked into the conference room. All eyes turned toward him.

"Hello, Cade. Good to see you," Jack said. He turned to Enid. "I asked him to come, as an Associated Press reporter, of course."

Enid looked at the three of them: Jack, Josh, and Cade. And then she turned to Josh. "Are you ready to start?" Josh nodded and Cade took a seat at the back of the room. Jack followed him to the back but remained standing, leaning against the wall.

Enid turned on the recorder and stated the date, time, and location of the interview. "I'm interviewing Bowman County Sheriff Joshua Hart." She looked at her notes. "Sheriff, I understand you plan to charge Frederick Peterson with the murders of former sheriff Bernard Waters and Fred's sister, Angelina Peterson. Is that correct?"

A collective gasp went around the room. Enid glanced at Cade, who gave her a discrete thumbs-up signal.

"That is correct. Based on information from Fred's father, Clyde Peterson, we were able to confront Fred. He confessed to both murders. The prosecutor is in agreement with the charges and will proceed immediately."

"What is Fred's health condition?"

"He's recovering from a GSW, excuse me, a gunshot wound, as well as a knife wound received during the home invasion of Dr. Jean Waters, but his doctors expect him to recover. He'll be well enough to go to prison."

A murmur broke out around the room. "Quiet," Jack said.

"What was his motive for these killings?" Enid asked Josh.

"Apparently, Sheriff Waters and his daughter Jean surprised Fred at the 7 Crows Farm. Fred thought Waters was there to arrest him and panicked. Waters had no idea Fred was at the farm, because it had been foreclosed years ago and the family had moved away. Waters had gone to the farm to see if whoever was staying there knew anything about the Peterson family or how he might reach them. Waters needed a DNA sample from someone in the Peterson family to compare it to the bones found at the inn. It was supposed to be a routine visit. Unfortunately, Fred and his accomplice panicked and killed Sheriff Waters. According to others who have come forward, Fred had an explosive temper and a long rap sheet."

"I want to come back later to his female accomplice, Darla Smith, whom you have in custody. But first, what was Fred's motive for killing his sister, Angelina?"

"Sadly, Fred had a history of mental and physical abuse against his sister and others. When she was around fifteen, he offered her companionship and favors to two county deputies in return for their looking the other way on his pot growing, as well as a laundry list of other petty crimes. The sister Angelina, known as Angel, was threatened with harm to their father if she told anyone what was going on, so she kept quiet. She moved in and out of the area several times and when she was twenty-four, I believe, she began dating Reggie Long. He encouraged her to leave with him to get away from Fred. When Fred found out Angelina was planning to run away with Reggie, Fred killed her."

"Did Fred sexually abuse his sister?"

"He admits to the physical abuse but says he never touched her otherwise."

"I don't want to accuse Sheriff Waters of any wrong doing, especially since he's not here to defend himself," Enid said. "But from what we've learned, he appears to have helped convict an innocent man of Angel's murder."

Josh lowered his head and stared at his polished black lace-ups. "We don't have all the facts yet, and I can't comment on SLED's investigation into the matter. I can say that there are allegations a former Bowman County deputy planted evidence to help get Long convicted."

"What about Reggie Long's conviction?" Enid asked.

"Since we now have a confession from Fred Peterson for the murder of Angelina Peterson, the Long family has hired an attorney to file a motion to vacate Reggie Long's conviction."

Enid glanced at the back of the room. Cade was no longer smiling. She took a deep breath. Dig for the story beneath the story, Cade had always told her. "Sheriff Hart, do you think racism had anything to do with your predecessor's actions?"

Josh started to speak, then stopped. He looked Enid directly in the eyes and spoke slowly. "I won't defend or condemn Sheriff Waters' actions without all the facts. We'll have to wait for SLED to determine what happened and why. Speaking as the current sheriff of Bowman County, I will say that this law enforcement agency appears to have failed the citizens of Bowman County, and as a result, an innocent man went to prison and died there. On behalf of this office, I apologize to our citizens and to the Long family. And, I assure everyone that justice will be done."

Enid glanced at the clock on the wall. "I know you have to leave soon, but I'd like to ask a final question. Who is the accomplice under arrest?"

"The young woman who was an accomplice to Sheriff Waters' killing is Darla Smith. She is Angelina Peterson's daughter." The room gasped again, and Enid tried not to show her own surprise. "The father listed on her birth certificate is David Smith, which may be a false name."

Josh continued, "We're not sure who the actual biological father is, or where he is, but we will do our best to locate him. Fred Peterson claims he has no idea who the father was. When Fred found out Angelina was pregnant, he sent her to West Virginia. After Darla Smith's birth, Fred took her to live with relatives and brought Angel back to South Carolina with him."

"Have they lived at 7 Crows Farm all along?"

"No, the farm was foreclosed right around the time Angel went missing. Fred moved around the state staying mostly in abandoned houses. At some point, he went to West Virginia and brought Darla Smith back with him. They had been staying back at the 7 Crows Farm only a few months before Boogie was killed."

"Did Clyde Peterson know he had a granddaughter?"

"I don't believe Angel's father knew about Darla. It's a tragic situation. Fred Peterson controlled his sister Angel, physically and emotionally, and then he went after her daughter. While it may appear Darla Smith willingly participated in Sheriff Waters' killing, she may also be a victim. She'll be examined by a psychologist for possible Stockholm syndrome and other psychological factors that may have contributed to her involvement. That investigation will continue also." Josh stood up. "I'm sorry, but I need to go now."

"Thank you for your time, Sheriff Hart," Enid said. After Josh left, she sat alone at the front of the room. The other reporters were talking in small groups, and Cade and Jack had their heads together. For now, she had to keep her focus on writing this article. In her world, this article would be a big deal, but it was hard for her to enjoy the situation when there had been so much tragedy all around.

CHAPTER 67

The DNA from Clyde and Fred Peterson provided the match to the bones found at the inn. What had been good odds that the bones were Angel's were now a certainty. With Lillian and Boogie gone, there was no way to know all the details of what happened. Who did Lillian overhear talking at the inn that led her to Pinewood Cemetery and Angel's bones? Was it Boogie or someone else? That secret might never be told.

After Enid's articles were published, the *Tri-County Gazette* got a lot of national attention. The series focused first on the bones found at the inn, and then the murder of Sheriff Waters. The final articles tied it all together.

In Madden, at least, Enid had achieved rock-star status, which made her uncomfortable. She avoided the diner, and when a *State* reporter asked for her interview, she insisted talking by phone. But this afternoon, she needed to go out. Angel's remains were being put to rest, and Enid would be there.

When Enid arrived at the small church where the service would be held, she recognized Clyde Peterson standing near the closed casket. Next to him was Darla, his granddaughter, with a Bowman deputy standing guard nearby.

Angel, Fred, and Clyde had led a complex life woven of lies, threats, and fear. And now, Clyde Peterson looked like a broken man. After years of carrying the heavy burden of untold secrets, he kept his head low. The church minister read two verses of scripture and said a few words about God's love triumphing over evil at the graveside service behind the church. He offered condolences to Clyde and Darla, who wept quietly. Clyde made no attempt to console her. They didn't share memories of birthday parties, family dinners, and other things that bond families. Instead, they were linked by death and unspeakable betrayal by one sibling against another.

After the minister's brief comments over the grave, the deputy escorted Darla back to the patrol car. Enid and Jack were there, as well as Jean Waters. Theo also attended, since Angel's bones had rested at the inn for years. No other family or friends gathered around to pay their respects to Clyde.

"Wonder what will happen to Darla?" Enid asked Jack after the service.

"At best, she might get off on manslaughter with a lenient sentence if they find she was victimized by Fred."

"It's such a tragic situation."

Jack nodded. "You ready to go? I'm in the mood for a chocolate milkshake. Can I interest you in one?"

"I'd love to, but I need to wrap up a few things. Can I take a rain check?"

"Sure. That is, if you're planning on sticking around."

Enid stopped walking and looked at Jack. "What does that mean?"

"Well, it means you've got bigger fish to fly than hanging around here with me at the *Tri-County Gazette*. And now that Cade's back in your life, you've got some decisions to make about Josh."

"I'm going to Josh's tonight for an overdue conversation. Can't say I'm looking forward to it. As for Cade, we'll always be close friends. But I don't think we can make it work, not as a couple. We've both changed over the years."

Jack opened the door of the pickup and helped Enid inside. "Well, if you change your mind about that milkshake, just give me a call. Rachel is coming home this weekend, and I can't wait to see her. I know she'd love to see you, too."

Enid stared out the window, watching Clyde by the grave as the workers began lowering the casket. "As much as I'd like to see her, I need some time alone, to think things through. Give her a hug for me and thank her again for me for helping us find Clyde. She's going to make a terrific cyber investigator."

• • •

Jean walked toward the grave where Clyde was standing. "Mr. Peterson, my name is Jean Waters. May I talk with you?"

Clyde lifted his gaze from the casket to look at Jean. "Did you say Waters?"

"Yes, I'm Bernard and Lillian Waters' daughter. I'm a cancer doctor in Memphis, at St. Jude's Children's Hospital."

"Guess those rumors were true, then. I never did ask Bernard outright about 'em. Figured if he wanted me to know he'd tell me. And then we kinda drifted apart in recent years."

Jean put her hand on Clyde's arm. "I just want you to know how sorry I am about everything. Perhaps if my father had . . . if he had done something when you told him about your son and about Angel..."

"That's not for you to take on, but I appreciate your kind words."

Jean dropped her hand. "I'll write a letter or do what I can to make sure your granddaughter is treated fairly. She's a victim, too."

"I appreciate that, ma'am, but you've already done a lot. They told me you paid for the casket and burial. I can't repay you."

"No need to. I can't make up for what happened to you and Angel, but I was glad to help."

"And I want to thank you for all the kindness Miss Lillian showed Angel. Her mother died when she was a baby, so Angel looked to Miss Lillian at the inn. They were close from the time Angel was a little girl, and I was glad she had someplace she felt safe." Clyde Peterson looked over to Angel's grave, where the workers were beginning to lower the casket. "I'm so ashamed of myself. I should have done more to protect her."

"We all have regrets. Try to forgive yourself. That's what Angel would have wanted, I'm sure. Now that you don't have to live in hiding from your son, what will you do?"

"Don't know exactly. Hadn't thought much about it. But I'll be fine."

Jean extended her hand to Clyde. "Goodbye, Mr. Peterson. Take care of yourself."

Clyde shook her hand. "You, too, ma'am."

CHAPTER 68

Enid watched Josh stirring a pot of spaghetti sauce on the stove. He had on a white cotton chef's apron that looked like it had been washed too many times. He turned around toward Enid. "It's almost ready. You hungry?"

"It smells delicious." Although, Enid wasn't hungry. "Can I help you with anything?"

"The wine is open on the table. Why don't you pour us a glass?"

Enid pulled the wine stopper from the bottle and poured a small amount of cabernet sauvignon in each glass. As soon as she finished, Josh walked toward the table with a steaming dish in his hand and sat it down where Enid usually sat.

"If that's for me, I can't eat that much," Enid said.

Josh leaned into her and kissed her lips gently. "Sure you can."

When they were seated, Josh raised his wine glass. "To you, and to your tenacity in solving the mystery of the bones at the inn."

They tipped their glasses, and each took a sip. Enid took a spoon and twirled several strands of pasta around it and then tasted it. "This is really good."

Josh grinned. "Thanks."

For the remainder of the meal, they talked about Madden, and how it was changing with all the new development around it. They also talked about Boogie. "I imagine you were hurt to find out Boogie wasn't the man you thought he was."

Josh scooped up the last spoonful of sauce from his bowl. "We don't know all the story, so I'm trying not to judge him. But on face value, it is disturbing."

Enid put her napkin on the table. "I'll help you clean up, but then we need to talk."

"Don't worry about the dishes. I'll get them later." Josh took her by the hand and led her to the large screened porch on the back of the house. He lit a candle on the table, and they sat in the two big chairs facing the woods. An owl perched in one of the big pine trees hooted, the sound eerily floating through the night shadows.

"I know you're upset because I didn't tell you what was going on with my brother," Josh said.

"Was it because you didn't trust me?"

Josh took Enid's hand in his. "Not at all. I trust you with my life. I've told you before I'm a protector. It's my nature. Besides, you were busy getting bones reconstructed and trying to find out what happened." He squeezed her hand. "I'm so proud of you."

"Is it all settled with your brother now?"

"Troy's got a good attorney, and we're working with her and the prosecutor to get a minimum sentence. And now I want to find my sister."

"What do you mean?"

"Your friend Karla knows Kimi, although she goes by Heather now."

"What? How is that possible?"

Josh told Enid about his conversation with Karla.

"Where is Kimi, or Heather, now?"

"I think she's in New Mexico. She paid Troy's bail, although he doesn't know it was her. I want to talk with Heather first, make sure she's the real deal, before I tell Troy."

"Did you ever find out where the tip came from, the person who called the media about you?"

"I put a lot of people away in New Mexico, some really bad people. It could have been any one of them. The story about my wife and then her killer getting killed was in all the papers, so it could have been anyone who wanted to cause me some trouble." He shook his head. "They sure accomplished that." He paused. "I may find out one day, but right now, I need to focus on moving forward, not looking back."

"Can you forgive Troy for not stepping forward earlier?"

"Troy will never grow up. He's an irresponsible, hotheaded kid. But he's my only brother, and I love him. I tell myself he wouldn't have let me take the fall for him, but truthfully, I'll never know."

Enid shook her head. "This whole mess is amazing. Real life really is stranger than fiction."

Josh turned in his seat to face Enid. "I'm going to rent Boogie's house from Jean for a while."

"I think that makes sense. You need to be closer to the sheriff's office."

"Have you thought any more about moving into my house in Madden? You could redecorate or do whatever you need to."

The owl hooted and flew into the darkness.

"We can talk about this later."

Josh leaned back in his chair. "I'm afraid I'm going to lose you. You have so much more to offer than Madden, or I, can give you. And then there's Cade. He's still in love with you. So is Jack."

Enid laughed. "That's ridiculous. Cade and I will always be friends, nothing more. As for Jack, he's . . ." She couldn't find the right word. He was more than a friend.

Josh smiled. "Aside from my competition, I think the biggest challenge we have to overcome is our jobs. I felt awful that I couldn't talk to you or give you information. I was even afraid of being seen with you while the investigation was going on."

"I think we need to give it a little time. If it's real, we'll work it out." She paused. "So when are you going back to New Mexico to find your sister?"

"Not right away. When I do go, will you go with me? There's so much I'd love to show you."

"I'll think about it. Actually, I've always wanted to go there."

"When you're ready, we'll go. Deal?"

"Deal. Now let's go clean up your cooking mess. I need to get some sleep."

"Are you staying over?"

Enid leaned over and kissed Josh. "Not tonight. I need to be alone to sort through some things. I hope you can understand."

"I'll take whatever I can get. Just don't leave me."

EPILOGUE

Enid watched Madelyn move from person to person at her victory party at the inn, working the room. She was clearly in her element. Even though Theo and Jack planned the event to celebrate Madelyn's election to the state senate, Enid looked around and realized that everyone important to her was in the room: Jack, Rachel, Josh, and Cade. And, of course, Madelyn and Theo. These people were her extended family now. The only person missing was Jean, who had returned to Memphis.

It had been more than a month since Josh had asked Enid to move into his house. The more she thought about it, the more she thought of it as his house. Her little rental house was home, for now at least. She planned to tell him she appreciated the offer but would decline.

"She looks the part, doesn't she?"

Enid turned around to see Cade behind her. "You startled me. If you're talking about Madelyn, then, yes. She's a natural politician."

Jack walked over to join Cade and Enid, while Josh talked with Rachel. Jack looked at Cade. "Well, did you tell her yet?"

"About what?" Enid asked.

Cade cleared his throat. "I was just getting ready to tell you. What Jack is referring to is that my boss wants you to come to work for the Associated Press. I should say come back to the AP. He's looking for another investigative reporter, and he respects your work."

Enid's hand flew to her mouth. "Oh, my. I wasn't expecting that." She gathered her thoughts. "Needless to say, I'm extremely flattered."

"And?" Cade asked.

"And, I'll consider it."

"I thought you'd jump on that offer," Jack said.

"If there's one thing I've learned, it's that promotions and bigger salaries don't necessarily bring happiness," Enid said.

Cade briefly shifted his focus to Madelyn, who was chatting with a small group of admirers across the room. Enid felt someone tapping on her shoulder and turned around.

"Hello, Enid."

"Phyllis, I didn't know you were here. It's good to see you."

"I was running late and just got here. Senator-elect Jensen invited me."

Enid exchanged knowing glances with Jack. Madelyn helped the Long family find a good criminal attorney to clear Reggie's name. She also made some calls to make sure the motion to vacate Reggie's conviction would get the attention it deserved, and that the family would be compensated. Of course, Madelyn would want to capitalize on a photo op with Phyllis, which would explain why the *State* newspaper reporter was here. Such was the life of a politician. Besides, the publicity would be good for Phyllis and her family as well. Reggie deserved some positive press.

"We're all happy the way things turned out," Jack said to Phyllis.

"Yes, it's great day for justice," Cade added.

"Thanks to all of you for what you did to help clear Reggie's name." Phyllis turned to Enid. "May I have a private word with you?"

"Of course."

Enid and Phyllis excused themselves and walked out on to the inn's porch. The weather was unseasonably cool.

"I won't keep you long," Phyllis said, rubbing her arms to stay warm. "I just wanted to say special thanks to you for what you did."

"That's not—"

"Wait, let me finish. I mean, you had every right to turn your back on me, the way I tried to deceive you in the beginning and then withholding information out of fear. I just thank God you didn't let my foolishness stop you from doing the right thing."

Enid took Phyllis' hands in hers. They were warm, even in the chilly night air. "I just wanted to help you find the truth. Nothing else mattered, then or now. I can't imagine the fear you must have had in coming to see me. You couldn't trust law enforcement after what happened to Reggie, and you didn't know me at that time." She squeezed Phyllis' hands slightly before releasing them. "I want to thank you, for your courage, and for doing what was right for your brother and your family."

"I'm so sorry I judged Angelina without knowing all the facts. I should have believed Reggie when he said she was a good person." Phyllis smiled. "I wish they could have had the life they wanted together."

"Maybe they will, in another lifetime, in another place. Now, let's go inside before we freeze out here."

A NOTE FROM THE AUTHOR

Thank you for reading *Secrets Never Told*. If you've followed the Enid Blackwell series, you know each of my books was inspired by an actual event that touched me profoundly. Following my experience as an alternate juror for a murder trial, I wrote *Secrets Never Told*.

This story touched on sensitive racial and social issues, which I attempted to explore in a respectful manner. Please accept my sincere apologies if I failed in any way.

If you enjoyed *Secrets Never Told*, please post a review on www.Goodreads.com or on www.Amazon.com if purchased it there. Reviews help other readers discover new authors, which enables us to continue writing for you. Your feedback is appreciated.

I invite you to visit http://RaeganTeller.com to learn more about me and my work, to leave comments, or to ask any questions you may have.

Thanks!
Raegan

ACKNOWLEDGMENTS

This page was the most fun to write, as I love to thank the people who helped make this book possible.

First and foremost, I want to thank my husband, the man to whom this book is dedicated. Without him, I would not be able to lock myself in Study Room 3 at Blythewood Library and write for hours on end. He manages our household, assists me in all phases of my work, and supports me unconditionally.

I also want to thank Dr. Bill Stevens, a Richland County Deputy Coroner and forensic anthropologist. He graciously walked me through the process for investigating "old" bones. Thanks to Major Harry Polis of the Richland County Sheriff's Department for connecting me with Dr. Stevens.

One of the great things about writing is that you learn so much in the process. Roy Paschal is an artist and former forensic reconstruction instructor at the FBI Academy. His presentation and reconstruction demonstration were enlightening and invaluable to my story.

A special thanks to my beta readers, who helped me refine the first draft of *Secrets Never Told*: Carol Allen, Martha Anderson, Jane Cook, Earl Craig, and Irene Stern, who was also my final proofreader. As always, my developmental editor, Ramona DeFelice Long, also an author, provided excellent feedback, suggestions, and encouragement.

To my friends and family who are with me on this journey, I offer my eternal gratitude.

ABOUT THE AUTHOR

Raegan Teller is the award-winning mystery author of the Enid Blackwell Series. She lives in Columbia, South Carolina with her husband and two feline investigators. Each of Raegan's books was inspired by a real-life event that touched her in some way. Since life doesn't always make sense, she uses fiction to provide answers and to bring closure where there was none.

Before writing fiction, Raegan was a business writer and copy editor, a communications consultant, executive coach, and insurance manager—among other things. While working her way through school, she even sold burial vaults at a cemetery. How apropos is that for a mystery writer!

Connect with Raegan at http://RaeganTeller.com

Made in the USA
Columbia, SC
19 September 2019